STONE
BLIND

ALSO BY NATALIE HAYNES

THE AMBER FURY
THE CHILDREN OF JOCASTA
A THOUSAND SHIPS

Non-fiction
THE ANCIENT GUIDE TO MODERN LIFE
PANDORA'S JAR

NATALIE HAYNES

STONE BLIND

MANTLE

First published 2022 by Mantle
an imprint of Pan Macmillan
The Smithson, 6 Briset Street, London EC1M 5NR
EU representative: Macmillan Publishers Ireland Ltd, 1st Floor,
The Liffey Trust Centre, 117–126 Sheriff Street Upper,
Dublin 1, D01 YC43
Associated companies throughout the world
www.panmacmillan.com

ISBN 978-1-5290-6147-5

1 3 5 7 9 8 6 4 2

A CIP catalogue record for this book is available from the British Library.

Illustrations by Hemesh Alles

Typeset by Palimpsest Book Production Ltd, Falkirk, Stirlingshire
Printed and bound by CPI Group (UK) Ltd, Croydon, CR0 4YY

Visit www.panmacmillan.com to read more about all our books
and to buy them. You will also find features, author interviews and
news of any author events, and you can sign up for e-newsletters
so that you're always first to hear about our new releases.

*To my brother, who was there at the beginning,
and the sisters I have found along the way*

List of Characters

STHENNO, EURYALE, MEDUSA – the Gorgons – are daughters of sea gods CETO and PHORCYS. They live on the north coast of Africa

ATHENE, warrior goddess; daughter of METIS – one of mythology's early goddesses – and ZEUS, king of the Olympian gods

POSEIDON, god of the sea; brother to Zeus, uncle to Athene

AMPHITRITE, queen of the sea; wife of Poseidon

HERA, queen of the Olympian gods; wife of Zeus

GAIA, goddess of the earth; mother of the Titans and the giants, including ALCYONEUS, PORPHYRION, EPHIALTES, EURYTOS, CLYTIOS, MIMAS and ENCELADUS

HEPHAESTUS, blacksmith god; son of Hera (but not Zeus)

HERMES, messenger god

HECATE, goddess of night and witches

DEMETER, goddess of agriculture and mother of PERSEPHONE

MOIRAI, the Fates

GRAIAI (the Greys) – DEINO, ENYO, PEMPHREDO; personifications of the spirits of the sea. They share a single eye and a single tooth

HESPERIDES, garden-dwelling nymphs charged with guarding golden apples that belong to Hera. They also tend to have everything you might need for a quest

NEREIDS, fifty sea nymphs of changeable temper

ZEUS, king of the gods; husband of Hera

Mortals

DANAË, daughter of ACRISIUS, a minor Greek king

DICTYS, her friend; brother to POLYDECTES, king of Seriphos, a small Greek island

PERSEUS, son of Danaë and Zeus

CASSIOPE, queen of Ethiopia; wife of CEPHEUS

ANDROMEDA, their daughter

ERICHTHONIUS, legendary king of Athens

IODAME, a young priestess of Athene

Other

CORNIX, a chatterbox crow

ELAIA, an olive grove in Athens

HERPETA, snakes

Part One

Sister

Gorgoneion

I see you. I see all those who men call monsters.

And I see the men who call them that. Call themselves heroes, of course.

I only see them for an instant. Then they're gone.

But it's enough. Enough to know that the hero isn't the one who's kind or brave or loyal. Sometimes – not always, but sometimes – he is monstrous.

And the monster? Who is she? She is what happens when someone cannot be saved.

This particular monster is assaulted, abused and vilified. And yet, as the story is always told, she is the one you should fear. She is the monster.

We'll see about that.

Panopeia

As far towards the evening sun as it is possible to travel, there is a place where the sea winds inland in a narrow twist. You are where Ethiopia meets Oceanos: the furthest land and the furthest sea. If you could fly above it, see it as the birds see it, this channel (which is not a river because it flows the wrong way, but you may see this as part of its magic), coils like a viper. You have flown past the Graiai, although you may not have noticed, as they keep to their cave to avoid stumbling on their rocky cliffs and falling into the wild sea. Would they survive such a fall? Of course: they are immortal. But even a god doesn't want to be battered between the waves and the rocks for all eternity.

You have also sped past the home of the Gorgons, who live not so very far from the Graiai, their sisters. I call them sisters, but they have never met. They are connected – though they do not know, or have long forgotten – by the air and the sea. And now, also by you.

You'll need to travel to other places too: Mount Olympus, of course. Libya, as it will come to be called by the Egyptians and later, the Greeks. An island named Seriphos. Perhaps this seems too daunting a journey. But the place you have found yourself means you are already at the end of the earth, so you'll need to find your way back. You're not far from the home of the Hesperides, but they won't help you, I'm afraid, even if you could find them (which you can't). So that means the Gorgons. It means Medusa.

Metis

Metis changed. If you had been able to see her in the moments before she realized the threat, you would have seen a woman. Tall, long-limbed, with thick dark hair plaited at the back. Her large eyes were ringed with kohl. There was a quickness in the way her gaze seemed to fall on everything at once: even when she was still, she was alert. And she had her defences, what goddess did not? But Metis was better prepared than most, even though she was not armed with arrows, like Artemis, or with thinly contained rage, like Hera.

And so when she sensed – rather than saw – that she was in danger, she changed into an eagle and flew high, the gentle south wind ruffling the feathers of her golden wings. But even with these sharp eyes, she could not see what it was that had made the short hairs pulling at the edge of her plait prickle when she was in human form. She circled in the air a few times, but nothing revealed itself to her and eventually she flew down and settled on the top of a cypress tree, curving her muscular neck in every direction, just in case. She perched there, thinking.

She dropped down from the high branches onto the sandy ground, her talons scratching small furrows in the dust. And then she was not an eagle any more. Her hooked beak retracted and her feathered legs disappeared beneath her. As one muscled body became another, only the intelligence in the slit of her eyes remained constant. Now she slithered over the stones, a brown zig-zag stripe along her dorsal scales, her belly the colour of pale sand. She flickered across the ground as quickly as she had flown through the sky. And as she paused beneath a large prickly pear, she pressed her body into the earth, trying to feel the source of unease that she had not been able to spot as an eagle. But even as the rats that lived on scraps from the nearby temple raced away from her, she could not feel the footsteps of the creature she should be fleeing. She wondered what to do next.

She stayed under the cactus for a long time, enjoying the heat of the ground, allowing her hooded eyes to move, but nothing else. She was almost invisible, she knew. She was faster than most other creatures, and her bite was venomous, devastating. She had nothing to fear. But still she did not feel safe. And she could not stay here, a snake for ever.

She uncurled herself from the base of the cactus, and moved into the shade of the cypresses. Suddenly she reared up, and transformed again. The zig-zag on her scales fractured and became spots, the scales themselves softening to a coarse fur. Ears sprouted, clawed feet appeared at the end of muscular legs. The panther was beautiful, swishing her tail to send the flies spinning. She moved slowly at first, sensing each individual stone beneath the pads of her paws. Again, she felt the ripple of alarm she produced in the animals nearby. But once more, she could not shake her own fear. She ran through the trees, weeds snagging on her fur as her speed increased. They did not slow her at all. She could catch anything. And what could catch her? Nothing. She revelled in her power. She felt almost weightless, pure muscle in pursuit of prey. And then she was caught.

Zeus was everywhere and nowhere at once. She could not outrun this bright cloud enveloping her. She flinched as her cat's eyes could not tolerate the glare, changed back to a snake as the cloud seemed to thicken and close in. She tried to slither away beneath it, but there was no beneath. The cloud emanated from everywhere, from the ground as much as from the air. She tried to speed away from it, but whichever direction she turned, it became more impenetrable. The brightness was intolerable: even through the brille that covered them, her eyes ached. She made one last attempt to free herself, changing forms again in rapid succession: eagle, but she couldn't fly above it; boar, but she couldn't gore her way through it; locust, but she couldn't consume it; panther again, but she couldn't outrun it. The cloud began to solidify and she felt herself squeezed. Her muscles began to throb from the pressure and she had no choice but to make herself smaller and smaller still: weasel, mouse, cicada. But still the pressure increased. She tried one last time: ant. And then she heard his hated voice, telling her she could not escape him. She already knew what she had to do to make the pain stop. Submit to another pain. Beaten at last, she gave in and reverted to her original form.

As Zeus raped her, she thought of being an eagle.

*

The only good thing about Zeus's sexual incontinence, his wife Hera had often thought, was its extreme brevity. His desire, pursuit and satiation were so short-lived that she could almost convince herself of their irrelevance. If only it didn't invariably result in offspring. More and more gods and demigods, each one appearing for no reason other than to confirm to her that he was virtually indiscriminate in his infidelity. Even she, a goddess with an almost limitless supply of spite, could barely keep up with the number of women, goddesses, nymphs and mewling infants she needed to persecute.

She did not usually have to turn her attention to his previous wife. Metis was someone she preferred not to think about at all, but if she did it was with a mild irritation. No one likes to come second, or third, and Hera was no exception. Metis had been wife to Zeus long before Hera had been interested in the idea. They had parted so long ago that people had forgotten they were ever married. On good days, Hera didn't think about it. On bad days, she saw it as cheating. It seemed particularly unreasonable that any goddess could claim priority over her, Hera, consort of Zeus, merely by having been there first. And since Hera had many more bad days than good days, she disliked Metis. But because she had so many other provocations to cope with, she usually ignored this.

It had been Metis, of course, who had advised Zeus in his war against the Titans. Metis who aided Zeus in his battle with Cronos, his father. Metis, who was so wily and clever, always hatching a plan. Hera was just as clever as her predecessor, she had no doubt. But circumstances forced her to use her plots against Zeus, whereas Metis had offered him her wisdom as a gift. Hera snorted. Much good that

9

had done her. Hera had replaced her: who now thought of Metis in conjunction with Zeus? Who doubted the superiority of his sister and wife, Hera, queen of Mount Olympus? No mortal or god would dare.

Which made it all the more infuriating that Zeus had betrayed her with his former wife. The rumour had flown between the gods and goddesses like a swirling breeze. No one dared be the one who told Hera, but she knew about it just the same. She despised her husband more with each fresh revelation, and she determined to take her revenge. Zeus had been very quiet for the past day or so, no doubt hoping that if he avoided his wife, she might somehow forget her rage. When she heard him returning, Hera sat herself on a large, comfortable chair in her chamber, deep within the echoing halls of Olympus, and looked idly at her fingernails. She draped her dress to reveal more than her ankles, and tugged it down a little at the front. 'Husband,' she said, as Zeus entered the room, a slightly shifty expression on his otherwise majestic brow.

'Yes?' he replied.

'I've been so worried about you.'

'Well, I was . . .' Zeus had learned over time that it was better to stop a sentence partway through than lie to his wife. Her capacity to unravel his deceits was one of her least appealing characteristics.

'I know where you were,' she said. 'Everyone's talking about it.'

Zeus nodded. Of course they were: no one gossiped like Olympian gods. He wished he had had the sense to render them all mute, at least the ones he had created. He wondered if it might be possible to do so retrospectively.

Hera sensed she did not have his undivided attention. 'And I was worried,' she repeated.

'Worried?' He knew there must be a trap, but sometimes it was just easier to jump right into it.

'Worried about your future, my love,' she murmured and shifted artlessly so her dress fell open a little further. Zeus tried to assess his situation. His wife was often furious and sometimes seductive, but he couldn't remember an occasion when she had been both at once. He moved a little closer, in case this was the right thing to do.

'My future?' he asked, as he reached out and pulled teasingly at one of her curls. She turned her head up to face him.

'Yes,' she said. 'I have heard such terrible things about the offspring of Metis.' She felt him stiffen, before his fingers went back to caressing her hair. He was trying very hard. 'It was Metis, wasn't it? This time?'

She could not keep the edge from her voice and Zeus quickly wrapped his hand in her curls. She knew he would wrench her hair from her scalp if she wasn't careful. 'I was just wondering if you can really have forgotten what she once told you about her children,' Hera sighed. 'That she would give birth to one who would overthrow you.'

Zeus said nothing, but she knew her barb had found its mark. How could he have been so foolish? When he had overthrown his father – with Metis's help, no less – and his father had done the same before him? How could he have forgotten what Metis herself had once told him when they were still married? How?

'You need to act quickly,' Hera added. 'She told you she would have a daughter who would exceed all but her father in wisdom. And after her, a son who would be king over gods and mortals. You cannot take that risk.'

But she was speaking to the ether, because her husband had already disappeared.

*

The second time Zeus came for her, Metis did not try to hide. She knew what was coming and she knew she could not evade him. The only thing left to her was to hope that her daughter (she would have known it was a daughter even without her prophetic gifts; she could feel it) would survive. Had she known this was how it would happen, when she'd told her husband long ago that she could bear him a daughter and then a son who could overpower his father? She knew Zeus's fears better than anyone. He would do anything to ensure that their son was never born.

Again she found herself surrounded by the brightest light, the inside of a thunderbolt. Again she felt the pressure to become smaller and smaller: panther, snake, grasshopper. But this time, there was no pain. Only a sudden, enveloping darkness as Zeus grabbed her in his huge hand. And then a strange sensation of being inside the black cloud that follows the thunderbolt. It was a darkness that would never end. Zeus had, she realized, consumed her, swallowed her whole. Now she and her daughter were inside the king of the gods with no means of escape. And even as Metis understood this, and accepted it, she felt something within her, within Zeus, resist it.

Sthenno

Sthenno was not the older sister, because they didn't think of time in that way. But she was the one who had been less horrified when the baby was left on the shore outside their cave. Euryale had been equal parts baffled and appalled: where had the child come from? What mortal would ever dare to approach the Gorgons' lair to abandon it there? Sthenno had no answers to her questions, and for a while, they both stared at the creature and wondered what to do.

'Could we eat it?' asked Euryale. Sthenno thought for a moment.

'Yes,' she said. 'I suppose we could. It is quite small, though.' Her sister nodded glumly. 'You can have it,' Sthenno said. 'I already . . .' She didn't need to finish. Her sister could see the pile of cattle bones lying beside her.

The sisters did not eat from hunger: Gorgons were immortal, they had no need for food. But their sharp tusks, their powerful wings, their strong legs: all were designed for the hunt. And if you were going to hunt, you might as well eat your kill. They looked at the baby again. It lay on its back in the sand, its head propped up on a tuft of grass. Sthenno did not need her sister to say the words out loud: it looked like a deeply unsatisfying kill. It wasn't running away, it hadn't even tried to hide in the longer grass.

'Where could it have come from?' Euryale asked again. She raised her huge head, her bulbous eyes searching the rocks above them. There was no sign of anyone.

'It must have come from the water,' Sthenno replied. 'Mortals can't find their way without divine assistance. And even if they could, they wouldn't dare to come here. The baby was brought to us from the sea.'

Euryale nodded, beating her wings. She scanned the ocean in every direction. No vessel could have sailed out of sight in the time it had taken the two of them to find the baby. They had heard a sound and it had roused them and they had left the cave together. No ship, no swimmer could be invisible to them so quickly.

'I don't know,' Sthenno said, hearing her sister's thoughts. 'But look.' She pointed at the baby and now Euryale noticed the circle of damp sand beneath the child and the seaweed-strewn trail leading back to the water's edge.

They sat in silence, thinking.

'It couldn't have been left there by . . .' Euryale glanced at her sister, not wanting to feel stupid.

Sthenno shrugged her broad shoulders, her wings catching the edge of the breeze. 'I don't know who else could have done it,' she replied. 'It must have been Phorcys.'

Euryale's bulging eyes widened. 'Why would he do that?' she asked. 'Where would he have got a mortal child from? A shipwreck?'

The Gorgons knew very little about their father. An old

god, he lived in the depths of the ocean with their mother, Ceto. They had many offspring besides Euryale and Sthenno: Scylla, a nymph with six dog heads and their six vicious mouths, who lived in a high cave over the sea from which she would appear to eat passing sailors. Proud Echidna, half-nymph, half-snake. The Graiai – three sisters who shared a single eye and a single tooth – who dwelt in a cave somewhere even the Gorgons would hesitate to go.

Sthenno and her sister were gradually closing in on the child. The sea whispered behind them. The baby had been left far above the tide's reach. Sthenno pointed to the wet trail that led to it: there were paired indentations on either side.

Euryale nodded. 'It was Father,' she said. 'Those are the marks of his claws, surely.'

As they drew nearer, Sthenno noticed that the child was sleeping on a messy pile of dead seaweed: had her father scooped it up to form a sort of bed? Everything she could see and everything she thought she knew were battling one another in her mind. The thought of Phorcys doing anything as – Sthenno hunted for the word – mortal as laying a baby in a handmade crib was impossible. And yet, here were the marks of his claws, each side of the wide path made by his fish tail. And there was the baby lying safely beyond the water, sleeping on a thick pile of translucent dead weeds. Like empty skins snakes left behind in the sand, she thought.

It was only when they were right on top of the child, and Euryale was eyeing it as an unwanted visitor and an undersized meal, that the two sisters understood that Phorcys had delivered it to them for a reason.

'She has . . .' Euryale dropped into a low crouch, tilting

her head for a better view of the child's shoulders. They could see only a little of her back through the seaweed, but her sister was right. The baby had wings.

*

It took the Gorgons a whole day to accept that they had acquired another sister, a mortal one. It took them several more days to learn not to kill her by accident.

'Why is it crying?' Euryale asked her sister, prodding the baby with her hand, talon curled carefully into her palm so she wouldn't injure her.

Sthenno looked at her sister in alarm. 'I don't know,' she said. 'Who knows why mortals do anything?' Both tried to think of mortals they might have seen behaving similarly, but neither could bring one to mind. In fact, they couldn't remember seeing any human children, but Euryale suddenly thought of a cormorant's nest in the rocks nearby. The cormorant had chicks, she told Sthenno, who nodded as though she remembered.

'The chicks made a terrible noise,' Euryale said. 'And the mother fed them.' Her wide mouth split into a grin. She flew a little way inland until she came to the nearest settlements. She flew back with a stolen sheep under each arm. 'Milk,' she said. 'They give babies milk.'

And so even though they were goddesses, they learned to feed their sister. After a while, Sthenno found she couldn't remember what their home had looked like without a small flock of curve-horned sheep scrambling over the rocky ground with ease. Even Euryale – who had once combed the skies searching for prey, seizing it in her mighty jaws and crunching its bones for the sheer pleasure of the sound – seemed to enjoy looking after them. One day, an eagle tried to pick off one of their lambs, and Euryale rose in the air to defend it. The eagle was too fast for her, and she returned empty-handed, a few of the bird's feathers falling to the sand behind her. But still it did not dare to try again.

In the early days, Sthenno wondered if Phorcys might return to explain his behaviour or to bring a message from their mother, Ceto, but he never came. The two Gorgons felt differently about this: Euryale was proud that their parents had entrusted the strange mortal child to them to look after. Sthenno wondered if her father had left the child with them hoping they would fail. It was impossible for gods to look at mortals and not feel some revulsion. Sthenno loved her new sister as much as she loved Euryale. But she still had to repress a shudder when she caught sight of her sister's horrifyingly small hands and feet, her revolting little fingernails. And yet, even if something had gone wrong with her birth, Medusa was a Gorgon too. And perhaps she would improve with time.

Because this was the next upsetting development. The baby kept changing: growing, shifting as they watched, like Proteus. No sooner had they adapted to some inexplicable feature of her than she developed a new one. They carried her everywhere because she couldn't move on her own, and then without warning she could crawl. They grew accustomed to that, and then she stopped crawling and started to walk. Her wings grew along with the rest of her, and it was a relief to them both to discover that even if she couldn't fly very well, she was not completely earthbound. Euryale confessed that the wings reminded her they were sisters, in spite of everything. They felt a brief surge of hope when her teeth appeared, but they were small and stayed firmly inside her mouth, not like proper tusks. She could use them to chew, but what use was that to anyone?

As Medusa would not stop changing, her sisters had to change too. Sthenno learned to make bread because milk no longer satisfied her. The three of them stared at the dough as it blistered and rose on the wide flat rock they had balanced over their fire. Euryale had been watching women perform the same chore and had brought back instructions and advice. The more time went on, the more they found themselves copying the humans who lived nearby.

*

Mortals had always feared the Gorgons, but the feeling was not reciprocated. Although their sisters, the Graiai, lived in a cave as far from humankind as they could, the Gorgons simply lived where they chose and people avoided them. Neither sister could remember why they had decided on this particular spot on the shores of Libya, but they had made it their home. They had a wide, sandy shore, bordered on both sides by large sun-bleached rocks, marked here and there by tufts of sturdy grass. The rocks formed great outposts: a hard climb but an easy flight for a Gorgon to reach the highest points and gaze out over the sea with its sharp-beaked birds diving for fish, or turn to face inland across the vivid red earth and the dark green scrub. And cutting across the furthest edge of the shore was a jagged scar in the rock, left by one of Poseidon's earthquakes which had almost torn the land in two. The ground was higher on the Gorgons' side of the breach, but not by much. Nonetheless, it gave the two of them an unspoken sense that they had picked the right part, the higher part, of the coast for themselves.

Libya was home to many creatures – cattle and horses were their closest neighbours, brought by the people who had settled nearby. Euryale remembered a time when there were no humans within a day's flying of their home. They used to be further away, but something had changed. She asked Sthenno if she could recall what had happened, but there was never any point asking Sthenno about these things. She always thought the world was as unchanging as they were. But even the Gorgons had changed, Euryale said: they had been two and now they were three. Sthenno shrugged and said, perhaps it was the weather. Humans worried about the weather, didn't they? Because they had animals to feed and crops to grow. And perhaps that was the difference. The land was drier, hotter than before. Euryale reminded her sister of a time when they had flown across great swathes of green, bursting with noise: the conversation of swallows, the call of bee-eaters and the song of crested larks. When they had landed beside a huge lake, and watched the storks bathing in the still water. Sthenno nodded uncertainly. She never disputed her sister's memory, but she didn't always share its clarity.

Gradually, Sthenno agreed, their neighbours had moved closer to the coast, closer to the sea. But their secluded shore remained private because it was too inaccessible, and anyway, men told each other stories about the creatures they believed they had glimpsed there. Monsters from the deep with huge mouths, vicious tusks, leathery wings: so fast and strong and always to be feared. They had manes like lions, or hair made from snakes, or bristles like wild boar. The Gorgons were everything and nothing to most mortals, Sthenno said. She might remember less than Euryale but she understood more.

And so men avoided their home, the beach and the sea, the rocks and the cave. The cave which Sthenno thought they must have chosen because of Medusa. Euryale knew they had lived beside it before Medusa was their sister, but she never mentioned it. The cave was Medusa's home, as soon as she was big enough to explore it. Gorgons loved the heat: Sthenno and Euryale could lie for hours in the scorching sun, unfurling their wings and allowing the warmth to seep through them. But Medusa would squint in the brightest part of the day, and her skin would become too hot. When she was still small, she found shade beneath her sisters' outstretched wings. But as she grew bigger, she spent long days learning the recesses of their cave – its many hidden tunnels and paths, and the way the jagged scar visible on the sands could somehow also be found underfoot in the blackness inside the cave – so intimately that when the sun grew too hot, she would kiss her sisters on their bearded cheeks and withdraw to the cooler air to sleep.

Sthenno had no daughter, but she felt like the mother of Medusa and she knew Euryale felt the same. And although she hadn't chosen the emotions she now experienced, she tried not to be appalled by them. The confusion and revulsion that Medusa had first provoked in both sisters had ebbed away. The anxiety, however, had not. Sthenno had never felt a moment of fear in her life before she was responsible for a child. What should she be afraid of, a Gorgon like her? Of men? Of beasts? The idea was absurd. And she had never experienced fear for another creature until Medusa. She had never felt the slightest worry when Euryale was away hunting or exploring: her sister could defend herself against any attack, just as she could. And then there was Medusa, who could be hurt by anything, even a stone.

Did all children have such unsteady limbs when they were small? Did they all collapse with no warning? Did they all spout blood when they came into contact with anything hard? Forgetful as she was, Sthenno remembered one thing and that was the cold dread which shuddered through her when Medusa tripped over the grasses that their flock negotiated without hesitation. She had been playing up on the higher rocks, showing off the wings that had let her fly the little way she could not climb. Medusa's fall was sudden and brief as she dropped onto a jutting rock that pierced through the sand beneath her. Sthenno could not say how old her sister had been, but she was not even the height of Euryale's bony hip. The noise she had made: Sthenno and Euryale had exchanged a wordless glance, each knowing the other's thought. Was this the moment when their sister emerged as a true Gorgon? The moment when she finally made the same deathless howl that Sthenno could create if she merely opened her wide mouth and cried out?

It was not. This was not a display of strength but of fragility. The howl was disappointingly short-lived, as the little girl had to gulp for more breath to sustain it. Breathing was an awful weakness. And then the blood appeared, pouring in a vicious stream down the child's leg. Sthenno hadn't even known what it was at first, had no idea that her sister's veins ran with this sticky redness when she should be filled with ichor, like a normal creature. She and Euryale ran to their sister, lifted her in their arms, cradled their wings around her. Euryale licked the blood gently from Medusa's skin. The howls subsided and the tears that ran down her cheeks disappeared, faint salt traces all that was left of them until Euryale licked those away too. Medusa stared at the rock that had hurt her. Euryale didn't need words to understand. She drove a clawed foot into it, watching her sister as the rock fractured and smashed beneath her.

And every day after that, as the angry purple welt on Medusa's skin faded, she would look at the place where the rock had been as she rubbed the itching scar. And then she would smile, because it could not hurt her again. Euryale had seen to that.

When Sthenno summoned her sisters to her – Euryale swooping down from the skies, Medusa running out from her cave – she would greet them the same way: we are one, but we are many. Medusa would always reply as though she had asked a question (which she had not): three isn't many. And Sthenno would smile and reach down to stroke her sister's beautiful hair, curling in thick dark ringlets around her face. You are many all on your own.

'I don't know what you mean,' the little girl said. 'I'm just me.'

And then one day, she said, 'Are we always three?'

'What?' Sthenno didn't understand.

'Will we ever be more than three?' Medusa asked. She had been watching the sheep which this summer had five lambs between them. Last year there had been only two.

'No, darling. We'll always be three,' Sthenno replied. Medusa saw the shadow cross her sister's face, but she didn't understand it.

'Who gave birth to me?'

Sthenno looked at Euryale, who looked at the sheep.

'Ceto,' said Sthenno.

'Who is that?'

Sthenno shrugged and said, 'Your mother. Our mother too.'

'But I've never seen her,' said Medusa. 'How can she be my mother? I thought you were my mother.' She looked between the two of them. 'If she's my mother, why isn't she here?'

They had looked forward to her talking. But now Sthenno felt there should be more time between a child beginning to speak and a child asking questions of every single thing she could see or not see, from the birds in the sky to the wind in her hair. Why, why, why. Sthenno had tried to tell Medusa she didn't know why cormorants flew closer to the shore than other birds, or why their sure-footed sheep liked eating grass when it tasted bad to Medusa, or why the sea was colder than the sand when the sun shone equally on both. Sthenno had never even noticed these things. But a lack of answers didn't deter Medusa from asking more and more questions. Sthenno looked at her sister expectantly.

'They're in the sea,' said Euryale.

'Who is they?'

'Our parents. You have two parents, a mother and a father.'

Medusa frowned. 'Are they fish?' she asked.

Euryale considered the question. 'No,' she said. 'Not fish.'

The little girl began to cry. The two sisters looked at one another in alarm. They had grown accustomed to her precarious moods, but it still seemed odd to weep over not having fish for parents. The more perplexed they became, the harder Medusa sobbed.

'You wouldn't want fish for parents,' said Sthenno, putting her arm around her child. 'How would you tell one fish from another? You wouldn't know if it was your father or not.'

'But fish are the only things that live in the sea!' Medusa wailed.

'No they aren't,' Euryale said. 'Why would you say that? Because fish are all you have seen in the sea, because they come closest to the shore where you live. But the sea extends far beyond what you can see from here. It is wide and deep and full of creatures and places you have never imagined. Phorcys and Ceto live in the deepest realms of the ocean.'

'But I couldn't live there?'

'No,' said Sthenno quickly. 'You would drown if you tried. Promise you will never go past the rocks you know.' She pointed at the huge rocks that formed the sides of their bay.

Medusa nodded. 'I promise. Could you live in the sea?'

Every answer created more questions. Euryale flexed her wings. 'I don't think so,' she said. 'Wet wings would be too heavy to fly, I think.' Sthenno nodded in agreement, because she had no idea.

'And that's why we all live here together?' Medusa asked. 'Because we can't live in the sea and they can't live on the land?'

'That's right,' Euryale said.

'Even though they aren't fish?'

'They aren't fish.'

'What do they look like?' Medusa asked. 'Are they like you?'

Euryale thought for a moment. 'No, not like us,' she said. 'They are not Gorgons. Phorcys is a sea god, he doesn't have wings. He has scales. And huge claws instead of legs. Ceto is—' Euryale raised her bushy eyebrows at Sthenno, who had no answer for her. 'I don't know exactly how to describe Ceto,' Euryale said. 'We have never seen her.'

'Never?'

'She lives in the depths of the ocean, Medusa. None of her children have ever seen her.'

Medusa sat quietly, her questions finally stilled. And her sisters hoped once again that they had kept her from feeling what they knew to be true: that she was a freak whose birth had horrified both parents. Sthenno was immortal, Euryale was immortal, their parents, grandparents, siblings were immortal. Everyone was immortal except Medusa, and creatures that no Gorgon would ever pay any heed.

But now, here they were. Euryale tending her flocks like a shepherd boy. The two of them anxiously discussing the milk yield. Sthenno hanging the dried skins of cattle across the front of their cave so that Medusa could keep warm at night, driving them into the rock with her hard talon. Everything about their days had become different once they took on the task of raising Medusa.

And how could anyone have prepared Sthenno for the change it had caused? She did not know where to site the pain she felt; she resented feeling it at all. But somewhere in her body was a strange new ache, which she eventually concluded was fear. Fear! In a Gorgon! The idea was absurd, infuriating. But that was what it was; she could not keep pretending to herself it was anything else. She lived with this throbbing, this constant nagging twinge that Medusa might not be safe. So not only was she – a Gorgon – experiencing fear, but she was feeling it on behalf of another Gorgon who should be as impervious as she herself once had been. Euryale felt it too, though she was too ashamed to mention it. Sthenno could see the same fluttering anxiety in her sister that she saw in herself. No wonder Phorcys had deposited the baby with them. No sea god would want to feel so weakened. A shudder ran through Sthenno as she thought of what she had lost: the sweet sense of owning herself and her feelings, of having no concerns at all, or only the very mildest kind. All of this was gone, exchanged without warning for a cold, gripping panic whenever a child stumbled or hid or cried.

This, she knew, was love. And she felt it even though she did not want it.

Hera

Amid the lofty grey peaks of Mount Olympus, Hera could see that something was wrong. Zeus was irritable at the best of times, but he was not usually as malevolent as this. The king of the gods had stalked Olympus for days, threatening one deity after another for the most minor infractions. The rock beneath his feet had shuddered at his step, the pine trees lower down the mountain cowered together. Usually, Zeus could manage to be civil to Apollo and Artemis. And yet there had been the most spectacular argument between the three of them earlier. And over nothing, really: Apollo was playing his lyre, which was annoying, certainly, but hardly a novelty. And Zeus sometimes cared for music. Hera preferred silence to everyone fawning over the pristine archer, but unusually she hadn't started the fight.

Apollo had been playing the instrument quietly, with only his sister cooing at his skill. He was, Hera thought, being quite tolerable. Then he had played a wrong note and Artemis had laughed. Rather winsomely, in Hera's opinion, but when did Zeus ever mind that? And yet her husband had shouted with rage, had blasted one thunderbolt after another in their direction. They were so shocked, they didn't even mock him for his atrocious aim. The columns supporting their lovely colonnades needed a little repair work, and the oak trees in the distance were briefly illumin- ated then blackened. The stench of burning leaves angered Zeus still further. He had been so furious that Hera almost delayed her revenge for the Metis affair.

Of course he had done as she hoped, and wiped the smug goddess from the face of the earth. But Hera resented that it had happened at all. It was not enough to have punished Metis, she needed to punish Zeus. And she knew one way to do that. Well, she smiled to herself as she stared at her reflection in a shallow pool and found nothing wanting, she knew countless ways to do that.

Hera and Zeus were ideally matched, at least in terms of their capacity to antagonize one another. There were days when she believed he could scarcely rise from his bed without seducing or raping someone. The time and effort it then took her to harass every goddess, woman or nymph he had molested? Well, it grew no less draining the more she did it. Quite the opposite, in fact. And on this occasion, she had decided Zeus's punishment should fit his particular, habitual wrongdoing. He had impregnated Metis, even if the child, god or demi-god, had not appeared. Hera paused to consider the awful possibility that there was a bastard infant somewhere which she had failed to locate and per- secute. No. Her large brown eyes gave the misleading impression of a sweet-natured creature. A deer, say, or a cow. But she was as sharp-eyed as any predator. She had missed nothing.

So, where was the child? It infuriated her that she didn't know. But she could hardly ask him. And none of her usual sources of information (nymphs trying to keep on her good side, in case the worst should happen to them) had been able to give her an answer. She would puzzle it out. But first she would punish him.

*

Hera did not mention Hephaestus to Zeus for a day or two (actually, she was not sure how many days it had been, since they all merged into one so quickly for her and the other gods). But it seemed to take only a few moments for her son to change from infant to adult. Perhaps all mothers felt this way, she wondered afterwards. And shrugged, because how could she ever know the answer without asking one? And who could be bothered to do that? All that mattered was that one moment he had been tiny, the next moment he was grown. He had a limp, she was irritated to notice, which he must have got from his father because he certainly didn't get it from her. But since she would never reveal who the father was, no one would know. And Hephaestus was skilled with his hands: that had become clear straightaway.

In fact, if anything, he was too skilled. Because Zeus's wrath that his wife had produced an illegitimate child of her own was swiftly ameliorated by discovering how useful this new deity was to have around. When Zeus had finally noticed a limping god with so much affection for the queen of the gods that she could only be his mother, he erupted with his customary petulance. But Hephaestus – always so eager to please everyone, especially Zeus – was quick to placate him by sculpting a bronze eagle and presenting it to his stepfather as a gift.

The other gods looked on with interest. Apollo was holding his lyre, but his sister's hand was on his arm, advocating silence. Zeus scowled and grabbed the eagle, seemingly ready to hurl it at its creator. But as he raised it in his hand, the rays of the sun caught the bird. Hephaestus had somehow moulded the feathers in just such a way that when the light was on them, the eagle's wings were the dark brown of Zeus's favoured bird, but the feathered edges glowed gold, just as if Helios were catching the real bird in full flight. Zeus was on the verge of saying he had never seen anything more beautiful unless she was naked, when he caught sight of his wife's eyes, softening as she looked at her son and her husband, and decided that perhaps some thoughts were best left unsaid.

*

Hephaestus built his own forge, behind the halls in which the other gods dwelt. He was there more than not, happiest alone making things. He would create anything – from clay, bronze or stone – and it was always the most exquisite object. He remained as he had always been: disliking any kind of conflict unless he had built the armour for the combatants himself. And even then he only wanted to see how it fared in usage: whether his spear design could withstand the shield he had crafted, reinforced with layer upon layer of leather. He would indulge the whim of any god who asked. Artemis murmured to her brother that it seemed impossible anyone so amenable was related to Hera, and Apollo nodded as he admired his sister's new quiver and her beautifully weighted bow.

*

But Zeus's temper did not improve. He could be placated with gifts but the improvement in his mood was always transitory and the following day he would be as irascible as before.

'What?' Hera eventually asked him, when he reduced his cup-bearer to tears for the third time in a day. 'How can you keep being angry with the poor boy? He does nothing except fetch and carry for you, exactly as you desire. You're making him miserable and he isn't even nice to look at when he cries.'

'I know,' Zeus said. 'How is it that women cry so prettily and men don't?'

'I can't imagine,' Hera replied. 'But he's wept all over the floor, and if I slip and fall I shall blame you.'

'I don't care who you blame,' her husband replied. 'I don't care what you do so long as you do it quietly.'

'Are your ears hurting you?' she asked.

'No,' he said. 'Be quiet.'

'Is your laurel wreath too tight?'

'No. I don't think so. How could something made of leaves be too tight?' he asked.

'I don't know, I just wondered.'

'Do you think the king of the gods can be injured by leaves?' His rage was mounting.

'I think something is making you angry,' Hera snapped. 'And it isn't the quality of nectar that boy brought you.'

31

There was a long pause. His bearded face darkened with anger; her solicitous expression did not change.

'My head aches,' he said.

'I didn't quite catch that.' Hera leaned forward, turning one elegant ear towards him.

'I said, my head aches.'

'A headache? That's why you're in a filthy temper?'

His golden eyes glittered. 'You get enough headaches, and they put you in a terrible mood.'

'Well, thank goodness you always manage to find comfort elsewhere,' she replied. 'Why haven't you asked one of the centaurs for help?'

'Is that what you do?'

'They're good at herbs, aren't they?'

'I think so. Apollo would know,' he said.

'He might even go and ask them, if you stop screaming at him for the slightest thing.'

'You could ask him?'

'I'm sure that would help. Perhaps if I told him you were sorry you smashed his lyre?'

'I'm not sorry.'

'Perhaps if I pretended you were sorry.' They stared at one another. He loved her when she was like this. It was a pity she was so often angry.

'Very well,' he said. 'Pretend I'm sorry.'

'Yes, husband,' she said. And she kissed him gently on the cheek before walking away to explain to the archer that his help was required, broken lyre or no.

*

The centaur produced a concoction of uncertain origin and off-putting hue. Apollo brought it to Hera, explaining that he had only just acquired a new lyre from Hephaestus, and had no intention of losing this one also. She would have to take it to Zeus and suggest he drink it. Hera walked through the lofty halls and light-filled precincts until she came to a small dark chamber, which Zeus had now made his own. She had transferred the potion to a golden cup, to try and improve its appearance. As she poured it, she thought that if anything, she had achieved the reverse: the potion looked just as unappetizing, and somehow the cup looked worse.

'Husband?' she said.

He groaned in response.

'I have the centaur's medicine for you.' She pulled the thick curtain aside, and even the slight increase in light made Zeus groan again. 'Here.' He was lying on a couch, his head propped up on cushions, and she held out the cup.

He took it and drank in one long pull. His grimace showed her that it tasted at least as unpleasant as it looked. But he did not shout or hurl the heavy cup at his wife. He simply sank back into the cushions and waved her away.

Hera found herself in the upsetting position of being worried about her husband. She had no experience of this: the greatest threat to Zeus's wellbeing was usually her.

*

But in the days that followed his condition did not improve. The halls of Olympus – which always rang with music, arguments and chatter – had fallen silent. Hermes had found a sudden rash of messages to be delivered. Ares was fomenting some small war to keep out of the way. Aphrodite was distracting herself with a handsome lover somewhere. Artemis was away in the mountains hunting, Apollo had gone with her. Hera found herself wandering alone, hearing her footsteps echoing back from the surrounding mountain peaks. She was both anxious and bored.

She checked on her barely conscious husband in the earliest part of the day, when the bright glare of Helios would disturb him the least. And – with no one to talk to and a disquieting sense that she should be doing something she was not – she did not know what else to do with her time. Hera found herself returning each day to the forge to talk to her son. He was always happy to see her, always quick to offer her the curved chair he had made for her. He would listen to her for as long as she could talk. He made her little models of birds and animals, which she didn't need but she didn't want to hurt his feelings by refusing them. And anyway, who else was giving her presents?

One day, she wept as she told him her fears: that mortals would stop their sacrifices, that Zeus would never recover, that the Olympian gods were scattered to the winds. Her son could not bear to see her in pain.

'Let me come with you,' he said. 'I will talk to him. Perhaps I can help.'

Hera looked at the lame little blacksmith and did not have the heart to tell him that the king of the gods was not an automaton made of metal or wood. At least Hephaestus wanted to try, unlike the other gods who had made themselves scarce. She would still have refused his offer had she not realized in that moment that she wasn't even plotting revenge against the gods who were avoiding Olympus and abandoning her. What had things come to?

*

Hera and Hephaestus made slow, painful progress uphill from the forge. The uneven mountain paths were hard going for her son; Hera shortened her stride so he could keep up.

'Did you need to bring your axe?' she asked. Hephaestus flushed.

'I feel better if I have it,' he said. 'Or a hammer. In case someone needs something.'

Hera nodded, choosing not to embarrass him further. She led him past bright porticos and huge open halls. He was so used to the small forge, she thought. He looked uncomfortable in these larger spaces. But eventually they made their way to the chamber where Zeus lay. Hera reached out to pull the curtain aside and Hephaestus grabbed her arm in panic.

'You need to ask him if I can come in,' he said. 'I can't just walk into his room.'

'I doubt he'll even notice you're here,' Hera replied. Saying the words aloud made her feel more alone than when she had kept them to herself.

'Husband,' she murmured as the two of them entered. 'Husband, I have brought our son to see you.' Now seemed as good a time as any to amend the precise origins of the blacksmith god. Zeus let out a mighty howl.

'Good!' he said. 'Has he brought his tools?'

'I have,' said Hephaestus.

35

'Finally, some sense.' Zeus leaned forward and opened his eyes slightly.

'If you had asked for tools,' Hera began. But looking at the state of her husband, she decided not to continue.

'Where does it hurt?' asked Hephaestus.

Zeus pointed to the centre of his forehead. 'Here,' he said. 'It hurts as though my brain were at war with my skull.'

'That sounds agonizing,' Hephaestus said. 'Has it been getting worse?'

'Yes,' Zeus replied. 'At first it felt as though my jaw wanted to be rid of my teeth, and the pain spread from there through my whole head. But now, it has moved up and focused just here, above and between my eyes. My skull cannot contain whatever it is a moment longer.'

'I could take my axe,' said the blacksmith, 'and swing it right at that spot.'

'How would that help?' Hera asked.

'It might relieve the pressure of whatever is fighting to get out,' her son replied.

'You think there is something there?' Zeus raised his hand slowly, tracing his fingers across the crucial place. He could feel nothing. But that didn't mean there was nothing.

'I don't know,' Hephaestus said. 'Could you come into the light a bit more?'

'The light makes the pain worse,' Hera replied.

But Zeus closed his eyes and the blacksmith, who had moved so cautiously as they walked through the halls, bent down with a quick, efficient motion and lifted the couch – king of the gods and all – then carried it outside into the wide corridor. He moved in close and seemed to be examining each hair on the god's head.

'I think I can see something,' he said.

'I can't see anything,' his mother replied.

'What can you see?' Zeus asked him, eyes still closed tight.

'I don't know how to describe it. It's as though I can make out the shadow of something which is pacing about behind your eyes. It's angry and it won't stop moving,' he said.

'That is what it is,' Zeus agreed. 'Use your axe, set it free.'

'Are you absolutely sure you want to be hit in the head with an axe?' Hera asked. 'I think it's a marvellous idea,' she said to her son, before turning back to her husband. 'But I'm not completely certain I think it would make your head hurt less.'

'I have tried everything else,' Zeus said. 'Use the axe.'

Medusa

She had imagined her mother so many different ways.
Medusa sat on her favourite rock: smooth, shaded from the
brightest sun by a small outcrop above, an easier climb now
her legs had grown so long. She perched up here every
day, waving to her sisters if they glanced her way, so they
knew she was safe. She wasn't avoiding them exactly, but
sometimes she found she wanted to be on her own, so she
could consider things without having to explain what she
was thinking, or why.

Occasionally she thought about her father too, but she
knew more about him and anyway, she only had to look at
Euryale's flock to see that mothers were all that mattered
to their offspring, and the lambs were everything to their
mothers in return. If they became separated because one of
the lambs lost its footing, their distress was mutual. Euryale
would fly to help the trapped lamb, reunite them so the
frantic bleating would stop.

And that was what Medusa thought about as she sat
high over the waves, gazing out over the darkening sea. If
a sheep could be so devoted to its young, where was her

mother? Did she not know where Medusa was, or did she not care? Would she perhaps see her daughter if Medusa came to this high rock each day and sat there for a while?

The Gorgon girl looked out across the vast ocean and believed she could be seen in return. And she could, but not by her mother.

Amphitrite

Amphitrite, queen of the sea, swam among the dolphins in the cerulean shallows thinking about how her husband had wooed her. He had fallen in love with her voice, he said, which reminded him of water lapping at the shore. And she enjoyed his pursuit, the compliments and the gifts. But there was something about him that made her uncomfortable, so she did not succumb to his undeniable charms. If anyone had thought to ask her why, she might have said that the pleasure she took in his attention was always slightly tainted by the feeling she had that in addition to his charm, which was always on show to her, he was capable of devastating cruelty. She had heard faint rumours: never a whole story, but partial echoes of many, as though she were trying to hear them by pressing a seashell to her ear.

Eventually, her disquiet had exceeded her delight in the gifts and the attention and she fled from the god, and from the sea that was his domain. She hid herself away, picking a defender who she believed could keep her safe. Even the Earthshaker would think twice about taking on Atlas. The Titan had protected her from Poseidon's rage, but he could do little to keep her from Poseidon's continuing attention. Messengers were sent, every day, to beg her to return to the deep. If she swam, the fish would murmur that he loved her. If she stayed on the shore, the wind would whip the sand into patterns of waves. There was never a threat, save in the relentlessness of his pursuit. The dolphins, which Poseidon knew to be her favourite, were the next to come and plead his case.

He'll stop, Atlas said. One day he'll just lose interest and give up. And she smiled because she wanted it to be true, and because she wanted Atlas to feel that he was reassuring her. But she already knew what the Titan did not, which was that Poseidon would never give up. How does the sea win any of its battles? By attrition.

And over the days and months and years, Amphitrite felt the sharp edges of her resistance wearing down. Wouldn't it be easier, the dolphins asked (always so friendly), to return to the sea? And in the end, of course, it was easier. Easier to give in than to hold out. And Poseidon had been so delighted with her return, so pleased to make her his wife that he never mentioned the time she had kept him waiting, never hinted that it had been anything other than a delightful game of seduction from beginning to end.

And this was the pattern set for their marriage. Poseidon never showed his anger, and almost all traces of its expression were obliterated. If it weren't for the sudden darting fear she could sometimes sense in the creatures that filled the water around her, she could have believed everything was as he wanted it to appear. And certainly, he was far more careful of her feelings than Zeus was to his wife, Hera. Amphitrite had to make quite an effort to find out who her husband was pursuing, and – with one exception which she now somewhat regretted because her response had not shown her at her best – she rarely bothered. Hera was her inspiration in this: who seemed to be happier? Amphitrite, swimming with her dolphins in the bright blue waters of the sea, her warm skin stroked by the weeds and the fish? Or Hera, consumed with rage, lost in an endless repeating cycle of fruitless revenge?

So Amphitrite usually paid little heed to her husband unless he was in front of her, giving her another beautiful shell containing another glorious pearl. But on this occasion, she could not help knowing where his attentions were focused. He seemed to be idling in the Mediterranean shallows every day, returning to the same stretch of coast over and over again. She had almost swum into him twice, and it was unlike him to be so careless. But he had been watching the strange Gorgon girl for months now. At least, Amphitrite assumed it was the girl he was watching, and not her Gorgon sisters. The other two had been there for a long time, and Poseidon had never dallied in their waters before. It was the new one who had caught his eye. The Gorgons didn't fit anywhere, Amphitrite thought, except the lonely little beach they had chosen for themselves. But then, where could winged creatures, who were also daughters of Phorcys and Ceto, ever fit? Poor things. And yet, there was her husband spending every spare moment watching the girl who belonged half to the sea and half to the sky.

She didn't need to ask him where he had been when he returned to her that evening, but she did, for the pleasure of hearing him lie. Admiring the temple of Hera, he said, which had been built by the townspeople high on the promontory. The distance from the Gorgons was not so great as to make this an implausible answer: Amphitrite had seen the temple too. And she agreed, it was impressive even viewed from far away, in the sea. A second temple was being planned, Poseidon said, and he wanted these people to honour him. No, they were not a seafaring people, he admitted. They did not live on an island, their land was fertile, their cattle grew strong. But he wanted them to offer him a temple nonetheless.

Amphitrite nodded sympathetically and made the soothing sounds that had caught his interest so long ago: the waves of the sea breaking gently on soft sand. Of course he wanted a temple. Of course he must persuade them. Of course, of course, of course.

And as she teased her fingers through his damp, salty hair and agreed with his every wish, she wondered if she should warn the Gorgons of the danger their sister was in.

Athene

'Use the axe,' Zeus said again. 'Do it now.'

Hephaestus stepped to one side, transferred his weight to his back foot, and tested the axe in his hand. Everything was right. He swung the blade and then dropped it as a deafening voice bellowed at him to stop. Suddenly the halls were full of noise: every Olympian god had returned at once. It was the god of war, he thought afterwards, who had shouted. But as he looked around him, he saw a wall of faces judging him.

'I asked him to do it,' said Zeus. 'Don't interrupt him again.' He squinted a look of pure loathing at Ares.

'You asked him?' Apollo said. 'Have you lost your mind? Has he lost his mind?' he asked Hera.

She was standing behind Zeus, and she replied with a shrug.

'I must have lost it,' Zeus said. 'To give any credit at all to your half-horse friends and their half-cooked potions. How many poisonous draughts have you sent me? I have drunk the lot and the agony in my head has not eased at all. Now, here is a god who is actually trying to help me, and you all decide to interfere?'

'If you had said you wanted someone to split your skull with an axe,' Ares remarked, 'I could easily have done that for you months ago.'

'But you didn't,' Zeus said. 'You disappeared, all of you. Skulking in your temples, avoiding Olympus, avoiding me. You cowards. He,' he waved at Hephaestus, who was standing awkwardly, his axe limp in his strong hands, 'he stayed behind and offered to help. Now let him do what I ask.'

'Very well,' said Apollo, turning to Hephaestus. 'As you were.'

Again, Hephaestus raised his axe and shifted his weight back. And this time when he swung it down, no one intervened. There was a blinding flash of light and a crashing sound of metal on metal. Every god closed their eyes and covered their ears. Even Hephaestus was paralysed: bent forward, resting his weight on the handle of his axe, his force spent.

And before them all stood a goddess. Fully formed, fully armed, a bright golden helmet glinting in the mountain sun, a long slender spear in her right hand.

'Thank you,' she said, more irritated than grateful. 'I thought no one was ever coming to let me out.'

There was a pause.

'I can't pretend I was expecting that to happen,' Artemis murmured to Apollo.

'Me neither,' he said. 'And I know centaurs.'

Their eyes – like those of every god around them – were trained on their newest addition, who looked back at them without enthusiasm. Her skin was almost translucently pale, so long had she been in the darkness. She had strong, slender limbs (though she wasn't tall – the helmet added to her height), and deft hands. Her expression was that of someone lacking patience but trying to hide it. Ares shifted from one foot to the other, uneasy at the sight of this warrior goddess. Artemis wondered if she knew how to use that spear. Hera said nothing, her face a mask.

It was Hephaestus – so accustomed to seeing a dazzling creation before him – who looked behind the new goddess to see what had happened to Zeus. The king of the gods was gazing at his new creation in wonder and rubbing his forehead with relief. There was no trace of a mark to show where Hephaestus had struck.

'Daughter!' he said, grandly.

The new goddess turned and looked at him appraisingly. 'Is that right?' she said.

Medusa

Euryale liked humans. She knew Sthenno preferred to avoid them, finding their fragility strange and unpleasant. But even before Medusa came to them, Euryale used to fly inland and watch them. She liked the way they were so prone to anxiety and haste. She liked the houses they made for themselves to sleep inside. She liked the huge temples they managed to build. She would return to the coast to tell Sthenno of all she had seen, but she knew her sister was only listening because she was kind.

But Medusa was different. She asked for the stories over and over again, correcting Euryale if she changed any detail. She pestered both sisters to be allowed to see people whenever she could. She loved seeing children, just as she loved it when their horned sheep produced lambs. And as she had grown older, her love for mortals only increased. 'They don't even have wings,' Sthenno said, one morning when Medusa was pleading for the three of them to go and see the new temple, which had been built a little way along the coast. The Gorgons could see it from the top of their own rocky heights, though it was on a loftier promontory. 'I wonder how they got the columns up so high.'

'We could ask them if we went to look,' Medusa said. 'Please.'

'Not today,' Sthenno said. 'There are things I need to do today.'

'But—'

'Another day,' Euryale said. The sheep needed milking and she had a feeling one of them was sickening with something. She had penned the little creature away from the others, on the far side of the shore.

'I could go on my own,' Medusa said.

Her sisters looked at one another. She could go on her own. She was of an age when humans did things alone, Euryale realized. And although it took a physical effort to remember, she was no longer a baby.

'How many summers have you been here?' Sthenno asked, suspicious.

'I remember thirteen,' said Medusa. 'How many do you remember?' she asked Euryale.

'Three more,' Euryale said, after a moment of counting. She thought of her flock of sheep growing through the years, the first lambs, the first deaths. She remembered Medusa being there each time: crawling, then standing, then walking unsteadily, then running. 'Yes.' She nodded at her sceptical sister. 'She has been with us for sixteen summers.'

'If I was mortal, my parents would let me go and see a temple,' Medusa said, turning from one sister to the other. 'Please. I think they're starting another one, I'm sure I saw them marking out the space. I want to see.'

*

Medusa wasn't afraid to be travelling alone. She was often on her own in the caves where they lived, or on the rocks around their patch of the shore. She was never far from her sisters, and she enjoyed the brief sense of solitude she felt when she left them behind. She unfurled her wings and flew the short distance to the temple precincts. Now she was close to it, she was even more dazzled by the ingenuity and grandeur. Vast sturdy columns were topped by a brightly painted frieze, and Medusa wondered how mortals standing at their base would ever be able to see the story of the war between Gods and Titans – a story her sisters had told her many times – without craning their necks. The whole edifice seemed to have been designed to be admired by someone who could fly. She fluttered up to look more closely at the painted figures, which ran all the way around the outside edge of the roof: the blues, reds and yellows each catching her eye in turn. She followed the story around, panel by panel: the Titans rising up against Zeus, the Olympian gods banding together to subdue them. When she landed back on the ground, she wondered where the mortals were: she could see none. She wanted to look inside the temple, but Sthenno had taught her to be careful of scaring humans who were apt to scream and run away if they saw a Gorgon. Perhaps they had already seen her approaching the temple and hidden. Still, she stood behind a column and pushed open one wooden door, just a little, hoping not to alarm anyone. She peered inside, her eyes accustomed to the darkness of her cave. She saw a pair of bright unblinking eyes staring right at her and she gasped before realizing they belonged to a statue.

She smiled as she pushed the door further, and stepped

inside. The statue was so impressive: no wonder it had made her jump. The goddess sat proudly on her grand chair, her skin glowing white, her helmet, spear and shield painted gold. Her eyes were remarkable: Medusa didn't know what could have made them such a piercing blue. She had never seen such a thing and yet she knew it was a perfect likeness, and that the goddess had just such eyes herself. She crept a little closer, admired the drapery of the statue's dress, reached out to touch it, but pulled her hand back when she heard a noise behind her.

'Don't stop on my account. I must say, it's rather a good likeness of my niece.'

Medusa turned to see who was speaking. A tall, well-muscled man was standing in the shadows of the colonnade by the door she had just used. He must have been waiting to follow her in, she thought, when he could simply have spoken to her outside. He had long black hair, curling down past his neck. His eyes were dark green and cold.

'Your niece?' she said. 'Is that who it is?'

'Of course,' he replied. 'That is Athene. Can't you tell from the helmet and the spear?'

'I didn't know she had those,' Medusa said. 'My sisters don't always mention what people are wearing when they tell the stories.'

He laughed, but she could tell the laughter was false. It did not sound like Sthenno laughing, when she caught herself doing something ridiculous, or like Euryale when she was entertained by the antics of their sheep. It sounded like – Medusa searched for the words to define something unfamiliar – like the laughter of someone who wanted to be thought amused, though they were not.

'Why are you pretending to laugh?' she asked.

The man stopped laughing immediately. 'I wasn't laughing at your sisters,' he said.

'You weren't laughing at all,' Medusa replied.

'I was thinking how funny it is,' he continued as though she had not spoken, 'that you are the daughter of a sea god and a sea goddess, and yet you only know your immortal kin through stories.'

Medusa did not know what to say to this, since the man was lying to her, and she had no idea why. She found herself wishing suddenly that Euryale had left her sheep for a while and come with her. Or that the priestess of the mighty goddess Athene were present. Or that the tall man wasn't so close to the door.

'How do you think I should know them?' she said. She moved to the side of the statue and the man moved silently in the same direction, so the distance between them was lessened.

'I think your sisters should have taken you to Mount Olympus to meet your ethereal family,' he said. 'Or perhaps they could have brought you to my kingdom instead. My borders lap up against your shore, after all.'

'Are you my father?' she asked. And this time his laughter was real, but again it sounded wrong. She realized it was because it was tinged with contempt. 'No, child. Phorcys is a very minor god, compared to his king.'

'Poseidon,' she said. 'Don't you usually have a trident?'

'Do I need one?' he asked. 'I thought your sisters didn't mention what the gods wear and carry.'

She stared at him, wondering why he didn't like her sisters.

51

'I don't know what you use it for,' she said.

'Attacking Titans,' he replied. 'You saw me on the frieze outside.'

'That's why you don't have it, then? Because the Titans were overthrown.'

'Exactly. So now I only carry it because I am used to it,' he said. 'But sometimes it gets in the way.'

'When you visit temples to look at your niece.'

'That's not quite why I'm here.'

Medusa opened her mouth to ask why he was here, before realizing she didn't at all want to know his answer. 'What's she like?' she asked instead.

'Athene? She's . . .' He thought for a moment. 'She's sharp. Sharp-eyed, like you see here. Sharp-tongued, often. Sharp-edged. She's quick to take offence and ruthless when she takes revenge. Zeus spoils her, and it makes her less pleasant than she might otherwise be. She's very quick to go crying to him if she doesn't get her way.'

Medusa looked back at the statue. 'I wonder what she'd say about you,' she said.

'I'm sure she would say that I am handsome and charming and that you should stop wondering if you could reach the door before I reached you, because you already know the answer is no.'

There was absolute silence. Medusa thought of the sheep and the eagle that had tried to steal one and again she wished Euryale was with her now.

'It wouldn't make any difference anyway, would it?' she said.

'Not really,' he replied. 'I am wherever the sea is, and you can't be with your sisters all the time.'

'So what happens now?'

'Now you submit to a power greater than your own.'

Medusa was never aware of it when she was with her sisters, because there was always the sound of the sea and the wind and the gulls and the cormorants and their flock. But in this silent space, she was conscious of being the only one whose breath could be heard. It made her feel weak. 'What if I don't want to?' she asked.

'You will want to,' he shrugged. 'Why wouldn't you want to? I am one of the Olympian gods. You should feel honoured that I am singling you out in such a way. It is a privilege you have done nothing to earn. I have seen you and decided to bestow my favour upon you. It wouldn't occur to you not to want to. It will occur to you to say thank you, I suppose.'

Medusa could not say why she suddenly felt less afraid, though her dislike of the god was in no way diminished. It was, perhaps, his tremendous self-regard, which meant that even though he was so much more powerful than her, and so intent on exploiting the disparity between them, she felt rather sorry for him. Imagine being a god, she thought, and still needing to tell everyone how impressive you were. 'You cause the earthquakes,' she said, 'that make the sand shimmer on the shore.'

'I strike my trident on the bed of the sea,' he agreed, 'and the earth trembles at my command.'

'Why do you do it?' she asked.

Again, she thought she saw a glint of weakness, as Poseidon straightened his back but somehow managed to look slightly shorter. 'Because I can.'

'Could you smash this temple and send it tumbling into the sea?' she asked.

He nodded. 'The columns would shatter and the roof would collapse,' he said. 'Although it's probably too far from the edge of the cliff for it to fall into the sea. The columns might roll, I suppose.'

'I'm not asking you to prove it,' she said.

'I don't need to prove it,' he snapped. 'The humans are building my temple now, to Poseidon Earthshaker. You must have seen the site as you flew here.'

'Oh, is that going to be a temple to you?' she asked. 'I wonder why they did this one first.'

'I imagine they were honing their skills,' he said.

'Do you think so? I would have thought they would do the most important gods first. But then, I suppose they would have built one for Zeus first, wouldn't they?'

'Not necessarily. Not everyone thinks that Zeus is the god most worthy of honour.'

'Oh, don't they?'

'No. Seafaring people have always built temples to my majesty.'

'Well, yes, I suppose seafaring people would. But these people obviously value you, because they're building your temple now.'

'Of course.'

'I suppose they just honoured your niece first because they value her skills, and perhaps they don't travel much by sea.'

'They have little need to travel anywhere,' he said. 'Their land is fertile, their livestock are strong.'

'Perhaps they should build a temple to Demeter next?'

'You're trying to make me angry.'

'I wouldn't have thought I had that power.'

He stared at her, his green eyes glittering in the half-light. 'I'm beginning to wonder if you do. Where did you learn to be so brazen?'

'I didn't know I was,' she said. 'And I'm sure you know the answer already, since you seem to have been watching me. My sisters taught me to be like them.'

'But you aren't like them, are you? You don't have their physical power, you don't have their immortality. There is only a pair of wings differentiating you from any other girl. Your sisters are monsters, with their tusks and their snaking manes of hair. You have very little in common with them at all.'

'My sisters aren't monsters.'

This, then, explained why he did not like them. He was appalled by their appearance. Medusa wanted to laugh but she was still afraid. As if anything that was important about Sthenno or Euryale was visible in their teeth or their hair.

'Aren't you loyal?' he said. 'Can love really have blinded you so much?'

'You're the one who is blind, if you can't see anything beyond a pair of tusks.'

'Euryale has two sets of tusks, I believe.'

'It doesn't matter what you believe,' she replied.

'You cannot possibly fail to see what anyone else could see,' he said. 'Why do you think I have picked you and not one of your sisters? You know you are beautiful, you know they are not.'

'I know when you talk of beauty you mean something different from what I mean.'

'I see.' He took a step towards her, and she forced herself

not to take a step back. 'So what do you mean by beauty, little Gorgon?'

'Euryale tends every one of her sheep like it is a child. Sthenno learned to cook so she could feed me when I was little. They care about me and protect me. That is beauty.'

'Neither of them is protecting you now.'

'You waited until I was alone.'

'I did. Very well, if these qualities are so valuable to you, if you really claim to believe that caring and tending are beautiful, when it is so common it is not even limited to humans – any animal cares for its young – then prove it.'

'How?'

'Come here,' he said, and he strode towards her, grabbing her hand. She wanted to pull away from him, but she knew immediately that however strong she was, he was much stronger. There was a clamminess to his touch, a smell of seaweed emanating from his skin. He dragged her to the columns closest to the sea, and pushed his hand against her back, forcing her to look across the wide promontory.

'Look,' he said. 'Out there, towards my temple. What do you see?'

She was sure the group of girls had not been there when she entered Athene's temple.

'You already know what I can see,' she said. 'I see a group of girls, talking and laughing together.'

'Are they beautiful?' he asked.

'Yes,' she replied.

'Why?'

'Because they are young and happy and together,' she said.

She could feel the irritation in the fingers that pressed against her.

'They are ordinary,' he said. 'Look again.'

And she did as he demanded but she could not see what he saw. 'It's because you have spent all these years with no one but your sisters for company. If you had grown up with other girls your own age . . .'

'If I had grown up with other girls my own age, you would have thought me ordinary too.'

'Not true,' he said. 'I would have admired those ringlets and those arching eyebrows. I would have approved of your long, straight nose and the way your wide mouth is ready to smile. I would have desired you in just the same way if you had grown up among all these girls. You would still have been extraordinary.'

'You're just guessing,' she said. 'You can't know that, you just think I want to hear it.' She felt the tension in his muscles as she said it, and she knew she was right. He was so very sure of his own charm. 'But I don't.'

'Very well,' he replied. 'Have it your way. You are nothing more than an ordinary girl with ordinary immortal sisters, and everyone is equally beautiful because you say so. Is that right?'

He grabbed her by the shoulder and spun her to face him. She could feel the pillar pressing against her back, and the smell of salt and anger on his face. 'You value them all so highly, you think caring for the weak is so important. Prove it to me and to yourself.'

She stared at his dark green eyes and loathed him.

'You can't prove what you believe,' she said. 'You can only believe it.'

'That is obviously not true,' he said. 'You believe you can fly, and I believe it too. We could prove it by taking you to the edge of the cliff and pushing you off it.'

'Flying isn't a matter of opinion,' she said.

'Nor is beauty.'

'I don't agree with you.'

He leaned close and hissed into her mouth. 'I will take one of those girls, Medusa. Any one, you can choose. I will take her to the deepest part of the ocean and I will have her until she drowns. Do you understand? I will rape her and she will die of it, because that is what it means to be weak.'

'They will knock down your temple and never worship you again.'

'Men will worship me across the world.' He shrugged. 'These ones hardly matter.'

She saw all his vanity and pettiness, and wondered why mortals worshipped any god like this.

'Or,' he said. 'Look at me.'

She could not bring herself to meet his eyes, but he reached out and took her chin, held her face so she could not look away.

'Or I will have you. Here, now, in the temple. You've made your disdain for the idea quite clear. So let us see how much you love these mortals. How much you value caring for the weak, like your sisters do.'

She stared at him in disgust. 'If I agree to this, you'll leave them alone?'

He shrugged. 'I might.'

'Then yes,' she said.

'They will never repay your affection. Do you understand that?'

She nodded.

'They will fear you and flee you and call you a monster, just like they do your sisters.'

'It doesn't matter what they think of me.'

'Then why do you want to protect them?'

'Because I can,' she said.

Euryale

When Medusa returned to their cave that night, she was quiet and scared and neither of them knew what to say to change it. She stayed inside the cave the following day, and didn't want to come out. She didn't want to see the light, she said. Didn't want to talk, or fish, or swim. She wanted to sit in the darkness as far from the sea as she could get.

'Come outside,' Sthenno pleaded.

At first, she replied that she was busy, then that she didn't want to. Then she stopped replying altogether. Sthenno and Euryale didn't know what to do. Sthenno was hurt that their girl was avoiding them, worried that she had said or done something wrong. Neither of them knew the labyrinthine caves well enough to find her if she didn't want to be found. But Euryale was less prone to self-doubt. Unable to imagine what might have provoked their sister to withdraw from them, she behaved as though Medusa were an injured sheep: she kept her distance, left food on a small flat rock just inside the cave entrance. The food was gone the next day, but still there was no sign of Medusa.

On the third day, Sthenno was so distressed that Euryale

agreed to go and look for her. She crept into the cave,
waiting for her eyes to adjust to the darkness. The further
she went, the darker it became, and she found herself
reaching out a clawed hand so she could follow the cave
wall. Beneath her feet she felt the sand thinning and hard
rock poking through. She became suddenly worried that
she might lose her way altogether, and turned to look back
at the way she had come. There was a faint light behind
her, she was relieved to see. Though when she turned back
to the darkness, it seemed blacker than ever and she had
to wait again for her eyes to adapt. She was peering into
darkness within darkness, trying to assess whether she was
looking at a tunnel which Medusa might be hiding within,
or whether it was simply a small recess that led nowhere.

'Medusa,' she called. Her girl wouldn't ignore her now
she had come into the caves, she was certain. And she was
right.

'Please leave me alone.'

'I can't, my love,' said Euryale. 'Sthenno is so worried.'

'You can tell her not to be.'

'I can, but it doesn't help. She needs to see you and talk
to you. You know what she's like.'

'I know.'

'Please will you come outside?' Euryale asked. She had
no idea how far she had travelled, but her feet were now
walking on solid rock, no trace of sand left.

'I can't,' said Medusa.

'Why not?'

'I'm afraid,' she replied.

No one could see Euryale, as she stood in the blackness.
Medusa was further along the path, which twisted and

turned, and even with a torch she would have been unable to see her sister because solid rock separated them. Sthenno was outside pacing, fretting on the shore. The rays of Helios could never penetrate this gloom, and the waters of the ocean could not reach it. But in this moment – though no-one could know it – Medusa was proved right. Her sister was indeed beautiful. Her jaw softened, her solid brow creased, her bulbous eyes filled with tears.

'Afraid, my love? Of what?'

'Of the sea,' Medusa said.

'Of the sea? But you are a child of the sea.' Euryale was confused. Medusa had always loved the water. One of Euryale's fondest memories was of the child running into the waves and out again, her wet feet picking up tails of dried seaweed and dragging them along behind her, a watery comet.

'Afraid of him.'

Euryale had been edging forward, hoping to find her sister by touch. But at this moment, she stopped dead. She asked nothing more; she knew who Medusa meant and what she had endured. 'Come to me,' she said quietly.

In a moment, Euryale found her arms filled by her sister's warm, shaking body. She could not see her eyes swollen with tears, but she felt the wetness soaking her breast. She stroked Medusa's hair, unfurled her wings and wrapped them around her, like a shell. 'Let's go to Sthenno,' she said. 'She misses you so much.'

Medusa nodded through her sobs. They made their slow, steady way back to the cave entrance, back to the light. When they reached it, they found Sthenno peering inside, desperate to know what was happening, but staying where she had promised Euryale she would wait. She did not say anything when Euryale put Medusa in her arms, she simply held her, and shushed her, and told her everything would be alright.

Euryale was unrecognisable from the softened creature she had become in the darkness. She stepped away from her sisters, and flew across the shore. She stood at the scar that ran along their beach and she turned to face the sea.

'You will never touch her again, do you hear me?' she screamed. The winds did not dare to answer her, and the seabirds kept their silence. 'Never.'

And with this, she raised herself in the air and smashed her feet onto the scarred rock. There was a tremor, and the sea itself felt fear. She rose again and smashed the scar a second time. This time, the tremor was greater. Once more she drove her mighty Gorgon heels into the ground, and the rock finally gave way. There was an almighty crashing sound as the water rushed away, and a terrible scraping shriek, as the rock split in two. The sky seemed to darken but it did not want to challenge her. She stood triumphant as her portion of the shore rose up, conquering its rival.

The sea had now retreated: it flooded over the lower expanse of rock but could only lap at the pedestal Euryale had created. The Gorgon shore was raised; the sea had receded into the distance, damp weeds and gasping fish left in its wake. She flew back to her sisters.

'There,' she said. 'You never need to be afraid of him again.'

Stone

The first statue is a mistake. But the little bird has been caught so perfectly that you would never know. It is perching on a branch, its small talons wrapped tightly around. It is sleek, and looks soft to the touch: its downy chest feathers have been particularly well done. It sits up, its eyes alert, its beak poised to eat any insect that flies too close. Its wings seem to slot into its long tail feathers, like parts of a child's toy.

Because it is made of stone, it is missing the colours of the real bird: the beak and the stripes across the eyes should be black, the back a deep red brown, fading to a pale orange. The chest and wings are bright blue, and the throat is saffron yellow.

If someone were to paint these details onto the little bird, it would be exquisite. Even as it is, you can barely resist the temptation to reach out and stroke it.

Part Two

Mother

Danaë

Danaë never doubted for a moment that her father loved her, which is how it was so easy for him to imprison her in a small room with thick walls and almost no light. He didn't tell her that he had consulted the Oracle, nor did he mention the prophecy it had shared with him: that his daughter would bear a son who would one day take her father's life. Acrisius was a vain man who had always enjoyed having a daughter and never wanted a son, though he didn't admit this: he could not have tolerated watching his own body become frail as his son grew stronger. But a daughter was different, and the passage of time pained him less as he watched her grow to adulthood.

He had visited the Oracle in good faith, he told himself, wanting to know that although he had no son, he would have a grandson to inherit his kingdom of Argos. His city was powerful and he was both proud and defensive of it: he did not want to die and have it fall into his brother's hands. He would rather see it go to a stranger. But most of all, he wanted it to go to his own heir. And so he rode the rocky paths to Delphi and made his offerings to the god and the priestess and asked what his future held. And what he heard was that his daughter's son would kill him.

He left Delphi a sorry man. As he rode slowly home along the dusty stone-strewn paths, he wondered if he might have preferred not knowing. His daughter was unmarried; he might have spent many happy, unworried years with her and a grandchild not yet born. Perhaps he would be old when the child finally killed him, old and frail with his mind wandering, in need of release. Perhaps it would be an accident: his grandson's horse rearing, the branch of a tree onto which the child had climbed falling. Acrisius's own horse trod wearily on beneath him as he thought of how he might die. The Oracle had ostensibly given him an answer, but it had raised a much larger question. He listened to his horse's hooves striking the ground, and with each sound all he heard was when, when, when. By the time he was nearing home, he had barely spoken for three days. He did not want to die, not now, not soon, not at all. And so he locked his daughter – the only person he had ever loved – in a small cell beneath his palace so she could not produce a baby who would hurt him.

Danaë heard this story through a small gap in the thick walls of her cell. Her maid brought her food each day, liberally seasoned with her own tears: Danaë was loved by everyone, even the men who had bundled her into the cell and walled her up. Her maid interrogated the slaves who'd accompanied her father to Delphi and reported back to his bewildered daughter. Had the king lost his mind, had the Oracle demanded this cruellest of punishments?

Gradually, she came to understand that her father's fear

of death – which had always made him hate his brother, since he looked at his twin and saw an ageing mirror – was the cause of her unhappiness. And because she was a loving daughter and a kind-hearted woman, she sympathized. No one could help being afraid of something. And being afraid of dying must be especially awful, because there was no hope of avoiding it. She knew too that Acrisius – never a sociable man – must be lonely, sitting in the palace with no one but slaves for company and the only person he had ever loved locked away beneath his feet. And yet, she found her sympathy had its limits. How could her father be so afraid of death that he would refuse to live? And how could he be so afraid of his own death that he would hasten his daughter to hers?

She began to wonder how she might free herself from this prison. Bribing the slaves was the most obvious place to start. But then she heard from her maid that the king had freed the slaves who knew his daughter, replaced them with others to whom she was only a name. Each day she was locked away, she could feel herself becoming smaller and paler, more forgotten. She found it increasingly hard to keep track of time, and quickly found she didn't know how long she had been in the cell. Her grasp on what was and what was not became less and less sure. Certainly, when Zeus appeared above the small cot on which she slept, she was not as surprised as she might have expected to be.

'How did you get inside here?' she asked, having opened her eyes to find a large figure glowing gold beside her.

'I rained in through the gaps in your roof,' he said.

'I see,' she replied. 'And you are –?'

'Zeus,' he said.

'Have you come to free me from my prison?' she asked.

'I hadn't,' he said. 'But I could.'

In his palace, on his own, Acrisius was steadily falling apart. What was the point in seeing, hearing, tasting anything if there was no one with whom he could share it? The old slaves – the ones he had known since his youth – had all been thrown out; the new ones shunned him because his temper was so unpredictable. Only now did he fully understand the choice he had made: he was alive, but not living. Daily, he thought of asking to have his daughter returned to him. But then the fear of death would rise up again and he would see the father of his future assassin in every man's face. He wanted to believe in his daughter's virtue, and he did. But he would not bet his life on it.

Danaë heard of her father's declining spirits from her maid, but she could not spare a great deal of energy for it. Her affair with Zeus had been briefly pleasurable, and the resulting pregnancy was not unwelcome. She too had missed having someone to talk to. But her loneliness had been assuaged first by Zeus, and then by the baby that she proudly carried. The cell no longer held her: Zeus had made short work of that. But she could not return to her father's side, nor did she want to. Would he try to imprison her again? Or worse? Would Zeus allow it? She was now visibly expecting a child, which could only make the fearful king more agitated. The slaves who had worked at the palace before his ill-fated trip to Delphi were pleased to help her though, and she found herself living with her maid in a small house nearby, where the women spoke of the king as though he were already dead.

Danaë spent several happy months with these women until the day her son was born. Her maid lived with her mother and her unmarried sisters. The married ones lived nearby and there was always company. In many ways, she preferred life in this bustling little home – always full of women and children and food and laundry spilling outside to bleach in the sun – to the empty life she had known in the palace. The more time she spent away from her father, the more she began to realize that his Delphic trip had only aggravated what had always been true of him. He had always been defensive, had seen every stranger as a potential threat rather than a possible friend. Their beautiful, light-filled palace had always felt cold. Surrounded by these women who understood her pregnancy better than she did herself, she felt nothing but joy when she contemplated the birth of her child. Zeus would not let anything go wrong, she was sure.

And her confidence was rewarded. The women all said it was the easiest birth they had ever witnessed: her son was beautiful and alive, and so was she. In the fuzzy aftermath of it all, as she looked at his tiny closed eyes and fists, she thought she would take him to meet her father, and that he would see he had been mad and wrong to fear this tiny, perfect boy. And then she remembered the darkness in her father's eyes on the day he had her locked away, crazed with fear of something that would never happen. She didn't trust him any more, and never would. So in the moments after becoming her son's mother, she ceased to be her father's child. Still, she should have guessed that someone would betray her to the king.

Danaë felt nothing through the whole terrifying experience of discovery and retribution. She was numb, as though it were happening to a stranger and she was watching it from far away. She must have spoken to her father, must have pleaded with him, and with the men who grabbed at her and dragged her outside. And somewhere in her memory must be the final words she said to her father, or that he said to her, but they were lost to her for good.

All she was sure of was that she had been cocooned in a haze of love and fatigue, and then there had been shouting and wrenching and glaring sun and an open sea and then darkness. And the only constant through this time was the weight of her soft child in her arms, her chin tucked down to protect his head, the faint smell of sour milk as she inhaled. And then she was lost for ever on the ocean waves.

Athene

'You need to intervene if you're going to save that girl you like, Father,' Athene said. The new goddess no longer felt new. She had settled into life on Mount Olympus with ease. She didn't like anyone particularly, and none of the other gods seemed fond of her either, except for Zeus. Athene assumed his favour was what caused the others to be so aloof, and it only made her more prickly.

But Olympus was a nest of temporary alliances and rival irritations, so she fitted in perfectly well. Yes, Hera despised her, but Hera despised everyone save Hephaestus. Hephaestus stared at her as though he had carved her himself from gold and marble, but was too afraid to speak to her. Ares was threatened by her, she could tell. Poseidon – when he was there – assessed her and then dismissed her. Aphrodite never noticed her, no matter what she did. Apollo and Artemis always ignored her. Demeter was kind enough but lacked any interest; Hermes feigned interest but couldn't be bothered to feign kindness.

But Zeus loved her. He was proud of his clever, argumentative daughter, and often took her side in disputes with the other gods. And since Athene would always rather be right than happy, and would rather win than be right, this worked out well for everyone. In return, she tried to help him with his affairs. And on this occasion, that meant noticing something Poseidon should really have seen first. Which was that one of Zeus's offspring (and one of his lovers) had been set loose on the open sea in what looked – at least from up on the heights of Olympus – like a wooden chest.

'Which girl?' Zeus asked lazily. He assumed that Hera was busying herself turning one of his favourite girls into a cow or a weasel or whatever, which meant it may well be too late to intervene and save her. Although there was always the possibility that the world had just gained an attractive new cow, so all was not lost.

'Danaë,' Athene said.

'Which one is that?' he asked.

'The one whose father was keeping her in a prison cell so she couldn't get pregnant,' Athene replied.

Zeus frowned. 'Did it work?'

'No. You turned yourself into golden droplets and rained down on her through the gaps in the roof.'

'Oh yes!' He smiled. 'That was a good one. She was lovely. Young, pretty, desperate for company.'

'I imagine she was.'

'What happened to her?'

'You got her pregnant.'

'Marvellous. Will I have a new demi-god roaming the earth?'

'You already do.'

'That's wonderful.'

'He's about to drown.'
'Oh. Let me—'
And in a small whirlwind, Zeus was gone.

Danaë

The chest in which Danaë's father had shut her and Perseus – another prison cell, smaller and more dangerous than the last – came to rest on the shore of Seriphos. Danaë didn't know it was an island, nor that it was in the middle of the Aegean, nor that Zeus had asked Poseidon himself to guide her and her baby to safety there. She didn't even know for a while that she had reached dry land: the swell of the ocean was in her bones now, and she would always feel it.

She had lain quite still in the chest for so many hours, perhaps days. She knew vessels capsized and sank, and she had no idea what provoked or prevented this: she had never even been on a boat. Unable to swim, she did not dare move. So she was lying inside when the chest was cautiously opened. She blinked hard into the dazzling sun, still holding her baby tight. The dark silhouette of a man moved quickly to one side, blocking the light from her eyes so she could see.

'I didn't mean to blind you,' said the man. 'I didn't know someone was inside.'

She tried to tell him that it didn't matter, and of course

76

he couldn't have known she was inside a chest, and to ask him who he was and where she was and if it was safe, but her throat was too dry and all that came out was a croak.

'Wait,' he said, and reached beneath the edge of the chest, where he must have placed his belongings before using both hands to open the lid. He brought a wineskin into view, and offered it to her. She wanted it desperately but could not let go of her son to take it.

'Here,' he said. 'Let me help you.'

She flinched as he reached into the chest and his hand brushed her hair. 'I'm sorry, if we can just get you sitting up, you can drink,' he said. 'If I give it to you as you lie there, I'm worried you'll choke.'

This was such a sensible, normal thing for someone to say that Danaë forgot her fear. This man did not want her dead. He pushed his hand beneath her shoulders, and helped her to sit. She drew her knees up, to protect the baby. The man undid the stopper of the wineskin and held it closer, so she could take it with one hand. She snatched at it and he stepped back. She was relieved to discover that she was drinking water, not wine, and she drank it greedily.

'You're safe now,' the man said. 'Let me get you some more water?'

'Yes please,' she tried to say, but she couldn't make a sound yet, so she just nodded, and felt herself coming back to life.

The man disappeared for a few moments but returned with a fresh skin of water. She drank again, trying to finish it all before he took it away.

'You keep that,' he said. 'We can refill it at the spring up there, when you are recovered enough to walk.' She didn't loosen her grip on it. 'If you can't walk up there, I will go and get you some more,' he continued. 'There's no need to worry. You won't be thirsty now.'

She nodded again. Her throat was still too painful for speech.

'I'm thinking, given how thirsty you are, that you might be hungry as well,' he said. 'When you've had time to adjust to not being thirsty, or seasick, or afraid. So this is what I suggest we do: I give you my hand to help you out of your little boat.' He smiled at her, and she tried to smile back, but her lips cracked and she stopped. 'You can wait on those rocks while I build a fire and I will cook you some of the fish I caught today. Or we can go to my house – it's just up there, on the ridge, you can see the roof from here – and then you can have bread with your fish, if you'd like. I also have clean tunics, because you might want one of those as I reckon the one you're wearing is probably scratching your skin now. Salt water is an itchy thing once it dries, isn't it?'

She nodded.

'And as and when you get your voice back, you can tell me your name and the name of this handsome young hero,' he said. 'I'm Dictys, fisherman and finder of women who wash up on the shores of Seriphos.'

Some hours later, full of baked fish and fresh bread, Danaë managed to tell him her name, and the name of her son. He gave her a room to sleep in, with a proper bed and a small window. He found a flat basket and a blanket, so the baby could sleep comfortably by her side. When she woke in the night – which was often – she would jump up from the bed to listen to her son's breathing, and then look out of the window to check the stars were all still there and that the blackness of night was not total. She would do this every night for the rest of her life.

*

It took several days for her to tell her story to the fisherman. He would leave silently before she was awake and return after the middle of the day, carrying his catch. Only when she had begun to recover from her ordeal did she notice the appearance of the man who had freed her from her second prison: stocky, hair bleached by sun and salt, bright green eyes shining from his leathery face, nose bent from an old break. In her Argive life she might have described him as kindly and paternal, but her perspective on these matters had shifted. He lived in this spacious house alone with no company. He cooked his fish and his bread each day and drank his wine well watered. It was such a simple life that Danaë almost choked on a fishbone when – after listening to the story of her father's descent into paranoia and cruelty – he told her that he had also witnessed insanity descend upon a king.

'There's nothing to be done when it strikes them,' Dictys said. 'Any attempts at reasoning with them just make it worse. Because they convince themselves you're the threat.'

'I didn't have the chance to reason with him anyway,' she said, thinking again of the raging glint in her father's eyes and the fear behind them. 'It was all so fast.'

'It is natural for a man to fear for his life, I suppose,' replied Dictys. 'But to turn on his only child? And to be so afraid of an infant who could not possibly do him harm?

It's hard to imagine what could make a man behave in such a way. The gods must have sent him out of his wits.'

Danaë wondered if she should tell her rescuer that she knew from an unimpeachable source that the gods had had nothing to do with her father's madness, but she decided she had probably told him enough for now, and changed the subject.

'What happened to your king?' she asked.

Dictys reached for the ladle and served them both more wine. 'He believed his younger brother wanted to displace him.'

'And did he?'

'No.'

'Did he hear a prophecy like my father?'

'No.' Dictys leaned over the table and looked hard at his cup. 'No, he didn't need one to rouse his suspicions. He was always angry with his brother, even when they were both boys.'

'Why?' She tried to read his expression, or at least work out what he was studying on the wine cup.

'Who knows? Brothers don't always get on, do they?'

As he turned the cup in his hand, she saw it showed Prometheus stealing fire from the gods.

'No, I suppose they don't,' she said. 'So what did the king's brother do?'

'As you see.' Dictys smiled as he gestured at the room in which they both sat, plain but comfortable with everything he needed in its place.

'You're the brother of the king?' she asked.

'I am,' he said, dropping his head in a small bow.

'But you're a fisherman.'

'You of all people, Danaë, know why. At the palace I was putting my brother on his guard and myself in danger. I like the sea, I enjoy my own company. I'm happier living this way. It's much safer than a wooden box.' She shivered. 'Ah, I'm sorry,' he said. 'But your tale has brought back painful memories for me.'

'When did you last see him?' she asked.

'Years ago,' he said. 'I live a quiet life here. And you and your boy are welcome to stay for as long as you'd like. If you'd prefer to be in the town, I will take you inland and find you somewhere safe.'

'Thank you,' she said. 'We'll stay here for now. You're very kind.'

'Fishermen have a rule that if you find a shipwrecked sailor, you have to offer him a safe haven,' he said. 'If I failed to extend that courtesy to you, the fish would swim away from my boat and I would starve.'

She saw he was smiling and also serious. And she knew now that Zeus had protected her after all.

Athene

'I want a thing,' she said to Zeus. 'Everyone else has one.'

'What sort of thing, dearest?' asked her father.

'You have thunderbolts,' she said.

His chest puffed up. 'I do,' he replied. 'You can't have thunderbolts. They are indivisible from my nature. People call me Zeus the Thunderer.'

'I don't want thunderbolts,' she said. 'I want something of my own. Like Apollo has a lyre and he has a bow. He has two things. I don't even have one. Artemis has a bow and a spear.'

'You have a spear and a helmet,' Zeus said.

'Ares has a spear and a helmet!' she cried. 'I want something that is just mine!'

'Does Hephaestus have anything?' he asked.

'He has a whole forge,' she said. 'And everything in it.'

Zeus nodded slowly. He supposed that was true.

'Does Aphrodite have something?'

'Aphrodite has everything she wants,' Athene snapped. 'Whenever she wants it.'

Zeus nodded again. That did sound like Aphrodite.

'What sort of thing would you like?' he asked. 'Does Demeter have something?'

'She has a daughter,' Athene said. 'She's either with her or she's complaining about not being with her. All the time. So she doesn't need anything else. And if she did, she could always have some sheaves of corn or something. It's not about her, anyway. It's about me.'

'You could have a loom,' Zeus said, stroking his beard. 'You're very good at weaving.'

'I can't carry that around with me, can I?'

'I suppose Hephaestus can't carry a forge around with him either,' said her father.

'I said it wasn't about anyone else! It's about what I want!'

'Well, dearest, you're skilful and warlike and wise. You have your spear and helmet, so that's the warlike bit taken care of. Your weaving skill is less portable, so we're putting that to one side. So that leaves wisdom. What would convey that?'

'I don't know,' she said.

'An animal? Would you like an animal?'

'What kind of animal?'

'Well, I have the eagle, of course. So not an eagle. You could have . . .' He thought for a moment. 'How about an owl?'

There was silence.

'The owl is just mine?' she asked. 'No one else will get an owl?'

'The owl will always be your symbol, my dear, and yours alone.'

'Then yes,' she said. 'I'll have an owl.'

Danaë

Danaë swept the floor, which otherwise became sandy as the wind blew the outside in. Her hair was tied back in a loose knot because even after all these years, she could not tolerate any sense of constriction. She wedged doors and windows open, though it filled the house with sand. Dictys never complained, nor even questioned it. And so every morning she swept. She smiled at what it would look like to a stranger: the daughter of a king doing housework for the brother of a king, while her son – the son of the king of the gods, no less – helped the old man with his fish. But there was no stranger to witness their life, except the other fishermen and their families who lived near the shore, to whom it seemed perfectly normal. And anyway, they never asked questions so had no idea who anyone's father was. Having grown up in a palace that was always humming with gossip (until her father lost his mind), it had taken Danaë a long time to grow accustomed to the lack of curiosity here.

She looked out of the doorway as she swept, less anxious now her son had been accompanying Dictys for a year or more. He had pleaded and pestered and she could not keep refusing him as he grew older, not when they both knew the old man wanted his company (although he never weighed in on the argument, always telling Perseus that he must wait until Danaë thought he was old enough).

At first, she had said no with such vehemence that her son – who was not prone to outbursts – wept with anger and hurt, and ran out of the house. He never cried, she reminded herself, but then she never shouted. She blamed herself for upsetting him, and also for not foreseeing it. Her son had no memory of any man but Dictys and the other fishermen. Of course he would want to follow them to the sea. Perseus couldn't remember their terrifying journey to Seriphos, the certainty of death, of sinking, and drowning, being eaten by a whale or some other monster of the deep. He had been only a baby, he had not learned to fear. Danaë would have stepped onto Dictys's boat if her son's life had depended on it, but otherwise nothing could have persuaded her. Sometimes when she ran to meet the men as they came in with their catch, the dry sand would shift beneath her feet and she would experience the same terrible lurching sensation she had felt so long ago as she lay in the box on the waves, frantically praying to her lover to save her.

But she could not keep her son away from the sea indefinitely, nor did she want him to fear it as she did. So she swallowed her concern, or tried to, and said yes. The first time, she watched them from the house all the way down to the shore, staring at the two silhouettes, trying to understand how or when Perseus had grown as tall as his adopted grandfather. She sat on the step of the house that whole day, long after the boat was out of sight, long after all the boats were out of sight. She could not concentrate on anything, did not eat or drink, did not notice hunger or thirst. She simply sat resting her hand on a patch of seagrass, twisting the strands between her fingers until they snapped off. When she saw Dictys's boat coming back to land, she could not allow herself to believe it was them. Even as she strained her eyes against the sun to see two figures tying up the boat and making the nets safe, she could not accept it. When the two dots began to climb the hill towards her, she allowed herself the tiniest scrap of hope that her boy was safe. But she didn't really feel it until she could make out his distinctive stride and the way he was trying not to run ahead so he could tell her everything. Dictys could cover the ground as quickly as a man half his age, but even he could not keep pace with her excited boy. And yet, as she felt the relief sink through her body she felt something else – pride – that Perseus would not abandon the older man. The sun glimmered off his salt-crusted skin and she wondered how anyone who saw him could fail to guess he was the son of Zeus. Her beautiful, strong boy, carrying the fish he had caught in the ocean he didn't fear. Unbidden, she had a memory of her father, sitting alone in his echoing halls. She wondered if he was even still alive. He had convinced himself that he would be killed by Perseus, of course, but he would certainly not be the first king to be tricked by an oracle. And his once-devoted daughter realized she did not care if he was alive or dead. She looked back on her childhood as she might a story. Her true home, she felt, must always have been here.

Now – many months after Perseus's first day fishing – as

she swept the sand from her floor, she still found herself looking out at the water, keeping one eye on his boat until it was too small to see. But her fear had subsided, and she watched from habit as much as anxiety. Her boy went to sea, unafraid. His mother was unafraid too, until the day the men arrived.

Athene

No one remembered who started the war, but it was definitely one of the giants. Athene had heard it was Porphyrion, trying to rape Hera. But someone else said it had been Eurymedon. And then there was the other claim, that the attack on Hera happened during the war, so couldn't have caused it. In that case, the war had been started by Alcyoneus pilfering cattle that belonged to Helios, the sun god. Looking at Helios's perpetually smug expression, Athene thought, you wouldn't imagine he had it in him to go to war over anything. And who cared about cows enough to start a war? She stroked the wing feathers of her owl jealously.

Whoever was to blame, one of the children of Gaia – whom the gods all knew to be boastful and arrogant – had behaved in such a way that even their mother could not save them, though she tried. The giants were determined to offend Zeus, Athene thought. Hurling rocks at Olympus was one thing, but setting oak trees aflame and sending those heavenwards was a mistake. Zeus was fond of oak trees.

The Olympian gods would descend to Phlegra for a battle

88

Athene relished. The giants were a serious threat: huge, aggressive and with the immense power of their mother on their side. Everyone knew that giants were impervious to attacks from the gods, and could not be killed. But the gods consulted an oracle and found there was an exception they could exploit. If a mortal fought alongside the gods, the giants were vulnerable after all. So the only thing the gods needed was a mortal willing to fight giants: one who was loyal or foolish, or ideally both.

Hera suggested one of Zeus's sons before any of the others had time to open their mouths. Zeus looked a little put out (Hera had been trying to kill this one since he was a baby, which not everyone considered a fair fight). But they did need someone and he couldn't protect them all. He sent Athene to ask him herself.

She shimmered into view among the tall pine trees that grew outside the man's palace, but even if you had been looking straight at them, you wouldn't have seen her appear. She wasn't there and then she was, and it seemed as though she always had been. She found him training in his court-yard, his skin painted with oil and coated with red dust to protect against the sun. She paused for a moment to admire his biceps as he raised himself up and down.

'Zeus needs you,' she said. The man collapsed to the ground, and Athene tried not to snigger.

'Are you . . . ?' The man grabbed at his throat as though someone were choking him.

Athene frowned, trying to make out the words. 'Am I . . . ? A goddess? Yes, Athene. Good to meet you. Could you come and help us fight the giants?'

The man nodded vigorously, but still couldn't speak.

'You'll probably die,' Athene said. It was best to be honest, she felt. 'But we need a mortal and we chose you, so it will be a very noble death.'

The man's expression lost some of its enthusiasm.

'And quick!' she added. 'If you get trodden on by a giant or a god – which wouldn't be intentional on our part, incidentally, but in the heat of battle one of us might step in the wrong place and there you'd be . . . Well, would have been. Anyway, it would be painless. Probably very painful just before it was painless, but not for long.'

The man looked her up and down in confusion.

'Yes,' she said. 'I'm actually quite a lot bigger than I look to you. But I didn't want to scare you so I decided I would appear to you mortal-sized. I can change my appearance at will, you see. We all can. I wonder how Zeus appeared to your mother. Well, we probably don't have time to get into that, do we? Because there's a war we need your help with and it can't start until you and I get there.'

'Where?' the man asked. Athene almost squealed with delight.

'Listen to that!' she said. 'You can talk. I thought perhaps you were mute for some reason. But you can talk quite well if it's just one word at a time. Well done. We fight the giants at Phlegra. I'll take you. Are you ready? I suppose you are, aren't you? It's not like you can really prepare yourself for fighting giants. If you've got any weapons you might want to gather those up, I suppose. Hurry, though.'

The man ran to a large wooden chest in the corner of his courtyard and grabbed a spear and a sword, a bow and arrows. He held them with practised confidence, and Athene thought perhaps Hera hadn't been wrong when she suggested they use this one.

'Wonderful,' she said. 'Come on. If you do die, I'll put in a word for you to get a constellation. Promise.'

Gaia

While Athene was recruiting the mortal, Gaia was plotting against the gods. She too had heard about the oracle, about the decisive role that would be played in the upcoming conflict by some human. She scoffed at the very idea she might fear such a man, given that he and all his fellow mortals depended on her for their lives and homes. But she decided her offspring might need help, just to be on the safe side. She knew that somewhere in her green expanse was the herb she needed. She just couldn't quite remember where. Was it in the mountains? Did it grow under the trees? Near the sea? Among the crops? If only she could think. Gods weren't used to doing things in a hurry. She needed a little time to look around for it: she could almost smell it – a tangy scent that made her think it must grow deep in the forest among the spores and the fallen pine cones. But did it flower? What colour was it? She began her search, aware that her children's lives depended on her.

But she had barely begun before she was plunged into darkness. She looked up, blinking: had Helios travelled across the sky more quickly today? Not a sign of the sun.

She looked the other way: then where was Selene? There were plants that only flowered by the light of her moon. Was that what she was looking for? But there was no moon so she could not find it. Angered, she turned again to look for Eos. If Helios was absent and Selene was missing, it must be almost dawn. Her pink streaks must be just about to light up the sky. Which would give Gaia enough time to find this precious plant. But the sky didn't lighten, and it did not turn red. Gaia had little idea of the passage of time – even less so than the other gods, perhaps – but she knew the sky had been black for too long. And she knew what had happened.

Zeus had moved against her. She cursed his name. The sun, the moon and the dawn were all hiding. By the time it was light enough to see, he would have stolen the plant for himself. She wept fat, flooding tears. Her children were about to go into battle unaided against all the Olympian gods. And now they could not even rely on her protection.

Gigantomachy

It was the mortal who made the first strike. He and Athene had arrived on the Phlegra peninsula; she was only just getting a sense of where the battle would be fought. She was standing on a broad high plain, a dark curve of trees falling away to her left and a steep drop of scrub down the hillside to her right. Far ahead of her was a gentle slope but she could not see it, because between her and its distant trees, the giants had made their battle line. These children of Gaia were vast, as big as the Olympians, near enough. And ranged out across the plain they would intimidate anyone except the gods they had come to fight. Huge torsos, strong arms, bulging thighs. But then – Athene looked again, she had heard them called snake-footed by her father but she hadn't realized what this would look like – each thigh became a scaly, muscular coil. The giants had the heads and bodies of men but they slithered along the ground. Athene was both appalled and compelled by their monstrosity. This was the war she had been born to fight, this and every one that came after it. She could feel the thrill rising within. The giants drew their strength from the earth, from their

94

mother: she knew that. And yet she felt as though she was doing the same. The fertile soil beneath her feet was full of power, full of life. And all of it was for her. She lifted her head; the sun glinted off her helmet. She turned, looking for the owl who was always perched on her shoulder, or on a branch nearby. She did not want him to be scared by what was to come. But then she remembered, she had left her owl on Olympus, murmuring to him that he should stay there out of harm's way. The thought of him being injured made her almost dizzy with rage. If one of those snake-giants even thought about her owl she would—

But her thought went unfinished, because the giants had begun advancing towards her. She had positioned herself as near to Zeus as she could, although Hera – her chariot pulled by four winged horses – was between them. Athene turned to look at them all – the Olympians and the other deities who had come out alongside them – lined up to crush this impudent rebellion. Every one of them was ready to fight: Apollo and Artemis with bows raised and arrows nocked, their mother Leto beside them with a blazing torch, Ares in a chariot, brandishing a spear. Even Demeter had a wooden stave made of a fat tree trunk and you could hardly call her a fighter. Rhea was riding on the back of a huge lion, Nux had brought a vat of snakes. They had spread themselves across the width of the plain: no giant would escape them. As Hera's horses flew forward, Athene caught sight of her father, his expression one of concentrated anger. Small sparks of lightning were glittering in Zeus's hands as he readied himself.

But in spite of all their prowess, all their weapons, the mortal was the first to claim a kill. Athene had almost forgotten about him as she revelled in the strength of her comrades and the imminent death of all their enemies. She had brought the man here, set him down away from lions and chariot wheels so he would not be crushed by mistake. And like a gadfly, he had all but disappeared from view, before suddenly stinging a creature far larger than himself. Before a single thunderbolt had struck, the giant Alcyoneus was grabbing at his side, roaring in pain. His eyes were on the Olympians, none of whom was close enough to have hurt him, save the Archer and his sister, and neither of them had yet loosed an arrow. Alcyoneus was shot twice more before he collapsed, writhing on the ground. Only now did he see who had shot him and his face creased in fury. And in shock. His mouth was gaping as he tried to breathe but could not: the arrows had pierced his lung. The mortal looked up at Athene, craving her approval. She shook her head and let her voice carry across the distance between them.

'No,' she said. 'Look.' And as they watched, Alcyoneus wrenched the arrows from his ribs and started to revive. He began to sit up. 'You see?' she said. 'He draws his strength from Gaia: they all do. You see the rocks over there?' She pointed at a craggy place off to the side of the battlefield. The mortal nodded. 'Drag him to the rocks,' she said. 'Separate him from the earth.' And the man raced off to do her bidding. Athene watched him with surprise: he was remarkably strong for a human. And though she didn't really care whether the man died or the giant (since the man would die soon and the giant would die today), she found herself cheering on the mortal as he hauled Alcyoneus onto the rocks. The giant's borrowed strength ebbed away:

his arrow wounds proved fatal, now he had lost Gaia's help. One down, Athene thought.

She heard a deafening crack from far across the battlefield, and the sky split in two. Zeus had hurled a thunderbolt at Porphyrion. The giant had attacked Hera, pawing at her as she tried to take her chariot out of his reach. Zeus would never let this stand: he accosted his wife on occasion, but no other creature would do so and live. A second giant down.

An anguished cry now rose up nearby: Apollo showing off his perfect precision. The Archer had shot Ephialtes, first through the left eye, then through the right. Doubly blinded, blood streaming from his blackening sockets, Ephialtes fell to his knees. Not even Gaia could save this one, Athene thought. She could give him back his strength if she wished, but he would still be blind on a battlefield. Beyond Apollo, Athene watched Dionysus as he clubbed Eurytos to death, his blows falling too rapidly for the giant to parry or evade. His brains spilled out on the fertile soil. To Athene's right was Hecate, who lobbed her dark torches at Clytios and set him ablaze. His brows were drawn in pain and fear, but she didn't hesitate, wielding her sword to separate his sorrowing head from his burning torso. Even the limping blacksmith god had found a way to fight, Athene noticed. Hephaestus lobbed huge gobs of molten iron at Mimas, who screamed as he burned.

Three, four, five, six.

Athene smiled as she surveyed the carnage before her: gods in the ascendancy, where they belonged, and half the giants slain when the fighting had scarcely begun. She could wait no longer or it would all be over. She had already picked her mark: Enceladus, a thick-necked giant ahead of her. He was pushing his matted hair back from his forehead, trying to untangle it from his beard so he could see better. But nothing would help him with what was coming.

Athene liked her spear too much to throw it at one of these filthy giants: what if he dirtied it with his blood, bent or broke it with his falling carcass? She knew Hephaestus would make her another, just as good, but she wouldn't take the risk. Not yet, not when she didn't need to. Instead, she picked up a huge triangular rock and hurled it at Enceladus. He could not escape its trajectory and was crushed into the ground. Athene wondered if he might try and draw on his mother's power to aid him, but it was far too late for that. Moving closer she saw that he had been obliterated by her throw: his body buried beneath the rock. Seven.

She experienced a rush of exhilaration to have made her first kill in this most mighty of wars. But even as she felt it, she felt something else too. A strange sensation, like ants were crawling all over her skin. One was not enough, she needed more. She could not leave this battlefield having done the same as Apollo, as Dionysus. War was supposed to be her speciality, not theirs. All around her she heard the crashing of thunder and the clashing of metal. But the chaos only increased her focus; her senses had become tuned to the noise and speed. She watched as Poseidon chased one giant right off the plain and into the sea. Athene rolled her eyes. What kind of idiot tried to evade Poseidon by running into the sea? The giants had strength and size in abundance, certainly, but they were still not worthy opponents. This fool might as well kneel down and offer his throat to the trident. She looked away, still searching for her second conquest. She already knew how Poseidon's fight would end. Eight.

Athene had moved closer to Artemis as she followed her uncle's battle in the sea. But an ear-splitting howl made her turn her attention inland. The hunter goddess had just shot another giant, her quick arrows bringing him down to the ground, his snake legs slithering and squirming beneath him. Perhaps Gaia was reviving him, but Artemis had brought her hunting dogs into battle. Athene felt a brief pang for her owl, but no regret for having left him on Olympus. She would not see her bird's beautiful wings sullied. Still, she had to admire the way the dogs launched themselves at the fallen creature. Teeth fastened around his throat, and this would make nine.

Athene couldn't see Hermes anywhere on the plain, but she knew he was there. Wearing the cap of Hades, which he had borrowed (or more probably stolen), the messenger god was invisible, even to her bird-sharp eyes. He was also invisible to the giant who flailed and bellowed into what looked like the breezes. But it wasn't the wind that pierced his skin time and again, slicing through his hide from every direction and none. Screaming, the giant tried to grab at where he thought the god must be, but Hermes was nothing if not quick. And the giant was getting slower as blood poured from wound after wound: forearm, shoulder, neck, thigh, belly. That was ten.

And then over to her right were . . . Athene could scarcely believe her eyes. The Moirai, the three all-powerful Fates, who spent their days spinning the threads of mortal lives, and cutting them when deaths were due. They weren't half as good at weaving as she was, Athene thought, but no one ever mentioned that because people lived and died with the length of yarn they spun. But no mortals were dying today, because the Fates had walked away from their spindle and their wool weights and their sharp knife. They were here on the battlefield, using bronze clubs to batter two more giants to death. Where did the Fates keep those handsome weapons in the normal run of things? Athene wondered. Did they have them hidden under their wool just in case? For the first time, she felt a grudging respect for the sisters: and that made eleven, twelve.

As the gods each pursued their enemies, Zeus was above them all showering Phlegra with lightning, one bolt slamming into another without pause. The fields would be alight for days after the giants were defeated: the trees were blackening everywhere she looked. And with so many duels taking place in every direction, there was, as far as Athene could see, only one more giant left for her. She could not imagine how the other gods had ignored him because to her he seemed to glow as he stood in the middle of the plain, lightning bolts illuminating him from all sides. Athene looked at him and felt something she had never felt before, and would rarely feel again. She had a ravening hunger for this giant.

The huge creature was swinging his club, shifting his weight from foot to foot, looking for an Olympian to attack. But he could not seem to move in any direction: he was either distracted by the carnage of his brothers or blinded by the lightning that exploded around him. And knowing he was hers and only hers, Athene moved across the battlefield so quickly that even the other gods did not see her coming. This one last giant could not fall to any other hand. She hurled her spear as she ran, all concern for keeping it pristine suddenly gone. Her aim was true and its elegant point pierced his throat: he staggered back under its momentum. He grabbed at the site of the pain but there was nothing he could do now. The force of her throw saw the spear penetrate right through his neck and as he collapsed, it came to rest upright in the hot earth onto which he fell. Athene was beside him a moment later. The deafening clashes of metal and blazing bolts of light faded and finally, in this moment, she felt as though she and the dying giant were the only two people in Phlegra. Dark blood was gushing from his throat and bubbling out red between his lips. Athene found herself appalled by the ugliness and yet she could not stop looking. This was what she was made for, she reminded herself. This was what it meant to fight a war. But that didn't explain the conflicting urges which raged behind her calm face: to look away from the death she had caused, to lean in and lick the warm blood from his lips. She watched as his eyes lost first their anger and then their fear. His mouth moved as though he wanted to tell her something and she bent down to try and make out the words. But all she heard was the last breath leaving his lungs, the last red globule pop, leaving a thin veil of blood in a perfect circle on his upper lip.

She looked up at the battle around her and saw it was now all over. She didn't know if it had taken a long time or no time at all. But as she watched, the mortal loosed his arrows into every giant but this one, her one, as the prophecy had demanded. Every giant must sustain an injury from the man if the gods were to win the day. Athene watched him busying himself around the place, and wondered how he had shot Enceladus, crushed beneath her enormous rock. Perhaps a snake scale or two had stuck out somewhere. She knew the man would soon be here, despoiling this kill. And she felt a rush of protective anger. Her giant was dead by her hands, and hers alone. She required no help from god or mortal, no matter what the oracle had claimed. She would not see the body damaged. Instead, she drew a sharp knife from her belt. Zeus had always said the giants had hide like leather. And she had always wanted a breastplate just like her father had.

She skinned the giant herself, like a cobbler preparing the skin of a heifer. In this way, she would keep her kill beside her for ever, wear him next to her breast. His raw body lay on the ground, unrevived by Gaia, who was scarcely able to comprehend the scale of her loss. Every one of her children cut down in a single battle.

It was just as Athene had always known: mothers did nothing to protect their offspring. His mother had not kept him safe, in spite of all her foolish promises. She had failed him. But Athene had not.

Danaë

The day Polydectes arrived was the same as any other until the thud of many feet brought Danaë out of the house. Perseus and Dictys were not yet back from the sea, but they would be soon – she glanced up reflexively – if Zeus willed it. She could see a group of men approaching the village from higher ground: they came not from the sea but from inland. She could hear the clank of metal but she was not yet afraid. They weren't wearing helmets, so they weren't planning to fight. They had short swords for self-defence, she concluded, as her father's men would have carried when they travelled any distance. She felt a sudden surge of panic that her father might have discovered she and her son had survived his attempt to kill them both. She tried to breathe evenly and make the fear subside. She could see the sky, Perseus was safe, Zeus would not let her father kill him. And then as the men drew nearer, she saw their tunics were not the same kind as the ones she had seen men wear when she was growing up.

The women who lived in nearby houses also came outside

to see what all the noise was about. The fishermen never made this cacophony: this was the sound of city-dwellers invading space that was not their own. They looked at the approaching men with suspicion but not hostility. The men stopped at the nearest house and asked a question. A jerk of the head was their only reply. So they kept walking, ever closer. Danaë found herself looking down at the sea, like she had done when Perseus was new to fishing. Where were the men? Were they returning home soon?

By the time the party approached her house, she could just see the little boats coming in to the shore. The men stopped and parted, like the guards had done when her father welcomed visitors to his palace. This was why they seemed so familiar, she realized, why they made her think of her former life. They were bodyguards to this man at their centre. Now they had stepped aside she could see him: greying hair, lines around his mouth betraying a lifetime of disapproval. He was a short man, broad-bodied with weak legs, and though she had never seen him before, there was something familiar about his expression.

'So you're his wife?' the man said, moving his eyes up and down her body as though he were trying to guess her worth.

'No,' she replied. 'I'm no one's wife. Who are you, sir?'

There was a bristling among the men as though they wanted to mock her ignorance but were unsure whether laughter would be punished.

'Does Dictys live elsewhere?' the man asked. His voice was slightly shrill and she wondered whether he always sounded so querulous.

'No, sir,' she said, looking straight at him. 'This is his home. But I am not his wife. He is unmarried.'

'I heard he had taken a wife. And you are here, by your own admission, in his house.'

Danaë suddenly knew who he was, just as she could see two men in her peripheral vision, climbing the hill from the sea. Dictys and her son would be with her very soon.

'He will be here shortly, sir. I'm sure you'd rather speak to your brother himself.'

The man's eyebrows rose sharply. 'I might tell him to find himself a housekeeper who is more polite to strangers,' he said. She gazed at him, tracing the echoes of Dictys's brow and nose and jaw on the king's face, and wondering how the same features could be so reassuring in one man and so off-putting in another. Now she saw the two silhouetted men hurrying to reach her. Dictys had seen the cluster of guards outside his home, and Perseus had broken into a run.

'I didn't intend to be rude,' she said. He snorted and opened his mouth to reply, before one of the guards noticed the fishermen returning and muttered something to his king.

Dictys's face was filled with concern when he finally appeared. Perseus ran straight to Danaë and stood in front of her. She remembered in a rush the first time she realized she couldn't see over his head any more, and then barely over his shoulder either. Her boy had grown so tall and strong, out on the water every day.

'Brother,' said Dictys. 'This is a surprise. What brings you so far from your palace?'

'I heard you had a family,' the king replied. 'A wife and a son, I heard. And I see it is true. Did you really think you could take a wife without asking your king's permission?'

'Danaë is not my wife.'

'I'm not sure that's something to boast about,' Polydectes snapped.

'She is my adopted daughter.' Dictys continued speaking as though he hadn't heard the interruption. 'Did you need this entourage to find that out? You could have sent a messenger.'

'Could I indeed?'

Danaë understood why Dictys had taken to the sea rather than deal with this brother. She would have been tempted to do the same herself, and she feared the sea like the River Styx.

'Yes, brother.' Dictys sounded exhausted. 'Although I'm delighted you came to visit. Please, come inside.'

Polydectes waved at his men, pointing at the modest house in front of him. 'You'll have to wait out here,' he said.

Danaë stepped back, her hand on Perseus's arm, so that Dictys could lead his brother into the house, but he smiled and shook his head. It was her home too. So she and her son turned their backs on the men and walked inside. Danaë could feel the tension pulsing from Perseus: he was angry and afraid of this man, she knew. He had grown up with only the fishermen for company, and a show of force like this was alarming.

She poured wine into a mixing bowl and set a jug of water beside it. They had two good cups, which she placed on the table as the men sat on either side. She stood back, nodding to Perseus that he should do the same. The men busied themselves with their drinks and she found herself looking at the king. He resembled his brother so closely one moment and then not at all. He was older, she knew, but she couldn't see it: years at sea were hard to hide. And – though she knew it must be in her imagination – she kept seeing traces of her father in the face of this stranger. Not in his appearance, exactly. Polydectes looked nothing like her father. But there was something about the irritated downturn of his mouth, as though the world existed only to disappoint. As the king finished preparing his drink, he looked up at her and she flushed, embarrassed to have been caught staring.

'Your adopted daughter?' said Polydectes. 'From whom did you adopt her?'

Danaë felt her whole body stiffen as this man spoke about her as though she could not hear. Dictys took a sip of wine before replying.

'Her father was sadly afflicted,' he said. 'She and her boy needed a home, which I was glad to provide.'

'The boy is not yours?'

'He is the grandson I wish I had,' said Dictys, and Danaë felt her son soften beside her and tried to do the same.

'Ha!' The king's laughter was intended to be unkind. 'For that to happen, brother, you would have had to desire a woman.'

There was silence. Dictys tilted his cup, watching the light flicker across the surface of the wine. 'Yes, brother,' he said. 'I would. But the Fates brought me a daughter and a grandson regardless.'

107

'You are a disgrace,' said the king. 'To have a woman like this in your house and take no pleasure from her.' He shook his head in disgust.

'I don't take pleasure from anyone unless they offer it freely,' said Dictys.

'You have always been weak.'

'I have always seemed so to you, certainly.'

'Where is the boy's father?' Polydectes turned to Danaë. 'Is he alive?'

This was a surprisingly difficult question for her to answer, since she did not want to blaspheme, but was unsure of the truth. Gods weren't alive, were they? They were something more than, or certainly other than, alive.

'No.' She spoke quietly, hoping this would make the king think it was a painful subject and stop pursuing it.

'I see,' he said. 'So you live here with my brother as a young widow, giving him the appearance of respectability he requires?'

'No, sir,' she said. 'Your brother was well-respected before I arrived here.'

'And will be after you leave, no doubt.'

'She isn't going to leave.' Perseus could no longer keep silent. 'We're going to stay here for ever.'

'What is your name?' The king turned to her son with the full force of his disdain.

'Perseus,' the boy replied. 'What's yours?'

The king ignored him, and looked back at Dictys. 'And you still go out on your boat every day? Live off the fish you catch?'

Dictys shrugged, and Danaë loved him for it. It was a small gesture to convey feelings too large for the words he had. Of course he went out on a boat every day: Dictys belonged to the sea. And of course he lived off what he caught: he and his fellow fishermen always did. If one of them had a run of bad luck, the others would share their catch with the man's family. No matter what the king said to make this life sound pitiful, it was not. It was – Danaë knew – full of a dignity that you would not find in the largest palace. Polydectes's men were all nervous around him: was that the enviable life? The quiet companionship Dictys had offered was the greatest gift any mortal could have given her. And now – she knew it even before the words were spoken – it was about to be taken away.

'This is no life for a woman like her,' the king said. 'She leaves with me.'

Dictys said nothing, but shook his head slowly, and Danaë saw her world fall apart.

'I am happy here, sir,' she said. But the words died in the air.

'You'll be happy married to the king,' he replied. It was clear to everyone that this wasn't a question.

Perseus looked at his mother and at Dictys, trying to comprehend how these two all-powerful people were suddenly incapacitated. Dictys could steer a course through a sudden storm, he could catch any fish the ocean chose to offer, he could out-sail the monsters of the deep. And yet there he sat, wordless. His mother could heal any injury, repair any break. But she simply stood in silence as their lives were smashed to pieces.

'She can't marry you,' he said. 'We have to stay here. I help Dictys with his catch.'

'How old are you?' asked the king. Danaë prayed to her son's father.

'Sixteen,' said the boy, trying so hard not to look like a boy any more, as Danaë tried to will him back to infancy. It was her fault, she saw. She had never taught him about men's cruelty, she had never wanted him to need to know. And here he was, sure that his answer would make this powerful man reconsider.

'Sixteen.' The king nodded. 'Old enough.'

'Old enough for what?' Perseus replied.

'You want your mother to stay here with you and him?' Danaë could almost taste the viciousness in the king's voice that her son could not even hear.

'Yes, I do,' said Perseus.

'Very well.' Polydectes turned in his chair so he could look the boy fully in the face. 'Then she shall stay while you go and fetch me something I want. You can sail, we know that. And you must be strong from carrying all those fish up the hill every day.'

'I am.' Perseus straightened a little, not seeing the trap.

'Good, then you can bring me something that would be impossible for an ordinary young man.' The king smiled. 'The head of a Gorgon.'

'Brother,' said Dictys. 'Please.'

'Of course I can,' said Perseus. 'She stays here until I return?'

'Well, I don't want to give you a reason to delay,' Polydectes said. 'So let's say a month, shall we? No, two months, because your mother looks so sad at the thought of you having to rush. That should be more than enough time for you to travel to the Gorgon lair and home again.'

He stood up and took a step towards the door.

'I'll return in two months,' he said to Danaë. 'You'll be ready to accompany me then.'

And having destroyed their home, he walked out of it.

Gorgoneion

You're probably feeling sorry for him now, aren't you? Poor little Perseus, the reluctant hero. Defender of his mother's honour. Boastful little fool: if he had simply kept his mouth shut while Polydectes was swaggering around trying to intimidate him. All he had to do was behave like any other of the king's subjects. Say yes sire, no sire, whenever he was spoken to, and the whole thing would have been over by now. Danaë would have gone to the palace and, what? What harm would have been done, exactly? Polydectes isn't a monster, he's just a pompous little man with an irrational grudge against his brother. Greece is literally full of men like this. Danaë only had to offer a few words of criticism of Dictys as she swanned around the palace for a few days, having other people sweeping the floors for a change and eating something that didn't have gills. Would that have been such an imposition? Food without scales. Most people would be relieved.

Polydectes would have lost interest in her in weeks, probably days. He only wants her because his brother had her: he's the king. He can have anyone he wants as his wife.

The second-hand wife of a dead man (as he believes Danaë to be) and housekeeper to an unloved brother? She's hardly the trophy he's looking for. Maybe if he knew about the Zeus connection, that might be persuasive? Although he might find that intimidating. (Do you really want to take the place of the king of the gods in a woman's bed? Even if that king of the gods was golden rain when he appeared to her?) It's often hard to say with men, isn't it?

Anyway, don't even begin to feel sorry for that brat. He isn't saving his mother from some awful torment. He's saving her from the mild inconvenience of travelling a day or two on horseback, making a few snide remarks about former lovers until the king – who isn't even interested in her, just spiteful – loses patience and sends her away again. Probably lending her a horse for the return journey.

The idea that Perseus is a hero is one I have taken exception to since – I can't even tell you how long it is. As long as I've known his name. He's arrogant and he's spoiled. You can't blame Danaë for it: she had such a traumatic start to his life. She's always let him do as he pleases. Dictys could have disciplined the boy better, I suppose. But it's hard with a boy who isn't your own. And he was so thrilled to have a child in his home, against all his expectations. Of course he indulged him: he followed Danaë's lead.

And none of that would even have mattered if Perseus had stayed in his little village, catching fish for the rest of his life, upsetting no one. Well, the fish probably wouldn't have liked him much, I suppose. But no one thinks about fish.

Certainly not Perseus who – you'll soon see – has no interest in the wellbeing of any creature if it impedes his desire to do whatever he wants. He is a vicious little thug and the sooner you grasp that, and stop thinking of him as a brave boy hero, the closer you'll be to understanding what actually happened.

Athene

Athene loved her new breastplate, loved it in the same way she loved her owl. She loved the way it gleamed in the sun, couldn't stop turning it in her hands and watching it catch the light. It wasn't bright and glittery, like metal. And not dull, like animal skin, only becoming shiny through use and wear. It had the beautiful soft glow of Parian marble gleaming in the evening light. Hephaestus had worked it into the perfect piece of armour for her, although he had a curious expression while he did it. Athene wondered what was bothering him – he made armour all the time – but she didn't ask because she wasn't very concerned so long as he made her what she wanted. And if he didn't want to know where she had found her skin, she didn't really know why he'd asked her. But whatever his reservations had been, they hadn't interfered with his work. Quite the opposite, in fact: he had made it more quickly than even she had anticipated. The fastenings were strong and it fitted perfectly.

She was wearing it now, as she thought back over the war. She had relived it many times already, but it never hurt to do so again. She revelled anew in the noise and dust and blood, and the smell of burning from each light-ning bolt Zeus fired. It was the first time she felt she really understood any of the other gods, when she thought about how they fought and killed. The coldness of Apollo and Artemis made more sense to her when she remembered them with bows and arrows in their hands. The shiftiness of Hermes wasn't directed at her, it was in his nature: that was why he fought using tricks and deception. Her father, raining his anger down almost indiscriminately. Poseidon cornering his opponent in the sea, where he was strongest. And then a small annoyance rose within her, when she had that last thought. She couldn't quite identify it. The sea, was it something about the sea? She allowed the sea to fill her mind, cast her nets around it. No, that wasn't it. Poseidon, then? Yes, the annoyance buzzed a little louder. Something to do with her uncle. But whatever it was hadn't happened during the war on the giants, had it? They had barely noticed one another, fighting in quite different parts of the battle. He hadn't said or done anything to her. And then the buzzing intensified again. Yes, it was something he had done somewhere else, to someone else. But it had also been done to her. He had injured her in some way. And then in a rush, she remembered.

He had taken some girl – mortal, nymph, she wasn't sure. But he had done it in her temple. Hers. Where her statue could look down and see it all. She felt an encom-passing rage. How dare he? How dare he when his temple was being built next door? He could rape or seduce whoever he liked there, Athene wouldn't interfere. But to profane her temple, and not even to consider the insult worth an apology?

She would have to find a way to get her revenge on him later. He was – as so often – away in his ocean kingdom: she could not harm him there. There would be an opportunity to humiliate him later, she was quite sure. But in the meantime, her anger was roused and she needed to expend it.

The girl. The girl would do.

Medusa

It happened at night, so that Medusa could never be sure if she had dreamed it or if it was real, or if there was any difference between the two.

She knew it was Athene who stood before her, anger consuming her lovely face, helmet tilted back, spear in hand.

She could see the goddess's lips move, but she could not hear the words, so that afterwards she felt that if only she had been able to make them out, she might have saved herself.

She was mistaken.

She felt a searing pain in every part of her skull, as though someone had wrapped her head in a cloth and then twisted and twisted it.

Her eyes were burning hot and seemed to be pulsing against their lids, so she believed she must be going blind.

She felt as if her scalp was tearing apart.

Afterwards, when she looked down at the place where her head had lain, there was a perfect halo of her curling hair left behind.

She reached up to touch her head and found she could not.

She screamed until her voice was gone.

It changed nothing.

Stone

This statue has never been seen, because it lies on the bed of the ocean. Perhaps that's just as well, because it would never stand up: it is too narrow at the base, top-heavy.

It's a cormorant, diving for fish, and it is just about to make its catch. Its beak is open, ready to snatch the fish from the waves. It seems impossible that the beak will not be filled in a heartbeat, that the cormorant will not rise from the water with its belly full. That droplets will not fall from its sleek, damp wings. But it is impossible, because this is only a stone bird.

But it looks so real. Its whole being is focused on its goal: wings folded back to elongate its body as it enters the water, feet tucked in beneath them, pointing to the sky. The bird knows that the fish have the advantage as soon as it breaks the surface, so it does everything possible to make itself faster, increase its chances. Besides, there is a whole shoal of fish. The cormorant only needs to get lucky once.

If someone had painted this statue, it would be black, but not a true black: there is a tinge of green beneath the blackness on cormorant feathers that only reveals itself in the brightest sunlight. Would the artist have captured that? A green that is almost black, a black that is scarcely green? The bird has glassy dark eyes; a membrane runs down the centre. It is represented by the slightest ridge in the stone.

Part Three

Blind

Cassiope

The queen of Ethiopia had every reason to admire herself as she stared into the mirror her husband had made for her. When they first married, he had been so dazzled by her beauty he had gazed at her all day and then demanded the torches be lit so he could continue to gaze at her all night. Cassiope told her mother he did this; her mother made a sign to ward off evil spirits. No man could maintain such intensity of desire, she said. Cassiope must ensure she was pregnant before his stupefied pleasure dissipated.

Cassiope had been very young at this point, she remembered, and prone to the fear that her mother might be correct. She wanted to have Cepheus's child before he could tire of her. And yet, she also wanted to continue their lives as they were. She didn't want to watch her body swell and distort. She was not ready for what the women whispered about when they believed their new queen couldn't hear. And her husband didn't seem concerned when she was not pregnant straightaway. Stroking her flat belly, he adored her as she was.

And, contrary to her mother's fears, Cepheus never

wearied of gazing at his wife's face. One day, he decided that the pleasure should be shared by her. She asked him what he meant and he smiled in a way which he intended to be enigmatic, but instead made him look like a small child struggling to keep a secret. Cassiope's mother had belatedly decided to keep her counsel but – within the confines of her home – she told her slave-women that the king was a child himself, and this was why the couple felt no urgency to produce an heir.

For a day or two there was a great deal of noise and slaves rushing around with cloths to remove dust and then Cepheus took his wife by both hands, and asked her to close her eyes. He walked her carefully – as though he were carrying a priceless object – from their bed chamber into a room that had never seemed to have much purpose. She followed him, keeping her eyes closed even when he told her there were two steps coming, even when he paused to check he would not walk backwards into the wall. Finally he stopped and told her she could look. She opened her eyes to see the palm of his hand, which he had placed a little way in front of them, so she wasn't dazzled by the bright torches. And as he watched her pupils contract, he moved his hand away so that she could see a large, very shallow pool filled to the brim. Now she could stare at her reflection for as long as she wished. She never found it wanting.

Her beauty was her proudest possession, more than all the gold and jewels Cepheus had showered on her when she became his queen. These things were intimately connected, of course: she would not have been chosen as queen had she not been beautiful. And not many queens had jewellery like hers. But none of the gems gave her quite as much pleasure as her long elegant neck, her perfectly poised shoulders, her smooth ebony skin. And none of those satisfied her as much as the frank intelligence that brightened her eyes. Her mouth was always quick to smile because she was happy with what she saw, and that gave her an expression which was both challenging and amused. Visitors to Cepheus's palace could rarely remember anything about the building, the furnishings, the food or the wine. They could hardly remember what they discussed with the king, although they had always enjoyed talking to him because he was a kind man, full of generous interest in his guests and their stories. But all of this was driven from their minds by the magnificent gaze of his wife.

Just as their subjects were beginning to murmur that a happy king was better than the other kind but that their kingdom nonetheless required an heir, Cassiope realized she was pregnant. The marriage was already a success in her mind, but now even her mother stopped carping. The midwife assured her it would be a boy, but sitting by the pool one night, illuminated by the flickering torches, she told the gods that she wanted a daughter. She wanted to watch another iteration of her beauty growing up, because nothing could stop her own looks from fading, she knew.

And when Andromeda was born – the midwives tense in the moments after her birth, in case their blithe predictions of a son were met with punishment – Cassiope looked down at her tiny face and saw exactly what she had hoped to see: a miniature perfect echo of herself. She did not resent her daughter's beauty (although no seller of unguents and creams ever went away from the palace with his goods untried). Rather, she relished her daughter's loveliness. Every visitor would always say that Andromeda looked just like her, then they looked away from the child so they could spend their gaze on her instead. And Cepheus never stopped telling her that her beauty was without equal in the whole of Ethiopia. So instead of resenting her daughter, Cassiope viewed her much as she viewed her glorious reflection in her pool. Another way of looking at herself and finding nothing wanting.

And if – as Andromeda grew into a woman – more young men stared a little longer at her, they still could not hide their admiration for her mother. Cassiope thought of her own mother – still handsome even now – and felt relief, even as she took a second darting look back at the water to check her jawline was as flawless as ever. Her perfection must appear – as it always had – to be effortlessly, divinely bestowed.

*

Andromeda loved her parents, and was proud to be their daughter. She would never have admitted that she found her mother's obsession with beauty – her own and Andromeda's – to be a burden. If it meant that her mother spent more time indoors, avoiding the harsh light outside, that only made her like any other woman of status in Ethiopia. And Andromeda was realistic. Her friends were always saying that every man looked at a girl's mother to see who she would become. No man looked at Cassiope – even now her daughter was of marriageable age – without holding his breath for a moment. Andromeda's whole future was brighter because of this: her friends never passed an opportunity to mention it. So she was at a loss to explain how she found herself betrothed to her uncle Phineus when she could surely have had any Ethiopian prince she chose.

Why did other suitors not come beating down her father's doors in their thousands? She tried not to feel hurt and angry. But the only important things anyone said in the palace were whispered in dark rooms to which she was not invited. Whenever she discussed matters with friends her own age, or with the slave-women who feigned ignorance, she found herself growing more aggrieved rather than less. When she could bear it no longer, she waited until there were no guests staying in the palace and cornered her parents while they were eating.

'Papa.' She knew she should at least pretend that her father made the decisions. 'I need to ask you a question.'

'Yes, my dear.' Her father was lounging back on his couch, a fat cushion beneath his elbow. Her mother sat on the couch beside him, from where the torches were best able to cast shadows of her elegant profile onto the ground.

'Why do I have to marry Uncle Phineus?'

The slave who was putting plates down onto the table between them froze – just for a moment – before continuing with his task, eyes fixed on the food.

'Andromeda!' said her mother. 'What kind of question is that to ask of a king? Why must you marry the king's brother? Who else should do it? Would you see some girl from another family raised up over us?'

'I don't think that would happen, Mother.' Andromeda knew her mother tended to start any dispute from quite a high pitch so she did not raise her voice in return. 'I think that Father is loved and respected by all Ethiopians, far more than his brother could ever be.' She took a sneaking pleasure in seeing her mother's eyes flicker with anxiety, having not anticipated this direction of attack. And now her father was preening himself, suddenly looking as plump as the cushion he was resting on.

'Of course that's true,' he replied. 'But your mother and I have always believed you can never be too careful. If something were to happen to me —' He broke off to make the sign warding off any cruel spirits who might be listening. 'I will be succeeded by Phineus. So you and your mother would be better off if you were married to him. We cannot afford for there to be a second branch to the royal family.'

Cassiope nodded. 'Phineus could marry some brat and produce five sons. Your father is looking after our interests. You would do well to remember that.'

'I'm hardly likely to forget it,' Andromeda replied. 'I just don't understand why I have to give up all hope of happiness.'

'Are you being a bit overwrought, my dear?' asked her father. 'You're very fond of your uncle, you have been since you were small.'

'As an uncle, yes,' she said. 'As a husband, I would prefer someone closer to my own age, and further from yours.'

'Well, I'm afraid we don't always get what we want,' Cassiope snapped.

'You do,' her daughter replied.

'What did you say?'

Andromeda knew the fight was lost but she wasn't prepared to let her parents pretend they weren't ignoring her desires. 'I said, "You do." Because you do. Father never disagrees with you about anything. He does everything he can to keep you happy. So do I.' She waved her arm wide. 'So does everyone. Everyone wants you to have exactly what you want because otherwise you make our lives a misery. We all go along with it. Until now. Because I don't want to marry a man as old as my father – who even looks like my father – to make sure you don't have to worry about being thrown out of a palace when you're old. If you're so worried about who Phineus marries, you marry him.'

She jumped up from her couch and as her weight pushed it back, its curved wooden feet screeched against the stone floor. 'I want suitors,' she said. 'I want men to come here and vie for my hand.' She was aware that she sounded childish and at the same time she wasn't sorry. She was barely past childhood, and her uncle was old. None of their explanations for this betrothal would change that.

*

Cassiope knew her authority was waning: her daughter would never have dared speak to her in this way before. She would talk to her husband about Phineus tomorrow, hurry the wedding along before Andromeda could persuade him to reconsider. She would not see her status diminish more than it had to. She was leaving nothing to chance: what if Cepheus died before her? What if he died soon? She would never be one of those old women sitting by the side of a dirt track, begging for scraps from travellers. Never. And now she knew she could not trust Andromeda to put her mother's needs first.

131

So in spite of what people thought and said, it was anxiety rather than arrogance that made her say the words that ruined her life.

Athene

Athene decided to leave Olympus for a while. She had grown weary of its quiet perfection. No wonder the other gods came and went – Poseidon to the sea, Artemis to Mount Cithaeron – to avoid the monotony of home. She walked around its precincts sometimes, half hoping she could find someone to talk to, half trying to avoid them because she could think of nothing they would say that would interest her. Sometimes she stopped by the forge and Hephaestus would pause his hammering to make her a gift of something. They were figurines, sculpted from marble or clay, wood or bronze. He would paint them in bright colours, pouring life into the tiny faces. Athene took them, usually, and admired them for a while as she walked. But then she would lose interest in them and drop them wherever she was standing.

Hephaestus never asked what became of his gifts, and it did not occur to her to ask why he kept making her these figurines when she never kept them. It would have surprised Athene if she had known that the blacksmith god watched her when she left the forge and kept careful note of how long it took her to lose interest in each gift, that he decided what to make next depending on which ones she dropped immediately and which ones she kept for a little longer.

It took him several attempts to make the one she eventually carried all the way back to the halls of Olympus. He'd never had trouble with the eyes or the quizzical angle of the head, but he'd struggled to make the tail feathers so delicate they looked real. Eventually, he found a way to carve the finest lines in the marble, so the solid stone looked capable of fluttering in the breezes. He painted the bird in a dappled pattern of cream on brown, its eyes flat yellow discs around huge black pupils. Its short beak was gilded and its small, strong legs ended with splayed feet and sharp black claws. He had caught the characteristic pose of Athene's own owl, head turned sideways.

When Hephaestus showed her the model bird, she looked briefly furious, as though someone were playing a cruel trick on her. Then she snatched it from him and he worried he had made the wrong trinket again and that she would hurl it to the ground or smash it against the walls of the forge as she had done once or twice before with other figurines she had not liked.

But once she had it in her hands, her expression softened. He watched in silence as she turned the model over and examined its folded wings. She lifted it to look more closely at its flexed feet, and then lowered it again to examine the beautiful soft brow line he had created. She scratched at the top of its head, cooed as though it could hear her. He said nothing. The model was so realistic that its living counterpart grow irritated and pecked at her fingers until she stroked him instead. She laughed to see the bird's jealousy.

This statue she did keep.

Euryale

Sthenno and Euryale never really slept, only tried to so that Medusa did not feel left out when she grew tired. So on the night she was cursed and her screams pierced the blackness, they were awake and they ran inside the cave to try to save their girl from whatever was hurting her. But there was no one there, no man, no animal. Euryale caught sight of a scorpion scuttling away in her torchlight and stamped on it just to be certain.

Their flickering light fell on Medusa, who had buried her face into the crooks of her arms. Her hands, though, were lost in a seething mass of snakes. Sthenno had given up hoping that Medusa would have snake hair like she and Euryale did, and yet here it was at last. But whatever had caused the change was clearly causing her terrible pain. Sthenno ran to her and put her arm around Medusa's shoulders.

'Darling, what happened?'

But Medusa could not reply, and Sthenno hugged her close. Euryale stood back, because Sthenno had dropped her torch and she didn't want them to be swathed in dark-

136

ness. It took her a moment to see that something had changed, that now there were two snake-covered heads together. She had always loved Medusa's tight black curls, of course. Medusa was beautiful, her hair perhaps more than anything. But now, with snakes writhing around her instead of hair lying inert, she looked . . . Euryale tried to put the thought into words. She looked right. She looked like her sisters, like a Gorgon, like an immortal creature.

Sthenno held Medusa and rubbed her shoulders. 'Don't cry, darling. I know, your beautiful hair. You loved it so. Don't cry.'

Euryale didn't want to scare these new snakes with fire (her own were well used to such things by now) so she still held back. But Sthenno looked up and beckoned her, so she drove the base of her torch into the hard sand, and approached Medusa slowly. She need not have worried: the snakes didn't rear or hiss. Her snakes – and Sthenno's, and Medusa's – tangled and untangled themselves contentedly, as though they all sprang from a single head. But Medusa still shuddered and wept. Even Euryale could see that although she preferred the snakes, Medusa did not.

And where had they come from? Their sister was mortal, they both knew it. And the only way you could tell she was a Gorgon by looking at her – unless you knew already – was if you noticed her wings. In all other regards she had always looked like an ordinary human girl. Had the snakes just sprouted fully formed from her head? Euryale couldn't imagine what it would be like not to have them. But then, she also couldn't imagine what it was like to feel pain. Unable to offer anything else, she took her sister's arm and held it to her chest.

Gradually, Medusa's sobs eased.

'Did the snakes just appear?' asked Sthenno.

'No,' Medusa said. 'She made them.'

'Who?'

'I'm not sure,' she replied. 'A goddess. She was here, in the cave. She was angry with me. It might have been . . .' Her voice died.

'We know who it was,' Euryale said. 'Vengeful and cruel, always blaming women for what men do to them. She has always been like this. You know she has.'

'Yes,' Sthenno agreed. She did know. So did Medusa, she just couldn't bring herself to say it. 'You'll grow used to the snakes, dearest,' she said, squeezing Medusa's shoulders once again. 'You've never minded ours. I know you'll miss your hair for a while, but it will be alright, I promise.'

'I know.' Medusa still buried her head in the crook of her arm, but her shoulders had relaxed a little.

'Do they hurt?' asked Euryale. Medusa's snakes shivered, as though they understood the possible threat.

'No,' Medusa replied. 'They did at first, a lot. Or it might have been my hair getting torn out that hurt so much. I couldn't tell: it all happened at once. But no, they don't hurt now.'

'There,' said Sthenno. 'So it's getting better, even though it isn't good.'

'It's my eyes that hurt,' said her sister. 'I can't open them.'

The Graiai

Perseus had left his mother and Dictys behind with a great show of confidence. Dictys had offered to lend the boy his boat, but Perseus had to refuse him. He could not deprive the old man of his livelihood: what if he never returned? There were no spare vessels among the fishermen, who tended to use all the materials they had to repair the boats they loved. And even if Perseus had a supply of wood available to him, he didn't have time to make a boat. He had less than two months to do the impossible.

Since no one knew where to find the head of a Gorgon, his mother suggested he ask his father for advice. Perseus did not know exactly how to do this and his mother could not really advise him. Danaë had attracted Zeus's attention while locked in a cellar, but Perseus had never managed to do so at all. In the end, he decided he should head inland, and try to find a sacred grove, or a temple. Perhaps then he could make his offerings to Zeus and receive help.

He set off across the island, avoiding the well-worn paths that would take him to the palace of the king, and asking everyone he met if they knew of a place sacred to the king of the gods. Some had no answer, one or two told him to keep walking and he would come to the place he sought. But after several days of slow and dusty travel, he felt no closer to his father or any answer to his problems. If anything, he felt further away. Wherever the Gorgons lived, he was sure it wasn't on Seriphos: why would Polydectes ask for something that was close to home? So travelling away from the sea had been a fool's choice. He berated himself for having wasted time discovering nothing.

*

He had been climbing steadily for days, but now the ground was falling away beneath him. He wondered if this meant he was heading back towards the sea. Had he crossed the whole island? He was filled with despair. The trees had thinned as the land grew higher, but now they seemed to be increasing again, and the undergrowth beneath them was thickening too. His way grew more difficult and he had seen no other travellers all day. Even the birds had stopped singing, as though they knew he was going the wrong way and couldn't bear to watch. He found himself in a small clearing. Large trees surrounded him, but one had lost a huge branch, which lay across the open space, tempting him to sit and rest.

He sat and unstopped his wineskin. The wine had long since run out, but he had filled it at a spring earlier and the water was cool and sweet. He looked down, idly kicking pine cones away from his feet. The branch had lain here for a long time, he saw. There was no smell of burning, but it had been sheared away from its tree by lightning: the end of the branch was still black. Curious, he moved closer to look at the damage, and saw smaller branches covered with burned pine cones: blackened on the outside, but still bright terracotta within. He reached down to pick one up and see if the soot came off on his hands.

'Do you think the pine cones can tell you where the Gorgons live?' asked a voice. Perseus jumped. He had heard no footsteps. When he was walking, that was all he heard: the sound of his own weight crushing twigs and seeds beneath him. But now he looked up and saw not one, but two fellow travellers. Except he knew somehow that they were not travellers. Afterwards, he wondered what had made him think that, but he couldn't be sure. It was something about their posture or lack of possessions, he didn't know. He had learned to assess travellers by how well or ill prepared they appeared for whatever was to come. These two looked like what was to come would have to prepare for them. Their clothes were pristine and their faces serene, showing no signs of fatigue: they had not lain down on a bed of leaves last night.

'No,' he said, staring at them. He assumed they had been sent by Polydectes to follow him and taunt him for this early failure. He did not want to give the king's servants – were they siblings? They looked similar and yet unalike, he could not quite make sense of it – the satisfaction of seeing his despair. He certainly didn't want the king to find out that he was doing everything wrong.

'No, of course not,' said the woman. A bird flew from one branch to another behind her. Perseus blinked because he would have sworn it was an owl, but he knew perfectly well they wouldn't be flying around at this hour. 'Of course we haven't come from Polydectes.'

Perseus was sure he hadn't said anything about the king. But then, he hadn't said anything about Gorgons either, and she had known about them. If these people hadn't come from the king, how did they know what he was looking for? A thought rushed into his mind and he flushed: did everyone on Seriphos know what he was doing? Had the king and his entourage told everyone they met to keep an eye out for the stupid young adventurer making a fool of himself? A second thought grabbed at the tail of the first: had the travellers he had spoken to on his way here misdirected him on purpose? He felt his eyes prickling with tears of rage.

'Well, don't cry,' said the woman, contempt accruing with every word. Perseus – used to the caring tones of his mother – flushed an even darker shade.

'We're here to help, son,' said the man. He wore a thin cloak which could not possibly keep him warm at night and a brimmed straw hat. His tunic was short and plain, and he rested his hand lightly on a staff. His boots were leather and laced up the front, the tongues curving down and the sides winging out at the top. He looked exactly like a normal traveller, and nothing like one at all. His sister, if that was who she was, wore a longer tunic, her cloak decorated with embroidered snakes. Her hair was bound into a knot at the back of her head: a simple band around her forehead held loose strands out of her eyes. Perseus looked again at the cloak. The snakes were so realistic, he thought he had seen one move. But it must just have been the way the light fell through the trees.

'What kind of help?' he asked. 'Do you know where the Gorgons are?'

The woman snorted. 'Of course we do,' she said. 'Is that your plan? To just go there and ask if you can have one of their heads? Really?'

Perseus felt smaller and weaker with everything she said. He should have thought of all this himself. The man flashed a look at his sister and she shrugged.

'We can help you to prepare yourself for the encounter,' the man said. 'You need guidance, don't you?'

Perseus wanted to say yes, but feared a further dose of the woman's scorn.

She muttered something about Zeus, but he didn't hear the rest. The man took a step towards him. 'She's right,' he said. 'You will die if you go into this unprepared. And that won't help your mother and it won't please your father.'

'My father doesn't know what I'm doing,' Perseus replied. 'I was trying to find him, but . . .'

The man reached out and put a restraining hand on his sister's arm. 'He does know,' he said. 'Why else would we be here?'

'Even the Graiai might not be able to help someone this stupid,' the woman said. 'I think he's doing it deliberately.'

Perseus started to ask who the Graiai were and, while he was at it, who he was talking to, but the man shushed him with a look.

'Your father sent us,' the woman said slowly and clearly. 'Though he probably didn't realize what he was asking of us, because he didn't know you struggled with such basic things.'

'I don't struggle with basic things!' Perseus could no

longer contain the humiliation. 'I don't know who you are. I don't know where I am. I don't know what a Gorgon is. I don't know how to find one. I don't want my mother to marry the king. I need help. I don't think that makes me stupid.'

'Oh, don't you?' she replied. 'That's fine, then, if you don't mind being nothing beyond an absence of knowledge or capacity. I can see how that might not be disconcerting for you. We just sort of assumed—' She gestured at her brother, and he nodded awkwardly. 'Assumed that you had some idea of what you were trying to do. But you were just – what were you doing, actually? Just climbing a hill and then going down the other side of it? Hoping a Gorgon might appear? Does that often work?'

'I was trying to find a sacred grove!' Perseus shouted. 'Where my father might be, so I could ask for help.'

'I see,' she said. Perseus was beginning to find her helpful interest more harrowing than her contempt. 'And you were planning to recognize the grove by . . . ?'

'I don't know!'

'Maybe a tree blasted by lightning?' she suggested.

He stared at her.

'Lightning bolts are something Zeus uses quite often,' she said.

The man said nothing.

'Lightning comes down from the sky?' she added. 'It's a very bright light. You might have seen it sometimes.'

'I know what lightning is.'

'Good, that's a start,' she said. 'So you know you're sitting on a branch that Zeus separated from this tree with lightning.'

Perseus felt his face grow red again. Of course he had noticed thc tree had been blasted by lightning. He'd noticed it when he first saw the branch. He had looked at the charred pine cones.

'I didn't realize this was a sacred grove,' he said. 'But now you've pointed it out, I can see it must be.'

'Well,' she said to her brother. 'He'll probably die before we get him anywhere near the Gorgons. But we did say we'd help him.'

'We did,' said the man. 'I'm Hermes, by the way. Since you seem to be struggling. This is Athene.'

Perseus opened his mouth and closed it again.

'It's lucky we already know who you are,' Athene said.

'I'm sorry,' he said. 'I'm not used to gods just wandering up to me and telling me they can help.'

'Gods have been helping you since the day you were born,' Hermes replied.

'You should pay more attention,' Athene said.

'I will now. Did you say we had to go to see someone else?'

'The Graiai,' said Hermes. 'Don't worry, we know the way.'

'And they'll help me?' Perseus asked.

The gods looked at one another. 'It probably depends how you ask,' Hermes said.

*

He was standing on a broad ledge, midway up the cliff face. Perseus had no idea how he had travelled from the sacred grove to this rocky outpost, where an angry sea battered the grey stone beneath his feet. Turning to look up, he had to grab at the rock beside him and steady himself. He probably could climb it, if he had to, but it was a long way to fall if he lost his footing. He couldn't have made his way here without divine assistance, he knew: even his year at sea had not taught him how to moor a boat against a sheer cliff. No wonder the gods had laughed at him. He looked left and right and realized he was alone.

He felt a sudden lurch of fear, and crouched down before his legs lost their strength. This was how Dictys had taught him to cope with seasickness when it had overwhelmed him on his first voyages. He breathed through his mouth, watching the horizon until it steadied. Gradually, he felt able to stand again, so he did. He decided he was more likely to find the Graiai above him than below, and followed the ledge up the side of the cliff.

It was a slow process, punctuated with occasional bouts of terror when the wind picked up and threatened to toss him into the ocean. Again, he would crouch down, shrink his body to create a smaller target, and press himself against the cliff. He traversed one section on hands and knees when he could see no other way to continue. And as he climbed he tried to believe that he was on his way to the first real part of his quest, and not that he was a plaything of the gods who were watching him from some impervious vantage point and enjoying all this.

He crept a little further up the ledge, wishing he knew what he was looking for. Did the Graiai live on the top of the cliff? Why had the gods abandoned him where they did? Or what if he'd gone the wrong way, and they had been just around the curve of the rock from where he began his climb? What if it got dark while he was perched here? The panic threatened to overwhelm him and he wished himself back on Seriphos, with his mother and Dictys to look after him. He cursed himself for the way he had tried to show the king he was a man, when he still felt like a child.

As he inched his way up the rock, he thought he heard something over the sound of the wind and the distant waves breaking beneath him. He stopped and tried to quiet his ragged breathing; he couldn't hear it now. But when he squeezed his way past another jagged corner, he found himself standing at the entrance to a cave. He ducked back and listened again. Perhaps he could hear a voice. No, two voices. He was afraid and he clung to the idea that the people he heard sounded old. Perhaps they would be slow and that would give him an advantage. Pausing, he tried to calculate what else was in his favour. The gods had brought him here, so he could suppose they didn't want him to die. Then he thought of what was against him. He had the short sword he had borrowed from Dictys, but he didn't really know how to use it. The Graiai certainly outnumbered him. And they had what he wanted. But hadn't Hermes said it depended on how he asked? So perhaps these things didn't matter.

He stepped out into the entrance of the cave, and heard the voices fall silent. They had seen him already. But then came a sudden shout.

'Why have you gone quiet? What's going on?'

'Shh, I think I can see —'

'Don't shh me. Just because you have the eye doesn't give you the right to shh people. Does it?'

'No, it doesn't. Not at all.'

'Let me see!'

There was a scuffling sound and then a squawk of anger.

'Give it back!'

'No, you weren't using it properly. Otherwise you'd see that a man has come to visit us and you would have said so.'

'I want to see.'

'You can see later.'

Perseus stared into the gloom. Gradually, he saw that he had been wrong: there were three figures, not two. He could just see their outlines, hunched and cloaked. Their heads were bound in scarves and only one seemed to be facing him. Her face was screwed up and she looked older than the rock she lived on, older than the sea.

'Who are you?' she demanded. And the other two women – if they were women – turned to face him.

'I'm Perseus,' he said. But his voice sounded weak and small and he despised himself. No wonder he was met with a cacophony of cruel laughter.

'You're Perseus,' said the one in the centre.

'Let me see,' screeched the one on the right. 'What does he look like?'

The one on the left said nothing.

'He looks young,' said the one in the middle.

'Could we eat him?' asked the one on the right.

Perseus was holding his sword, but he could feel his hands shaking.

'No, not that young,' said the middle one. 'Perhaps if we boiled him, but I don't think so.'

The one on the left suddenly delivered a sharp blow to

the middle one. There was a howl of pain and a flurry of cloaks and then suddenly the middle one went silent.

'Why don't you come closer?' asked the one on the left. Perseus grew cold, and tried to convince himself it was sweat from his climb that was making his back clammy and his hair damp. He took a small step nearer to the huddled bodies. 'That's it,' she continued. 'So I can see you.'

'Does Enyo have the eye?' asked the one on the right. 'Have you let her have it when it was my turn?'

The one in the middle hissed at her. 'I didn't let her. She took it. You heard her taking it.'

'But it was my turn,' repeated the one on the right.

'Be quiet, Pemphredo,' said the one on the left. 'You can have your turn later.'

'You always say that,' she wailed. 'I want to see now. Deino always lets you get your own way. It isn't fair.'

'She stole it from me,' said the middle one, whom Perseus presumed must be Deino. 'It was still my turn and it would have been yours next, if she hadn't stolen it.'

Perseus had no idea what to say. These strange old women, who could agree on nothing, were supposed to help him? The gods must have been playing a cruel trick.

'Well, you weren't telling us what was going on,' said Enyo. 'I needed to see for myself. You don't deserve to have the eye if you don't use it properly. No, Pemphredo, we can't eat him. He's a man, almost. What do you want?'

'The gods told me you could help me,' Perseus said.

'Help you with what?' said Pemphredo, her mood seemingly unimproved by the confirmation that their guest was not edible.

'Which gods?' asked Deino.

'Ones we like, or ones we don't?' said Enyo.

'Hermes,' Perseus said. 'And Athene.'

'Oh, I see,' said Deino. She turned to Pemphredo. 'Well, you like her, don't you?'

Pemphredo shrugged. 'She's not the worst of them, I suppose.'

'I don't like Hermes,' said Enyo. 'But of course you never remember that.'

'Why don't you like him?' asked Deino.

'Because he's a liar and a thief,' said Pemphredo. 'You shouldn't like him either.'

Perseus looked from one to another, and wondered who he should be addressing.

'They sent me to seek your help,' he said into the space between them. 'With my quest.'

Deino threw back her ancient head and laughed. The other two women joined in. Perseus wondered if mocking him was the only thing the old hags agreed on.

'With your quest?' said Enyo. 'What kind of quest would that be?'

Perseus straightened his shoulders. 'I seek the head of a Gorgon,' he replied.

All sounds of merriment ceased.

'The head of a Gorgon?' said Deino. 'Now what made the gods think we would help you with that?'

'I have to take it back to Polydectes,' Perseus said, in case they thought he was just greedy. 'Otherwise he demands that my mother marry him.'

'And why would we care about your mother's marital plans?' asked Enyo.

'She wants to stay with Dictys,' said Perseus, but he could feel his voice getting smaller.

'It doesn't matter what she wants if we don't care about her,' said Pemphredo. 'Mortals are all the same,' she said to her sisters. 'They think their concerns are everyone's concerns.'

'So you don't want to help me?' Perseus asked.

It was Enyo who replied. 'Why would we? What's in it for us?'

'What do you want? I could get it for you.' Perseus had no idea how he could get anything for these old women, not least because he didn't know how he could get away from their cliff or get back here with whatever it was they asked for.

'What do we want?' asked Deino. 'That's a good question. What do we want?' The three sisters muttered to each other for a moment and Perseus waited, hoping they might want something that was just outside the cave.

'Another eye,' said Pemphredo.

'Two more eyes,' corrected Deino.

'Each,' said Enyo.

'I'm sorry?'

'We want more eyes,' Enyo repeated. 'We share one.'

'I don't understand,' said Perseus. 'What do you mean, you share one?'

'It isn't difficult,' said Pemphredo. 'We only have one eye, and we have to share it. Some of us get less of a share than others.'

'How do you share it?' he asked, staring into the darkness. He had assumed that their eye sockets were wrinkled because they were old, but now that he knew he was looking

151

at empty space, he could see it. 'One of you just tells the others what she can see? Is that right?'

'No,' screeched Pemphredo, as she and Deino attacked Enyo together. There was a muffled fight and then it was Deino who stepped forward, and blinked a single eye in his direction.

'You see?' said Pemphredo. 'I never get a turn.'

'You had a turn yesterday,' snapped Enyo. 'You never remember your turns, so you always make a fuss about nothing.'

'I haven't had it once today,' Pemphredo replied. 'You and Deino have stolen my turn.' Deino rolled the communal eye. And Perseus realized the sisters were speaking quite literally. They took turns using one eyeball between them. He shuddered at the thought, and then hoped Deino hadn't noticed.

'Have you only ever had one eye?' Perseus asked. He had no idea where he could possibly find more eyes for these old women to use.

'Of course we have!' said Enyo. 'Do you think we had more eyes and put them down somewhere? Misplaced them?' She turned her unseeing face to her sisters. 'This is a waste of time. He won't help us. He can't. He's a fool.'

'I'm not a fool,' said Perseus, who felt he had been belittled enough for one day. 'I just didn't understand at first. I haven't met anyone like you before, and I was trying to learn more about you before I fulfil your demands.'

There was another pause, but this time – even Perseus could tell – it was different. There was no mockery, no cruelty in this silence, but something else: a scrap of hope.

'We only ever had one eye,' said Deino.

'And one tooth,' added Pemphredo.

'That's why we didn't know if we could eat you,' said Enyo. 'We have to take turns to eat and see. And no one can ever see what she's eating.'

'You can't have the eye and the tooth at once?' Perseus asked.

'Who would give them back if she had everything?' said Deino.

For the first time since he had walked into the cave Perseus felt something other than fear and disgust. To have so little, to live so pitiable a life that a partial share in a single tooth and eye could seem like everything. And just as he felt the surge of pity, he knew what to do.

'Could I see the eye, please?' he said. 'And the tooth?'

'Of course not!' screamed Deino. 'Of course you cannot. Why would we give you the eye or the tooth? You might take them and keep them and never give them back. Mortals are all the same: greedy, deceitful and cruel. Everyone knows. How dare you even ask?'

But Perseus noticed that the other two did not share her fury. Without the eye, they had less to lose.

'It would make it much easier for me to find more eyes for you if I've seen your eye properly,' he said. 'Otherwise I won't know exactly what I'm looking for. And I am sure that's why the gods sent me here today: so I could help you.'

'No,' said Deino.

'How about the tooth?' asked Pemphredo. 'Would it help if you saw the tooth?'

'Yes, of course,' said Perseus.

'Hand it over, Enyo,' said her sister.

'I don't want to,' said Enyo. 'I want to eat something first. The tooth isn't the same as the eye. You have to eat with it or there's no point having it. You're just minding it until the next meal.'

'We ate before the boy arrived,' said Pemphredo. 'I'm not hungry. Just give him the tooth.'

'No,' said Enyo.

'We can take it if you won't give it up,' Deino said. 'I'm not giving him the eye so you'll have to give up the tooth.'

'You can't take it. I'm stronger than both of you.'

'You're not stronger than both of us at the same time,' said Pemphredo. 'Not if we hold you and the boy takes the tooth.'

Perseus loved his mother with what he believed was a single-minded devotion but he hoped from his innermost soul that this was not the only way to find a Gorgon's head.

'Very well,' said Enyo and reached into her mouth. She took out one large tooth and held it up in her hand. Deino rotated her towards Perseus so she was reaching the right way. And – his whole body rigid to disguise his horror – Perseus stepped forward and took the tooth from her leathery fingers. He stepped back again and peered at it, holding it up to the dingy light.

'Ah, I see,' he said.

'Must be nice,' muttered Enyo.

'I mean, I think I know where I could find more of these,' said Perseus. 'Ideally you'd like one each? Or more than one?'

The shift in the sisters' mood was unmistakable. This silence dripped with hope.

'More than one?' asked Deino at last.

'Each?' said Pemphredo.

'Some people have more than one tooth,' said Perseus. 'It makes it easier to chew, I think.'

'It must do,' said Enyo.

'More than one,' said Pemphredo. 'Each. And eyes the same.' The other two nodded.

'That's right,' said Deino. 'Two eyes each, and as many teeth as you can find.'

'I feel confident about finding the teeth for you ladies,' Perseus said. 'But I don't know if I can manage the eyes.'

'If you don't,' Enyo said, calmly, 'Deino will kill you and I will take back the tooth and gnaw the flesh from your bones.'

'Please,' said Perseus. 'I want to find you more eyes, and I will if I can. But without the original eye I wouldn't know exactly what size I was looking for. There's no point my bringing you eyes that don't fit, is there?'

'Give him the eye,' said Pemphredo.

'No,' said Deino. 'You can give it to him when it's your turn.'

'I never get a turn. And if you give him the eye, we won't need turns.'

'She's right,' said Enyo. 'We would never have to share again.'

There was silence.

'Very well,' said Deino. 'But if he comes back with eyes that are too small and fall out, it's still my turn. Agreed?'

'Yes,' said Enyo.

'Yes,' said Pemphredo.

Perseus managed not to retch as he heard the jellied scoop of an eye being pulled from its socket. Deino held it out to him, and he took it from her. It was not the slimy texture that was its most revolting feature, he would remember in later years, but the warmth.

'There's only one more question, and then I will go and find what you need,' said Perseus. 'I know you could tell me when I come back, but I'm worried that in the happy excitement of new eyes, and teeth, I might forget to ask.'

'What is it?' said Deino.

'I need your help with my other quest,' he said. 'The search for a Gorgon's head.'

'To save his mother,' Enyo said. 'From death.'

'Was it death?' asked Pemphredo.

'Marriage,' said Perseus.

Pemphredo shrugged.

'You'll need what the nymphs have,' said Deino.

'The Gorgons are our sisters!' Enyo cried. 'Don't tell him that.'

'When did we last see them?' asked Deino. 'When did they last offer to find us a new tooth or an eye each? Each!'

'She's right,' said Pemphredo. 'The Hesperides can help you,' she said.

'And that's all you can tell me?' asked Perseus.

'They have what you need,' Enyo replied. 'Now bring us our eyes and our teeth.'

But Perseus had already thrown them into the sea beneath their cave, and by the time they realized he would never return, the gods had taken him far away and their howls of anguish were lost in the sound of the waves and the wind.

Gorgoneion

You are not. You're not still sympathizing with him. Why? No one asked him to touch the eye or the tooth. He asked to have them. He tricked the Graiai into handing them over. You saw that, did you? I suppose you thought it was clever. Clever Perseus using his wits to defeat the disgusting old women? Your own eyes aren't all that, you know. Oh, but at least they're safe inside your head. Well, lucky you. Would it kill you to be sympathetic about someone who isn't as fortunate as you are? Would it? No. So perhaps when you've finished congratulating Perseus for his quick tricks, you might spare a moment to think about how the Graiai lived after he was gone.

Blind and hungry.

Athene

Athene could tell that something was wrong with Hephaestus, but she didn't know what. Why was he standing in front of his forge with a strange smile on his face? Her request was not unusual. She wanted a new spear and a new shield.

'Why are you smiling?'

'Sorry,' said Hephaestus. He looked away.

'I didn't say you had to apologize,' she said. 'I asked you why you were smiling.'

'I'm happy to see you,' he replied.

Athene thought about this. 'I see. And you'll make the spear?'

'Of course, it would be an honour,' he said.

'Good,' she said, assuming he had finished. But as she spoke he opened his mouth again and said, 'I was speaking to your uncle.'

'Which one?'

'Poseidon.'

'Why?'

'He was offering me some advice,' Hephaestus said. 'You could sit down, if you wanted to.' He gestured at the broad stump of a tree, which had long ago been blasted to oblivion by Zeus. Hephaestus had carved it into a seat – a delicate pattern of leaves etched into its back – though Athene had never seen anyone here except him and he never sat on it.

'Why?' she asked.

'To test it,' he said. 'I'd like to know if you find it comfortable.'

She nodded, and walked over to the tree, which bore no trace of its blackened self. She sat on the gentle curve and leaned into the back. 'It's very comfortable,' she said.

'I made it for you,' he replied. Athene was growing bored of asking him why he kept saying and doing such odd things, so she decided to ignore this. She had never made any request for a chair. 'Would you like to know what Poseidon was advising me to do?'

Athene thought for a moment. 'Not really,' she said.

Hephaestus limped towards her. 'I'd like to tell you,' he said.

'I don't know why you ask me what I'd like if you aren't going to listen to the answer.'

'I'm sorry.' The blacksmith took another step closer. 'I was asking you as a way of introducing the subject. Because I didn't want to just tell you what he said.'

'Did he tell you to make me a wooden chair?' she asked. 'Because he might not have been giving you the best advice.' Hephaestus now stood in front of her and looked fondly at his handiwork.

'There's room for both of us,' he said. 'Look.' He spun awkwardly on his good ankle and sat down heavily beside her. Athene was beginning to wish she had asked another blacksmith, even a mortal one, to make her weapons. Hephaestus didn't normally behave like this and she didn't like it. She shifted away from him.

'Don't run away,' he said. 'Please.'

'I'm not running anywhere. I'm moving because you're sitting so close that your hip was touching mine and I didn't like it.'

'I'm sorry,' he said. 'Can I tell you about Poseidon?'

'Will it take long?' she asked.

'No.'

'Could you tell me while you're making my new spear?'

'No, I need to tell you here,' he said. 'Your uncle said I should ask you to marry me.'

She stared at the blacksmith god, her head slightly tilted as though she were trying to see what lunacy had crawled in through his ears.

'He was mistaken,' she said.

'He wasn't.' Hephaestus grabbed her hand in his, and held it. Athene knew she could easily outrun him, but his arms and hands were like the iron they worked. She wondered if it would be more effective to stamp on his good foot or the bad one.

'I don't like to be touched,' she said.

'I know,' Hephaestus replied. 'It's one of a thousand things I love about you.'

'But you're touching me, when you know I don't like it.'

'Because I want to be the one whose touch you like.'

'You aren't. No one is.'

'You don't mind when your owl flutters down and perches on your shoulder,' he said. 'You hold out your arm to him, so he can land more easily.'

'He's an owl.'

'I think you could love me like that.'

'I couldn't.'

He pulled her hand towards him. 'I've already asked Zeus. He approves the match.'

'It doesn't matter whether he approves it or not, because there isn't a match.'

'I want you.' He leaned towards her, pulling her closer. She could smell hot metal on his skin.

'I don't want you,' she said. 'Let go of me.' She wriggled to try and free her hand, and felt his body tense. She pulled harder and suddenly he let go. She jumped up, away from him, watching to ascertain if he would follow her or grab at her. But his whole body had gone limp. She saw a hateful satisfaction on his face and followed his gaze, glancing down at her tunic.

She felt the heat of his semen before she saw it, and she pulled at her cloak, tearing off a piece of the finely woven cloth. She swabbed her thigh clean, then hurled the wool to the ground in disgust. She wanted to scream that she hated him, and would never marry him, would never marry anyone, would go straight to Zeus and tell him what Hephaestus had done to her. But as she opened her mouth to say all this, she knew it was only half-true. She hated him and would never marry, but she was not going to tell Zeus what had happened, because she was too ashamed. She knew she was being ridiculous, because she had done nothing to be ashamed of. And yet, looking down at the slumped body of Hephaestus – his eyes closed, unworried – she could see that he felt no shame at all for what he had done. And yet, it was a shameful act and disgust and contempt were the proper response. If Hephaestus did not feel these things, then she must. They had to go somewhere.

And so she ran away from the forge, away from Olympus, hating Hephaestus and Poseidon and Zeus and herself.

Medusa

They bound Medusa's eyes with damp cloths, in the hope that the pain would die down, as the pains in her head had done. But it did not. If anything, the burning sensation grew stronger with each day. The dark mass of snakes swirled around her head, each of them somehow taking care not to dislodge the bindings. She relied on touch to find her way around the cave, which she already knew so intimately that it took very little time to learn without sight. Sometimes she felt cold and would move to the cave entrance, tracing her way along the wall with the lightest touch of her fingers. She would sit with the sun on her face, her back resting against warm rock, her hands buried in the piles of dried seaweed that littered the shore. Sometimes she would raise broken pieces to her lips, and taste the sea.

She didn't mind the darkness as much as the losses. She missed everything she could hear and many more things she could not. The constant cries of birds were a comfort, reminding her of the way they swooped and arced over the waves. She could hear the cormorants arguing with the gulls and she knew exactly which rocks they had perched on before picking their quarrel. She heard the sheep murmuring to one another, and smiled. Euryale herded a pair towards her, so she could lose her hands in the thick wool on their chests. She could feel the seagrass fluttering and the soft curves the wind left on the sand beneath her feet. She still had so much, she reminded herself.

But she missed the sight of fish darting around her feet as she stood in glittering water. She wanted to see the graceful birds in flight, not just hear them as they squabbled. She wanted to squint into the sun and witness the growing and changing of the seasons. She yearned for the bright pink of cyclamen petals instead of the dark, twisting red that was all she could see behind the bindings.

When the pain in her skull surged like a storm, she would press the heels of her hands into the sockets to try and calm them.

'What's it like?' asked Euryale. Neither she nor Sthenno had any real understanding of pain. Gorgons weren't capable of it, she didn't think. She had heard that some gods – some of the Olympian ones – could feel injuries, at least briefly. But Gorgons had leathery hides, fearsome faces, long sharp teeth. Who would dare to attack one, and what damage could they do?

'I don't know what to compare it to,' Medusa said. 'It's like the feeling of fire under my skin, except there's no fire.'

'I see,' said Euryale, who did not see, because she could put out a fire with her bare hands and feel nothing at all.

'Would it help if we took off these cloths,' Sthenno asked, 'and checked how your eyes look? We might be able to do something to help with the pain.'

Euryale nodded her agreement, and then felt foolish. 'I agree,' she said.

Medusa looked at her sisters through the darkness and imagined their faces. Sthenno's brow drawn in worry, her mouth slightly ajar, her shoulders raised ready to embrace and protect. Euryale looking away because she didn't want Medusa to feel outnumbered. Her guilty expression because she had forgotten and nodded. Medusa had felt the agreement between her sisters and wished she could explain to Euryale that she could hear their nods and gestures somehow, even if she couldn't see them. But she didn't want to make her sister still more self-conscious. And she could feel the tautness in Euryale because she wanted to fight something but could not attack those responsible for her sister's injuries.

How she would love to see them again, even if it was just once more.

Sthenno reached out her clawed hand and patted her sister's arm and Medusa knew they were both waiting for her to reply. She thought for a moment, but she could not take the risk.

'No,' she said. 'I think that would be the wrong thing to do.'

Gaia

Gaia, on whom the god's semen had fallen when Athene tossed it aside, was faced with a choice. She thought of her lost children, of all the giants the Olympians had slain, one after another. She thought of how she had gathered their broken bodies to herself when the battle was over, how she had held them, how she had wept rivers and lakes. If mortals were to stumble across the battlefield, they would find the ground scorched by lightning blasts. But no matter how hard they searched, they would not find the bodies of her children. Gaia had opened the earth to swallow their bones and keep them safe in death, as she had failed to do in life. She had examined every inch of them, knowing which god had damaged which child from the marks left on them.

She wanted to be able to avenge them, but she knew it was not in her nature to punish and destroy. She was the earth, she was meant to give life and sustain it. And yet. She thought again of the bodies of her sons – burned by thunderbolts, pierced by arrows – and she wanted to smash every tree on every mountain, to block every stream, to blight every crop.

But she knew this would only punish the mortals who loved her, and who had feared and revered her offspring. Would it do anything to injure the vicious gods who had done her such incalculable harm? It would not. Perhaps a temple or two would slide into the sea but they all had so many temples, so much greed.

And then here was the little scrap of wool, thrown from the goddess's hand to the earth. His seed, visible to all. Her touch, visible to Gaia alone. She thought of Athene running away from the blacksmith, her face distorted with contempt. Gaia saw the shame in the goddess as she skulked in her temples, the fury as she surveyed the sea and thought of not one, but now two cruel insults from her uncle Poseidon. The helplessness as she realized that there was not yet any way she could punish him for his encouragement of Hephaestus. And in her memory, she also saw the glowing joy that had suffused the goddess as she peeled the skin from Gaia's beautiful son.

She watched Hephaestus at his forge each day, wondering why Athene never came to collect her new weapons. She saw him pick them up, removing a speck of dust from the shield, checking again that the balance of the spear was perfect. She saw him try to distract himself by making, and she watched him fail.

And then Gaia – who could not destroy but only nurture – knew exactly what she would do to take her revenge.

Panopeia

Do you remember where you are? At the place where Ethiopia meets Oceanos: the furthest land and the furthest sea. Past the Graiai and the Gorgons, all of whom you know better now. These daughters of the sea are drawn to it and repelled by it at once. The blind Graiai say they fear for their safety on their grim grey island. And yet, no one forced them to take up residence there: they found it and made it their home. And Sthenno and Euryale wanted to stay on the coast, so their parents could reach them if they ever chose to (they have never chosen to). How much time must pass before you accept that no sea god is coming? Although, of course, Phorcys did make one brief visit to their little patch of the shore, when he gave them their strange mortal sister. Did they stay by the water in case he decided to bring another?

Medusa used to swim in the sea every day, and then she stopped. Some of the Nereids said it was Poseidon who drove her from the water, some say it was Athene. Cornered by one, cursed by the other. I think it was both. But even she stays by the sea, no matter what. Her sister reshaped the shoreline to please her, pushed Poseidon himself away. She doesn't leave, but she hasn't been out of the cave for a while. So she is still here, but you wouldn't know it.

Now, where was I? Or rather, where were you? You're at the furthest point you can sail to, where the ocean kisses the setting sun. It is beautiful and sad at once: it holds none of the promise that dawn brings, if you journey the opposite way. It is a place where things come to an end. Mortals don't belong here: it makes them melancholy.

But perhaps you are stubborn. Or desperate. Perhaps you have some pressing reason that overwhelms the natural antipathy you feel at being in the wrong place.

And so instead of going back to where mortals belong, you're following the narrow coils of the sea inland. It is not a journey you could make on foot: you would not survive the first part of it. It is a difficult and dangerous journey even by boat: every kind of peril would beset you. You really would be safer to take wing. And then you would arrive more swiftly at the place where the sea unfurls into one last large circle. There is an island in the middle of this final coil, and from the air you would not be able to tell which way the water flows. The island has never – at least not so far – been reached by any mortal creature. The narrow lick of sea guards it fiercely.

Even if you could find a way to be close enough to see it, you would not. Those sea coils shroud everything in a thick mist, no matter which wind is blowing or how hard Helios burns down. You would believe you had reached a miserable spot, this dismal lake where the sun never penetrates. You would wrap your cloak more tightly around your shoulders, and bow your head to walk into the wind. The relief you first felt – the land around it is arid and baked to a dark red – would soon disappear. You could not even slake your thirst because the only water you would find is briny and you would spit it out. You would hurry away from this place and vow never to return. You would follow the water back the way you had come.

And because you could not see the island, you would never be able to tell another soul that it was there. Its inhabitants remain uninterrupted by mortal men. Or at least they always had until now.

The Hesperides

No one was quite sure how many nymphs there were. Some said three, some believed four, and one enthusiast went as high as seven. But the disparities were easily explained: the Hesperides lived in an isolated spot, they did not travel and they never encouraged visitors. So most things that people repeated about them as certainty were not certain at all. Which was how Perseus had found himself at a loss for how to proceed, even with the Graiai's advice drumming in his mind as he climbed to the top of their cliff. He had no idea if this was the right thing to do, or how his divine companions might find him again, or why they couldn't just appear a little sooner, before he had scraped the skin from his hands clinging to the rock face and believing throughout the climb that he would fall into the crashing water, or smash onto the stone beneath him. But he could not stay where the Graiai could hear him, even if they could no longer see him or eat him. And clambering down towards the water seemed riskier – just – than climbing away from it.

When he finally reached the summit, his relief was immediately blown away by the gale which almost took him off his feet. He lay face down on the rock, holding on for his life. He had no idea how long he clung on, but it was more than enough time to believe he had been abandoned to this most desolate place for good.

'What did they tell you?' asked Hermes, when he and Athene arrived.

Perseus raised his head as far as he could without letting go of his rock.

'Why are you lying down?' Athene added. 'Are you tired?' She smiled at Hermes triumphantly, delighted to have learned something about mortals that she could share.

'I am tired,' Perseus said. 'It was a long and difficult climb.'

'Was it?' asked Hermes.

'Very. Also, Aeolus has set all the winds loose upon this rock, and I think if I stand up I will be blown into the ocean.'

'You see?' Athene was almost hopping with glee. 'They talk about weather. They like it.'

'I don't like it,' Perseus clarified, nervous as he was to contradict her. 'I just don't want to fall.'

'I think I understand,' said Hermes. 'But you spoke to the Graiai? Before you lay down here?'

'Yes, I spoke to the Graiai.'

'And did you manage to learn anything from them?' Hermes asked.

'The Hesperides have what I need,' Perseus replied.

'Oh, the Hesperides!' said Athene. 'We should have thought of that.'

Hermes nodded thoughtfully, while Perseus tried to blink the wind-pricked tears from his eyes. 'Yes,' Hermes agreed. 'We probably should have.'

'Is there a reason why you didn't?' Perseus was trying to sound interested rather than critical, but his fingers were going numb and he was finding it difficult to hold on.

'I don't know,' said Hermes.

'Could we go there now?' asked Perseus.

'Where?' said Hermes.

'Wherever the Hesperides are.'

'Didn't you ask the Graiai where you could find them?' said Athene.

'No.' A particularly belligerent gust almost sent him flying. 'No, I was hoping you would know.'

'We can't do everything for you,' she replied. 'Maybe you should go back and ask them for directions.'

Perseus thought he might just let go and allow the winds to take him to his death. 'I'm not sure they would tell me now,' he said.

'Oh, did you annoy them?' she asked.

'I tricked them,' he said. 'So they would tell me what I needed to know.'

'I see,' said Hermes. He and Athene exchanged a glance. 'We were hoping you'd do a little more.'

'I will try to do better next time,' said Perseus. 'If there is a next time.'

'I'm not sure I would encourage you to embark on other quests,' said Athene. 'You're not doing well at all, not even by the standards of a mortal.'

'I'm sorry.' Perseus was crying from the bitter cold, but if he hadn't been, he would have wept.

'What do you think?' asked Hermes.

'It's what Zeus wants us to do,' she replied. 'Help him.'

'I suppose we must,' said Hermes.

'Thank you.' Perseus could scarcely open his locked jaw to set the words free. But in a moment the buffeting winds were gone, and the salt spray was gone, and the sharp rock was gone.

*

He blinked and raised his hands to his face to wipe away the tears. His fingers snagged in his salt-rimed hair: even when he and Dictys had been caught in a storm, he had never found himself in such a state. He saw water in front of him, a gently flowing stream. He cupped his hands to drink and spat it straight back out.

'It's seawater,' Athene told him.

'I can tell now I've tasted it,' he said. 'I thought it was a river.'

'A lot of people would probably make that mistake,' she said. 'Because it flows so far inland. But it's still part of the sea.'

The gods had been entirely untouched by the wind and the ocean and Perseus now remembered that they would also be untouched by thirst. 'Is there fresh water nearby, do you know?' he asked.

'Probably,' she said. 'Somewhere.'

'I'll go and look in a moment if that's alright.'

'Of course it is,' Athene replied. 'You could refill your water-skin then, couldn't you?' She looked again at Hermes, delighted with herself.

Perseus had been concentrating so hard on not dying, and then on interrogating the Graiai, and then on not dying again, that he had completely forgotten he was carrying a water-skin. He pulled on the leather strap that had held it in place across his body. As the flask appeared by his ribs, he reached across for it and winced in pain.

'Are you hurt?' asked Hermes.

'No,' Perseus admitted. He had come off the Graiai's rock with cuts and bruises but nothing too severe. He felt the greatest discomfort in his biceps and his calves, and thought of all the times he had helped Dictys with his nets, or carried home their catch. He had believed himself strong, but his quest had already found him wanting. He unstopped the bottle and drank deeply. He wanted to pour water over his salt-crusted eyelids but he worried he would need it to drink later.

'Where are we?' he asked.

'The island of the Hesperides, of course,' said Athene. 'Where did you think we'd take you?'

Hermes shook his head slowly. No wonder he usually delivered a message from Zeus and then disappeared. Mortals were tiresome company.

Perseus looked around him. After the desolate island of the Graiai, he was relieved to see that the Hesperides lived in a more appealing location. Seagrass and prickly pears grew on the banks of the river which was not a river. Then came the soft sand on which he now sat, drinking his water and enjoying the warmth of the sun. He was a little confused by the way he could see the far bank of the stream, but nothing beyond it, as a thick fog obscured everything else. But he tried not to concern himself because when he turned to look the other way, he saw lush green of every variety. He saw fat-leaved trees growing above thick grass. Bright red and purple flowers sprang out from among the darkest leaves like the sparkling fish he and Dictys used to see in the deepest waters. Accustomed to living only on the sand and the sea, he didn't think he had ever seen so many colours before.

'What's he doing?' asked Athene.

Hermes shrugged. 'Looking?'

'What at?'

'I don't know.'

The two gods followed the young man's gaze, but they saw nothing remarkable.

Athene stepped closer to Perseus and leaned down. 'These aren't the Hesperides,' she said slowly. 'They're just plants.'

'They're beautiful,' said Perseus, scrambling awkwardly to his feet and trying not to groan as his calf muscles screamed.

'Oh, good,' said Hermes. 'The nymphs will be glad you like them, I'm sure.' He looked across the top of Perseus's head at Athene. 'We'll come back,' he said.

And the sea mist seemed to rise up and take them, because Perseus saw a blur and then an absence and realized he was once again alone. He had the feeling he was irritating his divine companions, but he didn't really know why, so he didn't know how to stop. It was a relief when they left, even though he was afraid of what he might find ahead of him.

He reminded himself of what the Graiai had said: the nymphs had something he needed. And nymphs surely wouldn't be as disgusting as those hags. He pushed away the memory of their warm, slippery eye between his fingers. He took a few steps inland and wondered which way he should go. If the island belonged to the nymphs, they could be anywhere. And how big was their island anyway? Seriphos was an island but it would take many days to search. And – he reminded himself as his thigh muscles pleaded with him to sit back down – he did not have many days. He stood still and listened. There were so many birds flitting among the trees, all he could hear was their song. He wondered if he would even recognize the voice of a nymph if he heard her. He could not know, of course, that the Hesperides already knew he was there, and were laughing as they hid from him.

*

The Hesperides were not hiding because they feared the arrival of this mortal man: they feared no one. They were hiding because they lived in paradise and they had long since run out of interesting things to do. The arrival of a man – or was he a boy? – had thrown their predictably perfect day into turmoil and they were all delighted. Some hid in the apple trees, others disappeared into the waters of the beautiful lake at the centre of the island. They watched Perseus crash around their flawless gardens looking behind rocks and up trees and they sniggered at his foolishness and ignorance. Had he never seen a nymph before? Perhaps he believed they were the size of a stoat. Occasionally, Perseus would stand still, look around him, take a deep breath, and shout, 'Show yourselves, nymphs.' This only made them laugh harder.

'Are all mortals like this?' one whispered to another. They persuaded the birds to start flying around Perseus in all directions, so he couldn't tell if he was being serenaded or assaulted. He eventually stumbled across their lake and gave up the search, gratefully drinking and refilling his water-skin while he had the chance. Staring at his rippling reflection, he decided he could take a few moments to bathe, since he couldn't seem to find the nymphs anyway. The salt was scratching every inch of his skin. He took off his sandals and untied his cloak, leaving them both on the bank. He stepped into the lake expecting it to be cool, like the water he had drunk. But somehow it now felt warm against his skin and he submerged his whole body, even plunging his weary head beneath the surface. He watched dappled fish dart away in every direction and felt unreasonably sure that they were mocking him, just like the birds. But the water was so calming, and the feeling of clean skin and soft clothes was so pleasing, that he could not maintain his annoyance. He swam a few strokes. It felt so good that he swam a little further and faster, enjoying the way the water tugged at his tunic. Let it have the thing if it wanted it so much. He straightened his arms and the tunic floated away. He could not remember ever feeling more free. He pulled himself beneath the surface once again, then pushed himself up hard, closing his eyes as the water rushed past his face. He burst up, shouting with delight and relief. And only when he opened his eyes did he see the Hesperides sitting on rocks all along the bank, as though they had been there the whole time.

Perseus blushed bright red and dropped back into the water to try and hide himself. But the water was so clear that he felt no less naked. He looked around for his tunic, which must surely be within reach. But somehow it was not. Perseus felt a rush of panic, which only deepened when he saw a fluttering white shape on the rocks in front of him, and realized that two nymphs were sitting on what looked a great deal like his tunic.

Moments ago, he had felt like the dolphins he used to see leaping gleefully alongside Dictys's boat. Now, as he tried to walk through the water towards the Hesperides, he felt like a man wearing rocks for shoes.

'It's easier to swim through water than walk through it,' one of the nymphs called out.

'He's scared we'll see more of his naked body if he swims,' said another.

'I don't think we could see more than we've already seen,' said a third. 'Although I am very happy to see it again.'

They all giggled and stared and Perseus did not know what to say or do. If he backed away from them, they might disappear again and he might lose his only chance to ask them for their help. The Graiai and the gods had seemed equally certain that he could not pursue his quest without their assistance. But they were mocking him, and one of them had taken his tunic. He blinked water droplets from his eyes. Another had, it seemed, stolen his sandals. On Seriphos men went naked whenever they wished, of course, but women weren't standing around watching them. Or lounging on their tunics. Or wearing their shoes and impersonating the inelegant way he moved. The nymphs were certainly much more beautiful than the Graiai, but Perseus was not sure he felt any safer in their company.

'I wonder if you'd mind passing me my tunic?' he said to the nymph who was sitting on it. All the others started laughing at the sound of his voice. He found himself unable to ascertain precisely how many they were, because every time he tried to count them, one seemed to disappear and reappear elsewhere, without him ever being able to catch the moment when she moved. They were each very beautiful in their own different ways. And yet he could not quite calculate how many perfect golden faces, long golden arms, or flowing golden hairstyles he could see. As soon as he tried to memorize one deathless beauty, he looked at another and she was so exquisite that he forgot who he had been staring at only a moment before. He wanted to line them up and look at each in turn and compare her with her sisters. But more than that, he really wanted not to be naked in front of them all.

'Would I mind?' said the golden nymph. 'No, I don't think I'd mind. But you see, it was all wet from the water, just like you. So we fished it out and stretched it over the rock here, to dry it for you. We thought you'd be happy.'

She turned her face downwards a little and gazed at him through long lashes. Perseus found himself terrified that he had upset her and she was about to cry.

'I am,' he said. 'I'm very happy. Happy and grateful. It's just that I don't have anything else to wear, so . . .'

'You aren't cold?' asked another nymph. At least, he thought it was another. She was certainly sitting on a different rock. But she too had huge limpid eyes that looked ready to fill with tears. 'Our garden has been admired by the immortal gods and goddesses for almost as long as time itself. And you find it cold?'

'No, no, not at all.' Perseus stumbled on a rock as he tried to move closer while covering some of his nakedness by hiding under large leaves that hung over the water from trees growing on the bank. 'I'm certainly not cold, your garden is perfect in every way.'

'What do you like about it most?' asked another nymph.

Perseus really wanted to be less exposed before he answered this. Not least because he seemed to upset them so easily. 'I like . . .' He paused to think of the honest answer. 'I like the birds, I've never seen so many kinds or heard so many different songs.'

'He doesn't like the flowers.' One nymph put her arm around her sister's shoulders. 'I don't know what more you could have done.'

'No, I do like them!' Perseus said.

'The fruit trees don't interest him at all,' said another. 'Though Hera herself keeps her apple tree here.'

'No, they do!' Perseus didn't know how he was getting everything so wrong. 'I admired them the moment I saw them. I wasn't sure what fruits they were, because I have never seen a golden apple tree before, but I was very interested in them in spite of that.' Seeing another nymph's face fall, he corrected himself. 'Not in spite of it. Because of it, really.'

'I suppose it's too much to hope that you noticed the beautiful soft grasses you lay on?' said another, and Perseus could no longer tell if she had addressed him before or if he was affronting a different nymph each time.

'I liked those too,' he said. 'Beautiful and comfortable.'

'But you aren't enjoying the lake?' said the one who was now sitting on his tunic.

'I am,' he said. 'I would just feel like I was addressing you more respectfully if I was on the shore alongside you and, you know, wearing clothes.'

'Oh, I see,' said another and he turned to try and keep track of her this time. 'You'd be happier if we were all in the same position, as it were.'

'Yes,' he said, just before realizing that he would actually feel a great deal less comfortable if they were suddenly naked and in the water beside him. He wondered if it was possible to die of embarrassment. The sound of an unspecified number of inhumanly beautiful women giggling at him was almost as upsetting as the sound of the Graiai quarrelling with one another. He tried to reach up to the rock and grab his tunic but now it was suddenly in the hands of a nymph who was using it to dry herself. Perseus wondered if they would keep laughing at him if he burst into tears and concluded that they certainly would.

'Please let me have my tunic,' he said. 'My mother made it for me and I might never see her again.'

'Oh, the poor boy,' said one. 'Losing his mother, so young.'

'When did we last see our mother?' asked her sister.

Fat tears flowed down the first nymph's face. Perseus wanted to comfort her but feared that if he left the water now, his intentions might be misconstrued.

'You've upset her,' said another of the Hesperides.

'I'm sorry,' he said. 'If I could just have my tunic—'

But none of the nymphs was listening. They flocked to their sister, embracing her. Not knowing what else to do, Perseus climbed onto the bank, discovered his cloak near where he had left it, and wrapped that around himself. When one of the Hesperides noticed, she too burst into tears, and had to be comforted by the others. Perseus wondered if he should ask again for his tunic, but he feared the response. He decided to try a different strategy.

'I am sorry to have caused so much distress,' he said. Sniggering broke out again. He knew he sounded pompous and foolish – if anything, he sounded like Polydectes – but he didn't know how to address the Hesperides. They were powerful but also beautiful; immortal but emotional. They had nothing whatsoever in common with the girls he had grown up with in the fishing village.

The Hesperides, meanwhile, were beginning to tire of their diversion. It had all been very entertaining, seeing this mortal man who Athene and Hermes had decided to bring to them. It had been fun hiding from him, more fun stealing his clothes and teasing him. But there was something so monotonous about mortals, which was one of many reasons why they usually kept their distance. The boy wanted something, and he would ask for it and they would either reward or deny him. But what did they get from the encounter?

They had quite enjoyed seeing him naked, but was he really more delightful than the creatures that lived in their garden? Aegle seemed to think so (she was always the most emotional one: this was how she could cry at will). But Arethusa would not have minded if he had drowned in the lake, so long as he gave the fish something to nibble on. Erytheia, meanwhile, preferred the snakes that twisted their muscular bodies around the golden apple trees, though she was enjoying wearing the man's shoes. Hesperie had not even bothered to come down to meet him: she would have to remove her lovely hairband if they were all to appear the same. And after going to all the trouble of acquiring it, and choosing one with such a beautiful chequered pattern, she was hardly likely to take it off just to play a trick on some trivial man. It had taken her the longest time to tie it just right, under her hair. Chrysothemis asked if she didn't want

183

the mortal to see it and admire her, but what did she care if he admired her hair or not? He would be dead soon, either way. Lipara, meanwhile, was sure that the man had broken a twig off her favourite laurel tree as he blundered through their garden. She was sitting beside Arethusa on the tunic, wondering if they should push him back into the water and hold him under. Neither of them could completely remember if this was fatal to mortals, but so much was dangerous for them that it might be worth the attempt. But then there was Antheia, standing beside the olive trees, gazing at the man with frank hunger. If he were to ask for an apple (generally, when anyone approached the Hesperides, it had something to do with the apples), she would have handed over a whole tree.

'What do you want?' Chrysothemis finally asked the boy and he mumbled something about the Graiai and a quest. He stumbled over his words and mangled his story at every stage, but eventually, the nymphs uncovered what had happened. He was on a quest to take a Gorgon's head to appease some mortal who would otherwise marry the boy's mother. Even Arethusa was intrigued by this element: what could the man possibly do with a Gorgon's head that would compensate him for losing a wife? Surely the more suitable gift would be a bride who liked him better than the boy's mother apparently did? The nymphs murmured among themselves, aware that the boy could not hear them unless they chose. The whole thing sounded so peculiar. What had the Gorgons done to be embroiled in this young man's family matters? Nothing, came the reply. As far as they could tell, he did not seem to have thought about the Gorgons at all. Ordered to fetch the head of one of them, he had simply set out to do so with no thought for how the Gorgon might feel about giving it up.

So did they send him away empty-handed? That was the most obvious response. And yet, Athene and Hermes had brought him here: two gods working together could only mean that they were carrying out the will of Zeus, surely? And although the nymphs largely shared a view on the subject of Zeus, they could not wholly disregard what the old lech wanted. Especially not if he was sending Athene – as observant as she was spiteful – and Hermes, who would tell tales if they ignored him.

And then there was the matter of the Graiai. The grey sisters were not easily impressed. And the boy must have done something to earn their help. He was rather vague about exactly what that had been. Hesperie – who had joined the debate even though she wasn't interested in the outcome – said he must have been very persuasive for the gods to help him, and the sisters too. So they should assist him in his quest, should they? Lipara was quite sure they should not, at least not until her laurel tree had regrown its missing branch. He had said something about the number of days he had left before the man married his mother regardless of his quest. But who could remember how many days it took a laurel tree to grow?

Whatever the nymphs felt about Perseus, they decided it could not influence their decision. The presence of the gods, the involvement of the Graiai: these things were too important to overlook. What did a mortal need to decapitate a Gorgon? There was evidently no point asking the boy what he required: he hadn't even known he needed the nymphs until the Graiai told him. So they worked it out among themselves, while he stood there, useless and hopeful. A sword, obviously. He had one already but it was like a child's practice sword, although all the Hesperides agreed that he had no idea this was the case. He carried his sword with great seriousness, but looked like a boy playing with his father's weapon. So he needed something suited to the task: a harpē, with its vicious curved blade, would be more appropriate. And something to carry the head, once he had it. They discussed the options. There was a kibisis hidden away somewhere: that would take the weight. Very well, the sword, the bag, what else? He would need to move a great deal faster than mortals usually could if he was to outrun the Gorgons. And he would need to hide from them. The nymphs considered these requirements for some time. Winged sandals, usually worn by Hermes, would be ideal: the messenger god could loan the boy his shoes. Hermes could travel perfectly well without them, they were just an affectation. But they did have one more item they could lend Perseus and after much discussion, they agreed they would. The nymphs had come into possession – none of them could quite recall how – of a cap that had once belonged to Hades. No one could imagine why he would have needed a cap which threw darkness all around it, rendering the wearer invisible. Hades was in the Underworld or – occa- sionally – on Olympus. In neither of these places would he ever need to go unseen. Perhaps this was why he had given it to whichever nymph had brought it to the island. Or she had acquired it, assuming Hades didn't need it any more. And while they were on the subject of who needed what, if Perseus was borrowing winged sandals from Hermes, the nymphs could surely keep his shoes. Should they ask, before sending him on his way? He had left them unattended beside their lake, on their island, so that meant the sandals practically belonged to the Hesperides already. One nymph had already worn them, another had put them safely beneath a rock. They glanced down at him, and it was perfectly clear that Perseus would leave barefoot rather than ask for his sandals back.

*

When Athene and Hermes arrived to collect him, Perseus was sitting where they had left him. His curly hair was mussed, his tunic appeared to be back to front. He had a dazed expression and was holding the straps of a golden bag in his left hand. It was large and sturdy, decorated with silver tassels. Neither god needed to ask what it was for. In his right hand, he held a curved blade which – again, both gods knew – had once belonged to Zeus. He really did prize the bratty child if he had let the Hesperides give him this sword. On his lap, the boy held a winged cap, which Hermes recognized, having worn it many times himself. Hades was terrible at keeping track of his possessions: he really should be more careful.

'Where are your shoes?' asked Athene. Perseus looked at his bare feet as though seeing them for the first time.

'I'm not sure,' he said.

'Typical,' muttered Hermes. 'They really will take anything.'

'That's why I don't usually come here,' Athene replied. 'They can't leave a single thing alone.'

'You'd have needed new spears if we'd stayed any longer,' said Hermes. Neither he nor Perseus noticed the expression of horror that appeared and disappeared on the goddess's face.

'I think they said you'd lend me your sandals,' said Perseus. He shook his head slowly, as though trying to dislodge a strange dream or remember a long-forgotten name.

'Did they indeed?' said Hermes. He looked at Athene and she shrugged. 'I'll have these back when you've finished with the Gorgons.' Hermes reached down and grudgingly loosened the ties around his ankles.

'Yes, of course,' said Perseus.

'I mean it.' The messenger god handed them to Perseus, jerking them away from him at the last moment. 'You don't bring them back here, do you understand?'

'Yes,' said Perseus.

'Because if you do, I might never see them again,' said Hermes. 'They take everything for safekeeping.' His tone did not suggest he considered anything to be safe with the Hesperides.

'Perhaps they'll give me my sandals back,' Perseus said. He looked behind him towards the places where the nymphs played and hid around their trees and their lake. He turned back to Hermes with doubt in his eyes.

'I'm sure they'll consider it,' said Athene. 'But you'll need something else to give them, and they might take that and keep the shoes anyway.'

Perseus tied Hermes's sandals around his ankles, stroking the wings that now sprouted on either side of his calves. Hermes glared at him. Athene held her shield a little tighter.

'Where are we going now?' asked Perseus.

'You're going to the Gorgons,' said Athene. 'We just came to make sure you had everything you need.'

'Are they nearby?' Perseus looked foolishly from side to side, as though a Gorgon head might suddenly hover into view.

'I'm not sure how long it'll take you,' said Athene. 'But they're that way.'

She pointed across the river which was not a river, to a direction lost in mist.

'I don't kno—' Perseus began, but he was speaking to the breeze.

A Nereid, Unnamed

Well. This might be the most egregious insult any of us has ever sustained, and we're immortal so there has been plenty of time. The Nereids are fifty in number and we are the daughters of the ocean. I'll repeat this, because it seems that not every mortal has been paying attention. Nereids are immortal, and we are fifty, and so if you insult us as a group, you insult fifty goddesses at once. Ask yourself if that sounds like something you want to do.

And then ask yourself if it might be a little arrogant to compare yourself with us. Mortals have a word for this kind of arrogance: the kind that makes a person think she can compare herself favourably to a goddess. The word is hubris. And while I am all in favour of using precision to describe something, might I suggest that you would be better off not doing something so dangerous so often that you need a specific word for it? Perhaps develop your self-control, rather than your vocabulary.

What could she have imagined would happen to her? Cassiope, I mean. Is it possible you hadn't heard? Cassiope, queen of Ethiopia. I'm sure you're aware of her. She's a famous beauty, apparently (by mortal standards). Married a king who doted on her, cherished her, indulged her. Allowed her to believe that she could keep her looks, no matter how many years went by. Since Cassiope believed this, she gained no humility as she grew older, only anxiety. She became more and more fearful that her beauty was slipping away, more in need of reassurance, more desperate to convince herself that the compliments she heard from her husband and her slaves were still true. And every day, she looked at her reflection and persuaded herself that somehow age had not touched her, the way it does every living creature. She looked at her daughter – who you might recall is named Andromeda – and believed they must look the same. While she was occupied with this delusion, she added another: she – and her daughter – were as beautiful as the Nereids. More beautiful, perhaps.

Can you even imagine? To have such a thought is madness and folly, equal and immense. To express such a thought? Tantamount to a death sentence.

Perhaps you are thinking: if the woman was so foolish, so deluded, what difference did her words make? Surely the gods would simply overlook them, because why would they concern themselves with the words of a stupid woman? If I know so much about her – about her frailty and her ageing – why am I angry? Carry on that way, and I'll lose patience with you too. Nereids are not minor deities, and we will not be treated as such. We are the daughters of the sea. I bet you can't even name one, can you?

You see, that is absolutely typical of you people. So you don't bother learning fifty names (don't pretend it's so difficult; you can count to fifty, can't you?). But I should just overlook any and all insults?

No.

The Nereids will not let these statements go unchallenged and unpunished. Cassiope is not now as beautiful as a goddess and nor was she ever, even when she was the age her daughter is now. Andromeda is not as beautiful as a goddess either. She is reasonable-looking, for a mortal. That is the best you could say about her. My sisters and I have convened and discussed the matter: we have come to several conclusions.

The first is that mortal women probably wouldn't have these delusions of immortal beauty if gods did not take it upon themselves to seduce some of them. Of course, it is still hubristic. But you can just about understand how they could convince themselves that one or another of them is a rival to our great beauty, if she is the object of desire to Zeus or Poseidon or Apollo. Just about. So it is Poseidon who will rise up to punish Cassiope. Because otherwise his existence will become a constant trial until he does as we ask. Yes, he is a mighty god, the ruler of the ocean. But there are fifty of us and we're all furious.

The second is that these slights against us must end. And therefore Cassiope will need to be punished in a way that resounds through the ages. Mortals have – it seems – forgotten the power of the Nereids. They will not do so again.

The third is that the best way to punish a mortal woman is through her child. Mortal women love their children. Even Cassiope – the most selfish of women – loves Andromeda.

The fourth is that the sea is home to more than fish, and Nereids.

The fifth is that some of them are hungry.

Medusa

Medusa waited until her sisters were both outside the cave before she loosened the bindings around her eyes. She didn't want them to see what was there in case they could not conceal their reactions. Sthenno would try, if she saw a pair of ruined sockets. She would press her lips together behind her tusks and then she would say that Medusa looked very well, so far as she could see. Euryale would be unafraid and she would not experience the horror that Sthenno would work so hard to hide. Medusa knew them both. And she did not want them to see.

So she waited until Sthenno was making bread for her and Euryale was away with her sheep, and she untied the knot at the back of her head. The slender, muscular bodies of the snakes moved aside, hissing softly. She unwound the cloth slowly, trying to measure any shifts in the pain she felt. As the pressure eased, she found that she could blink behind the cloth. So her eyelids were still attached: she had wondered. She reached up to touch them through the remaining fabric: was it odd that the bindings were dry? Tears had always flown plentifully for Medusa, but

194

no longer. She felt the last loops of cloth drop into her hands.

She blinked, then blinked again. Perhaps the eyes needed time to adjust to the darkness of the cave. She waited, but still there was only blackness. She wasn't sure exactly how far inside the cave she was sitting. She could test her sight in the lighter part of it if she could only work out which way that was. She reached in front of her and tried to orient herself from the rock she could feel. It didn't help her at all. This cave she knew so well – would have said she knew blindfolded – she no longer knew. She heard something scuttle past her and she turned her head, but she was too slow. Whatever it was had gone by, unseen. She could not have explained how she knew it was going into the cave rather than out of it, but she did. And so she moved slowly in the other direction, hoping the darkness would grow lighter.

But it did not. She began to doubt herself: perhaps she was further away from the light after all. But she knew she was not. She could feel the air growing warmer on her skin, she could smell the salt more strongly. She blinked again. Was that something? She could not be certain but the blackness was faintly tinged with red. She paused and allowed her eyes to grow used to the sensation. They still hurt. But the more she tried to see, the less she felt the pain.

There was red. And after she had waited for a long time, there was also gold, at the edges. Helios had not abandoned her after all: this was his light she could perceive. She moved her head slowly, hearing the snakes curl and uncurl around her. They wanted to be in the sun, she knew. This was the first time they had expressed any kind of desire to her, but the message was quite clear. The snakes longed for the warmth of the sun on their scales. They longed – and somehow now, she longed – to feel hot sand on their bellies. If she lay on her back on the shore, they would have that, and they wanted it, and she knew they did.

Gradually she saw more here: a brighter core and a darker circumference. When she moved her head the brightness did not move with her: it was not her eyes, but the image they saw that held the distinction. She was looking at the cave entrance then. Still she waited, and eventually the image developed further. Now she could see gold, and also a darker, cooler light. The sea.

She didn't know how long she had been standing here, gazing at her world and seeing only its faintest outline. But she could wait for as long as she had to. The snakes were patient too. She thought perhaps she could see a difference between the light at the bottom of her eyes and the light higher up. To the right was the sun, the brightest golden disc. And to the left? She moved her head carefully again. There was an unmoving line and she knew she was looking at the horizon.

She heard her name being called by Sthenno. She opened her mouth to reply. But then, with no warning, the snakes became a hissing writhing mass of fear and anger. She had no idea what had frightened them and they gave her no chance to find out. They pulsed around her skull, frantic and desperate. What? she asked them. What do you want? What can I do? The snakes continued their seething fury. Medusa was not afraid of them, and at the same time she knew she must do what they urged. But what was it? She could not understand. She raised her hands to her temples and felt a sudden surge of energy. Yes, that is it, yes.

She was still holding the bindings in her hands. And just as she knew that her snakes wanted to lie on the sand, she knew this. They wanted her to cover her eyes again. She did not attempt to reason with them. She didn't try to understand why they wanted her eyes to be closed, or how they were telling her that she must cover them up. There was no arguing with these snakes: they were a part of her now. She took the cloths in her hands and bound them lightly across her eyes. It wasn't enough to placate the snakes entirely, but they did slow their squirming. She wound another layer of cloth across her face, and another.

By the time Sthenno reached her, she was completely in darkness again. But the sun shone on the snakes, and it shone on her.

Cornix

Kra kra! You'll never guess what I just saw. Never, ever, not if I let you try all day. Go on, try. You see? I knew you wouldn't get it. Do you want another go? You can have as many as you want, but it won't help. This crow knows and you don't.

Alright, I'll tell you: Athene has a child. He isn't exactly hers, obviously: she is a virgin goddess, just like you thought. But Gaia gave the child to her and said she must take responsibility for it. Because she – Gaia – didn't want to raise another child, after losing all her beautiful giants in the war against the gods. That's her word, beautiful, not mine. I didn't think the giants were beautiful, to be honest. But that's not something I would say to Gaia because there's never any real need to say something hurtful unless you can't help it, which sometimes I can't but on this occasion I could.

The boy is the son of Hephaestus: you remember that time he tried to persuade Athene to marry him? And she said no and he grabbed her and held her until he ejaculated on her thigh? (Sorry – is that too much for you? Crows don't always know what is appropriate.) She took a piece of wool and wiped herself clean, but she threw the wool onto the ground so Gaia took it. Gaia can make life out of nothing, so of course she could make a child out of that. And she did, and then gave it to Athene.

And Athene didn't know what to do, at first. You can imagine it, can't you? What does she know about raising a child? What does she even want to know about it? I thought she might give the boy to Hephaestus and tell him to deal with it. Because why shouldn't she, really? But she didn't, she did something else.

She's very good at weaving, did you know that about her? She tells everyone, so you probably did. So she took the child to a river, and wove a basket out of willow branches. She hid the child inside: can you imagine that? Kept weaving until the basket was sealed shut. And then she took reeds from the water and used those to fill in every gap so that no one, not even a sharp-eyed crow, could have seen what was within. And then she gave the basket to the daughters of Cecrops: do you know about them?

I suppose you don't really need to know about them, beyond that they were who Athene chose to protect the basket. Cecrops was a king of Athens (with three daughters) and Athene likes Athens, which is probably why she went there and gave them the child. But if I'm honest I'm only giving you these details because I like you to know I know them. It doesn't make much difference to what happened next, except it does now I think about it.

Because the daughters of Cecrops are named Herse, Pandrosus and Aglaurus. Three daughters chosen by one goddess to guard one basket. She gave them an order before she left, which was that they were on no account to open the basket and find out what was inside. In case you're doubting my story and wondering how I know so much, I was hiding in an elm tree nearby and I saw the whole thing with my own eyes. And I heard every word too. Athene told them it was a secret and she trusted them to keep it safe.

And two of them did. You see, this is the part where I think maybe it does matter that she picked the daughters of Cecrops. If she'd picked someone with only two daughters, things might have turned out very differently. But she chose these, and Herse and Pandrosus did exactly as she'd asked. They hid the basket, ignored it and then forgot about it. Exactly what Athene was hoping for.

Wait – you look upset. Are you worried that the baby will die? Suffocate or starve or something? The offspring of the gods and the earth itself is not as fragile as a mortal child. Remember how difficult it was to kill the giants? Gaia's offspring are not made lightly. So don't concern yourself with the child's wellbeing, because in a moment you'll understand that you're worrying about quite the wrong person in this story.

Aglaurus wanted to know what was inside the basket and she wouldn't leave it alone. She went back, over and over, to look at it and turn it about and wonder what was inside. She couldn't understand how her sisters were so accepting of Athene's orders. She couldn't bear not knowing everything. She peered at the basket and held it up to the light, tried to push the reeds aside so she could just make out something of the contents. She told herself as she did this that once she had slaked her curiosity she would leave it alone.

But Athene doesn't weave in such a way that a woman can just peer through the gaps. She doesn't leave gaps. *Kra kra!* So Aglaurus couldn't see a thing. And you might think this would be enough to warn her of the danger she was in. If the goddess had meant for someone to see inside the basket, she would have allowed it. But – foolish girl – her curiosity only intensified. So she found the end of one of the reeds and she worked it loose. Just gently, pushing it and pulling until one little strand stood proud. She worked it a bit more, now she could grip it more easily. It was loose anyway, she told herself. She might as well undo it. But because she didn't dampen it first, the reed snapped between her fingers. A crow could have told her how to do that better: she should have asked me for advice. But she could always replace it, she decided, so she kept going. She unwove one reed and then another and then another. But even that wasn't enough for her to be able to see. Telling herself that she was the brave one and her sisters were cowards, she undid more and more of the basket, until the top looked like an abandoned bird's nest. Now it was open and she could finally see what was inside.

She screamed and dropped the basket to the ground. Her sisters came running, but it was too late. The snake slithered out and bit Aglaurus on the foot. Herse and Pandrosus ran to their sister who was grasping her ankle and crying out in agony. Their thumping feet angered the snake so much that it bit each of them as well, before disappearing into the undergrowth.

I took the news to Athene myself. She has always loved crows: she likes us because we're clever and she likes us because we know everything. But this time she wasn't pleased at all. She was angry with the messenger because she was angry with the message, I suppose. *Kra.* So she said that from now on, crows would never be as welcome to her as owls. Owls! Not just her owl, the one Zeus gave her. All owls. Even though they aren't half as bright as crows and don't see a quarter of the things we see because they sleep during the day. But she has made her mind up and crows must be punished for the crime of the daughters of Cecrops. So now I don't take any news to her. I bring it to you instead. *Kra kra!*

Stone

This one is small and I'm not sure you would want it. It has been perfectly caught as it runs along, its jointed legs seemingly frozen in time. It is not poised to attack, its sting is not raised. The sculptor wants us to think, I suppose, that it was caught unawares. If the sculptor thinks about his audience at all, of course. Perhaps these statues were not meant to be displayed, perhaps they were made just for the sheer pleasure of creating them. Perhaps they were not even supposed to look as realistic as they do: perhaps his skill surprised even him. But if you saw this one unexpectedly, you would fear for your life.

Gorgoneion

I'm wondering if you still think of her as a monster. I suppose it depends on what you think that word means. Monsters are, what? Ugly? Terrifying? Gorgons are both these things, certainly, although Medusa wasn't always. Can a monster be beautiful if it is still terrifying? Perhaps it depends on how you experience fear and judge beauty.

And is a monster always evil? Is there ever such a thing as a good monster? Because what happens when a good person becomes a monster? I feel confident saying that Medusa was a good mortal: has that all disappeared now? Did it fall out with her hair? Because I think you already know why the snakes were so anxious that she cover her eyes when they heard her sister approaching. (That's another question for another day, I suppose: do snakes have emotions? Are they capable of anxiety? But let's focus on the question in hand.) They knew before Medusa knew that her gaze was now lethal.

She found out a day or two later, when she tried again to remove the bindings from her eyes. She turned her gaze on something she could see moving across the ground in front of her. A quick dark streak on the golden sand. It stopped, mid-run. She reached out and picked it up, dropped it straightaway when she realized she was holding a scorpion. Picked it up again when she understood that it was dead.

It took her a moment to work out what was wrong. It was the wrong texture for a scorpion. She had – perhaps this shouldn't need saying, but just in case – never held a scorpion in her hands before. She knew their sting could be fatal. But she also knew how shiny they were, how slick their shells appeared. And this was rougher to the touch than a scorpion could be. And surely it was also too heavy, given its size? She took it and kept it and puzzled over it.

But she doubted her own eyes: who could blame her after they had sustained such an insult? She wondered if she hadn't seen it move, if it was a tiny statue of a scorpion that had washed up on the shore. Or perhaps one of her sisters had found it in a human settlement nearby and brought it to show her, and then forgotten to tell her about it. None of these explanations seemed to her to be less plausible than the truth, that she had looked at the scorpion and it had turned to stone.

It would take two more days and two dead birds – a cormorant, a bee-eater – before she understood the truth.

Part Four

Love

Athene

It was Hephaestus she most wanted to hurt. The days on Olympus – which had once all seemed the same – were now sharply differentiated because she spent each one wondering how she could exact her revenge. And so every day became a complicated journey around the labyrinth of possibility and impossibility: she must hurt Hephaestus because he had hurt her, and honour demanded it. And yet she could not hurt the blacksmith, because Hera and Zeus protected him.

It had not always been so, of course. Hera had despised her son when he had been born lame: Athene had heard the Archer and his sister discussing it more than once (immortality and excessive self-regard left them prone to repetition). So Hera felt no love for Hephaestus until he bribed his way into her affections with his endless display of gifts and fawning. But that time had passed long before Athene had been born from the head of Zeus, and there was no way back to it now, she reluctantly concluded, retracing her steps to the beginning of the maze.

But if Hephaestus was safe in Hera's affections, surely

Athene could isolate him from Zeus? He had turned on Hephaestus once, she remembered that. A time when the king of the gods had finally lost his temper with his queen; her conspiracies and criticisms had made him blind with rage. He aimed a mighty thunderbolt that would have maimed even a goddess. But he missed, which only increased his wrath. He advanced on her, roaring, determined to punish her somehow. The other gods shrank back, either because they were too afraid of Zeus to intervene or simply did not care if Hera was obliterated. Only Hephaestus, the loyal little hound, stood by his mama: threw himself between them, begged them to make peace. Zeus had picked up the blacksmith by his lame foot and hurled him from the mountain. Hephaestus had been quite badly injured when he landed – Athene shivered with delight to think of it. If she could only find a way to provoke her father's rage so he would do it again.

But how? This was the part of the puzzle that took her in circles: it looked so promising, but follow it for a few turns and she found a dead end, whichever way she went. What would provoke Zeus to such a pinnacle of fury? Only Hera at her worst. And why would she antagonize him for Athene's benefit? She did nothing for anyone but herself. Perhaps Athene could irritate Hera enough to create some friction between the two of them, but it wouldn't be enough. Could she trick Hephaestus into believing his mother was in danger once again? Perhaps he could be induced to start another fight with Zeus? But this threw up two further stone walls: Hephaestus would do anything to avoid conflict with Zeus, except stand by while his mother was in danger. He would never begin anything. And even if he would, she could not inveigle him into such a course of action without speaking to him, and she did not want to do that ever again.

And so she turned the labyrinth around and approached it from a new direction. If there was currently no way to harm Hephaestus, she would take her revenge elsewhere, and destroy something Hephaestus loved later on, whenever the opportunity presented itself. She had eternity to take her revenge. Yes, she wanted it now, but it could wait. Meanwhile, she would turn her wrath against a god who had now injured her twice.

Amphitrite

Of course Poseidon had done as the Nereids had asked. It was never really in doubt. Fifty insulted Nereids was fifty more than he could ignore. He tried, for a short while. Went away and hid somewhere. His wife had been unable to tell her sisters exactly where. Olympus? Athens? No one was quite sure, but no one was worried, because he had to come back to the sea sooner or later. It was his domain after all: he could not abandon it for long. And he couldn't ignore the Nereids either.

They knew just what punishment to demand because they all knew what Poseidon wanted. He had lost a tiny strip of his kingdom, when the Gorgon stamped on that fault line. Amphitrite was certain her husband deserved it, though of course she never asked him. But he returned to the same spot day after day, glaring at the risen shore and the receding sea. Every new grain of dry sand seemed to burn his eyes. Tiring of his dark moods, Amphitrite had done her half-hearted best to console him. All gods experienced an occasional loss of power, she told him. But he snarled at her and stalked off through the waves, leaving her with nothing but her large collection of exquisite pearls for company. One of her sister-Nereids suggested she preferred things this way, but Amphitrite did not reply. Even when Poseidon was absent, he had ways of hearing everything. Who knew which fish, which sea creature would betray her this time? She would not take the risk.

But the other Nereids discussed their plans in Poseidon's absence, even while Amphitrite allowed the waves to talk for her. If the sea god was so injured by the loss of a small part of his kingdom, then he would want to redress that hurt. And what better way to do it than by expanding his ocean elsewhere? If the Gorgons had rejected him and insulted him, then he could flood another land and improve his spirits that way. Meanwhile, the Nereids wanted their honour – insulted by the arrogance of the queen of Ethiopia who believed herself and her daughter their equal in beauty – to be avenged. So the solution was simple. The only difficulty would be in persuading Poseidon that it was his idea. And even that would not be very hard, because Poseidon was arrogant and had always believed himself as cunning as his brothers, Zeus and Hades. The Nereids – Amphitrite, in particular – had encouraged him to believe this. So now, all they had to do was suggest, and wait.

*

Poseidon roamed the sea, restless and irritable. He had nothing to enjoy, and nothing to look forward to. He counted his recent disappointments: the dullness of life on Olympus, which he had tried to improve by playing a trick on Hephaestus and Athene. But it had failed. The blacksmith god had not realized it was a joke but had really tried to propose to Poseidon's niece. None of the gods seemed to know exactly how she had refused him, but it had created a pall over the hallowed halls which would not lift. Hephaestus was wretched and Athene was furious. Poseidon could not share with the other gods that the whole thing had been his idea, because even he could perceive that it would not be seen as a triumph of wit. Athene, he was certain, was planning to get her own back and he didn't know how she would do so. Would her wrath be directed at Hephaestus alone? Or would the blacksmith have told her that it was Poseidon who had encouraged him? He briefly entertained the thought that Athene might think her uncle was sincere, that he wanted her to marry and thought the pair a good match. But whenever he summoned a memory of her scorn-filled eyes, he knew this was unlikely. He wasn't afraid of her, obviously. But he was queasily aware that if she turned her anger in his direction, he might not emerge entirely unscathed.

And then there was his disappointment that the Gorgon girl had not been dazzled by his wit or humbled by his power. Yes, he had taken her, but there had been little satisfaction in it. She hadn't enjoyed the game, or admired him, or given him anything of herself at all. She had made a choice to save the mortal girls from their deaths, and Poseidon – who he was and what he ruled and how he felt – hadn't entered her mind. He was a force of destruction to her, and nothing more. It had left him feeling angry and empty. Why did no one care about his feelings?

He regretted the whole encounter now. The girl had disappeared from his view once he'd raped her. He didn't even know if she was back with her sisters: there was no sign of her from the water. And that brought him to the next thing he was upset about: his shrinking ocean. He did not know how the Gorgons had done it, but somehow they had pushed his domain back, away from their shore and their cave. And though he had complained to Zeus that his kingdom had been diminished and that he had been insulted, his brother had displayed no real concern. Anyway, going to Olympus had been tiresome because his niece was staring knives at him whenever he caught sight of her. He had no idea what had made her so sour, nor did he see why he should ask. But this was why he had decided to play his trick on Hephaestus. And even that had backfired. Every simple pleasure was denied him.

He surfaced beside a large rock. Birds flew in every direction as seawater spurted into the air. He lifted himself out of the waves and lay on the warm stone. He had never questioned his grandeur before. And yet, as he admired his mighty trident glinting in the violent sun, he felt a brief shudder. What was that? It could not be that he was cold – gods did not feel hot, or cold. It certainly wasn't an earthquake: how could the ocean tremble if he, Poseidon, had not struck the seabed with his trident? It was something else, something internal. He felt – he frowned with the effort of trying to name this bizarre sensation – uncomfortable. As though he could see himself with Athene's eyes. This was clearly absurd and he dismissed the feeling. He looked magnificent: the king of all the seas, lounging atop this handsome rock, utterly at home. But then it came back: the odd feeling of something being wrong. For the briefest moment, he wondered if he looked like a lolling seal. But this was impossible. He was an all-powerful god and droplets of his beautiful ocean dripped grandly from his beard. And here was the thought again: he might resemble a lumpen seal basking on a rock.

He shook his head, sending water in every direction. A mighty god.

A damp, petulant sea creature.

He looked around him: eyes scanning the horizon. Athene was not there. Her contemptuous gaze was not trained on her uncle: she might be cunning but she wasn't usually invisible. So if she wasn't there, why did he feel that she was watching him?

He dismissed her from his mind, once and for all. He knew she was plotting against him, but he could do nothing about that until she revealed her plan. He must simply wait, and be ready for her.

He waited for the discomfort to subside. Poseidon had long trusted his instincts and now he had listened to them – and their advice to be wary of Athene – surely they would leave him in peace? She was going to try to take something he wanted, or destroy something he loved. Those were the only two possibilities. And now he was prepared.

He turned over to stare at the sun. The only eyes on the sea god now were those of Helios, flying overhead with his blazing light. He could enjoy this time above the water, away from his wife in the ocean depths, from his niece in the Olympian heights, from the rest of the Nereids who were angry about something some woman had said and demanding he punish her and her husband. He would have to give them what they wanted: even a god as powerful as him could not ignore fifty Nereids for long. They made so much noise.

The prickling feeling had not subsided. It was not Athene who had made him nervous. Nor Amphitrite. Nor the other Nereids. If he could be honest with himself, he knew whose eyes he could feel on him, though he didn't know those eyes had now been changed beyond recognition.

*

When Poseidon skulked back to his wife, she knew something was troubling him, but she did not ask him any questions or offer any comfort. He sighed and moaned, and Amphitrite ignored him. He lay beside her, resting his head on her shoulder, his greenish locks wrapped around her shoulders like seaweed.

'Are you comfortable, my love?' she asked. She shifted her arm a little, to see the dappled light move on her pale skin.

'Not really,' he replied.

She tried not to sigh, because she knew he took it personally. Besides, this was still an opportunity. 'You're melancholy again,' she said.

'I am,' he replied.

'Because you have been slighted.'

He edged a little closer. 'Yes.'

'No wonder your feelings are hurt,' she said. 'I have felt hurt on your behalf.' She ran her fingers gently through his seaweed hair, untangling it without snagging.

'Have you?' he asked.

'Of course.' Amphitrite knew he loved to feel her fingers on him. 'What kind of wife would I be, if I felt nothing when you are insulted and rejected?'

217

She felt him stiffen slightly, and realized that he was afraid she might know about the Gorgon girl. Poor, stupid Poseidon, she thought. Always so sure he was discreet in his pursuits, always so utterly mistaken. She continued, as though she hadn't noticed. 'How could the other gods be so unfeeling?' She felt him relax against her. 'They are jealous, my love.'

'Do you really think so?' he asked.

'Of course,' she replied. 'Your kingdom is vast.'

'Zeus's kingdom is bigger,' he said.

'I suppose that's true,' said Amphitrite. 'If you like that sort of thing. Empty skies. Weather.'

'The other Olympians do like that sort of thing,' he said. 'They think my kingdom is dark and damp.'

'That's because if they thought about what it really is – a vast world teeming with life, all ruled by you – they would be even more jealous. I suppose that might explain . . .' She stroked his hair, her voice faltering.

'Might explain what?' he asked.

'Why they are content to see you lose part of your kingdom to Zeus,' she said.

'The Gorgons stole my territory,' he snarled. 'Zeus will claim no responsibility for it at all.'

'I'm sure that's right,' she said. 'I don't suppose you could . . . No, I'm sure you wouldn't want to.'

'Want to what?' Poseidon sat up and looked at his wife. 'What could I do?'

'You could take something in exchange?' she said. 'Or somewhere.'

'You know what Zeus is like,' he groaned. 'He wouldn't let it go. We'd be at war for generations.'

'I suppose there is a way around that,' she said. 'But I'm sure you're right. Let's not think about it any more.'

'Let's not,' he agreed. 'What sort of way?'

'Perhaps if you were seen to be punishing a mortal for hubris?' she said. 'Zeus can hardly object to you doing that, can he?'

'No.' Poseidon shook his head so vigorously that waves smashed onto every coast, breaking distant fishing boats into flotsam. 'Zeus is all in favour of punishing hubris. Have you a particular example in mind?'

'Do you know, I have the perfect example,' she said.

Andromeda

Andromeda knew something terrible was about to happen, and she knew it in the same way that she knew when an earthquake was imminent, or a terrible storm was about to break. Her father used to say she was a seer, and although he laughed as he said it, he was only half joking. But Andromeda knew she had no special powers, because she was never sure exactly what terrible thing was coming, only that something was. At first, she thought this might simply be her rightful response to her parents' insistence that she marry her uncle, Phineus. But as the sun climbed in the sky, and the air somehow grew thicker, she felt it was more than that.

Cassiope was refusing to speak to her daughter, or anyone, having shut herself in her rooms. Cepheus had pleaded with her to open the doors, had sent slaves to offer her every sweetmeat she might want. On previous occasions when his wife had been angry, begging and bribery had worked.

'What shall we do?' the king asked his daughter, as they ate another meal amid jolting spurts of conversation.

Andromeda did not know what to suggest. She had always

placated her mother in the same way her father did: by giving her what she wanted until her mood improved.

'Do you know exactly why she's angry?' she asked. The words 'this time' hung in the air between them.

'I don't,' said her father. 'I know she was frustrated about you and Phineus, but I don't think she would have locked herself in her rooms over that. Not for this long, anyway.'

'She would have locked me in her rooms over that,' Andromeda said.

'Yes.' The two sat in silence for a moment.

'It's odd she hasn't done that,' Andromeda added.

'Yes.'

This time the silence lasted a while longer, as they both considered what could have happened. Cassiope had been so angry about her daughter's attitude to marrying Phineus, it was inconceivable that she would have allowed Andromeda her freedom. What if the girl had run away? Cassiope would never have taken such a risk. Even Cepheus couldn't pretend that she would have trusted him to take care of things without her.

The two of them were still lost in thought when they heard the shouts and the pounding of feet.

Elaia

It's true we weren't here at the beginning, but we were here at the end and which is more important? No one wants a beginning without an end. And we were there for the crux. In fact, we are the crux.

It all began when Athene wanted a place of her own. Gods are territorial, in a way we find difficult to understand. You're probably worrying now, are you, that we've insulted her? Don't be afraid: she would never harm us. And anyway, why would she be insulted? She knows it's true. We are everywhere, across Hellas and beyond. How could we understand what it means to call one place home?

And yet, if we did call somewhere home, it would be Athens, the city which is now hers. They named it after her: even humans probably know that. But what humans forget is that it wasn't always hers. She won it, fair and square.

That rustling sound is everyone agreeing with me, by the way.

Because Poseidon had his eye on Athens too, you know. Well, what doesn't he have his eye on? Oh, stop doing the

222

terrified expressions: he can't hurt you here. We're far enough from the sea and you can't seriously believe he could damage us with an earthquake? Well, I suppose you're more fragile than we are. But really.

And you know I'm right. He is never happy, that one. Never has enough, not even with all the seas at his command. Not even with his trident and his Nereids and his . . . Whatever he has. Who cares, when it's all underwater? No wonder he's so acquisitive. And when he heard that Athene wanted to make Attica her own, he demanded that it instead be given to him. Because, he claimed, he had lost some minuscule part of his kingdom to the Gorgons. What did they do, we asked? Drink it? How could he lose any of his kingdom? The seas are refilled whenever it rains.

Needless to say, Poseidon didn't see a need to answer us. His status prevented it, no doubt. And it doesn't really matter that he hadn't lost anything important: the relevant point is that – as usual – he was managing to feel aggrieved. So he wanted Athens and so did Athene, and Zeus didn't want to adjudicate between them. (No, don't worry: we have no comment on the king of the gods. His lightning can strike from anywhere, and even we respect that.) The Olympians would decide, Zeus decreed. Athene and Poseidon could both make their case. And then one god, one vote.

Even then, Poseidon demanded that he should go first. He hadn't even thought about Attica until Athene wanted it, but now it was such an urgent desire of his that he needed to make his case immediately. Perhaps he'd realized that half the Olympians would be quite happy if he withdrew to some distant underwater cave and was never seen or heard from again. There's a limit to how much complaining anyone wants to listen to, so whiners have to get their oars in early.

If Athene was annoyed by the way Poseidon shoved his way in front of her, grabbing at what she wanted, she didn't show it. Which, let's be quite honest, means she wasn't all that annoyed, because she doesn't often hide her feelings from us. Perhaps she knew she just needed to be patient. Again, not always one of her strengths but she can't bear Poseidon and she loves to win, so she held her temper.

He made exactly the kind of tedious, showy gesture you would expect from a god who demands everything but doesn't know why. He swept up to the acropolis, stood there for a moment to make sure everyone was looking at him, and slammed his trident into the ground.

The Olympian gods were trying to pay attention because Zeus had only just charged them with the task of deciding who should take Attica. Even Apollo and Artemis weren't yawning and that takes some effort. But when a new sea bubbled up beneath the trident (quite a long way beneath it, naturally: it takes a sea god to decide he should try and form an ocean at the highest point on a plain. But not everyone can be gifted in the same way), the archer gods began nudging each other and sniggering. Was that it? A little sea?

We felt much the same way ourselves, truth be told.

Poseidon spread his arms and shook his trident above his head. One of us believes he shouted, 'Behold!' but the rest of us are choosing to give him the benefit of the doubt. Anyway, we all beheld his new pond, whether he demanded it or not. It's just that most of us weren't wildly impressed.

Athene usually has quite a placid expression: you've probably noticed it on her statues, have you? She looks so calm and patient, spear in hand, helmet tilted back at that characteristic angle. You may not know this about her, but that is how she likes to appear no matter what is going on in her heart. How do we know? How do you think we know? She tells us a lot more than she tells her human petitioners and priests. She knows we support her and besides, we are excellent listeners.

Only if you knew Athene as well as we do, and were as well-placed to observe her as we are, only then might you have seen what we saw: a tiny flicker of scorn crossed her face. She had nothing to fear from this opponent.

She watched Poseidon sink into his small waves and she turned her attention to the acropolis where he had been standing moments before. She looked at the bare dry earth, and she saw that it was lonely. She saw the animals who wanted shade, and the humans who yearned for a new crop, one they would treasure above all else. She stared at the retreating sea and she said nothing.

And then she glanced at the other Olympians, who were mildly interested to see what she would do to rival Poseidon's bid. And all of whom were perplexed when she kneeled down to plant a tree.

How could a tree rival an ocean, they might have thought? But then, how could a god think anything so foolish? Attica was not short of oceans, but it was missing something, and Athene had seen what the land required. It needed the sound of the wind rustling slender green-silver leaves. It needed an elegant pale trunk, and it needed bright green fruit.

In short, it needed us.

Andromeda

Andromeda glanced to her left, and felt the strange sensation of seeing her own hand but not really believing it was hers. Because why would her left hand be bound to a tree? Looking to her right, she saw the same thing. A roped hand which seemed to be connected to her, but couldn't be hers because two days earlier she had been sitting opposite her father in the palace, discussing what was wrong with her sulking mother. And up until that point she had been a highly favoured princess of a wealthy country, which had never involved being fastened to a pair of dead trees, for any reason.

She wanted to scream and cry but there were so many people watching her. She did not want to humiliate herself any further, so she breathed in slowly and decided she would walk her way through the last two days, pace by pace. She would do it silently, and above all she would not look down. No matter what.

A breath out. She tried to remember which she had heard first: the pounding of leather on stone as men came racing through the palace halls? Or the terrified screaming as the waves pursued them? Or the sound of the water itself, suddenly and inexplicably filling the land between the sea and her home? The shouts and screams, she concluded. Then the sandalled feet. Then the angry tide. She felt a matching surge of fear rush through her, and tried to maintain her composure. Perhaps it had been the sea she heard first, she thought. But she hadn't been able to identify the deep rumbling sound – deafening and out of place – so she had not realized until afterwards.

A breath in. And then there had been the panic, the hard bright contagion that filled the palace faster than water, faster than running, screaming men. The water was briskly destructive, smashing everything it touched. And yet, when it licked her feet as she sat on the roof watching it rise with a fascinated horror, it was warm and soft. She had expected to die alongside her parents, in the moments that followed. But as quickly as it invaded her home, the water retreated again.

A breath out. It did not retreat far. The palace was left with piles of splintered wood, fractured ceramics, sodden, stinking fabric, and a thin jagged crust of salt crystallizing along the walls. But the palace was the least-affected part of their kingdom, certainly of the area that spanned Andromeda's home to what had once been the coastline. Much of this land was now underwater. Homes, livestock, people: all had been lost to the encroaching greed of Poseidon.

A breath in. Of course, they had tried to placate him. They had rushed to his temple, which the water had not even touched (skirting round the base of the hill on which it stood). Cepheus had given his priests whatever they asked for: cattle were in short supply now, but they sacrificed ten to the sea god straightaway. The king could hardly have done anything else, given that his surviving subjects were looking upon a vast plain of water that had swallowed their loved ones alive. What does the god say? Andromeda heard the panic in her father's voice again. A man to whom everything had come easily was not made to deal with a crisis on this scale. He was dwarfed by it, emasculated.

A breath out. And his wife – who had been saved by her locked doors, which allowed only a trickle of water into her rooms – watched the whole thing in uncharacteristic silence. Cepheus had asked for her advice, but this opinionated woman had offered nothing. Andromeda could see her father struggling to make decisions without her mother's customary contributions. Feeling that she should do her duty if her mother could not, Andromeda began to talk to her father about practicalities: where should people who had lost their homes sleep? How could they be fed now so many animals were gone? How would they be fed later, now so much grain was lost? She felt wholly unequal to the task of advising, but she knew her father needed her and she wouldn't let him down.

A breath in. And then that night, the three of them sat together in a dingy chamber she could not remember ever noticing before. From the seeds that lay on the ground in the corners (swept there with a hasty broom) this had been a storeroom until today. It was, however, drier than any other room she had checked, and the musty odour of damp was fainter. A jar of oil lay on its side by one wall, impossibly unbroken. The table had been nailed together by slaves in a rush, and Andromeda watched as her father reached for a dented goblet filled with undiluted wine, snagging his sleeve. Always so fussy about his clothes, Cepheus didn't even notice the tear. The palace steward brought them bread which had burned at the edges and a soup made from whatever had not been washed away: onion, caraway, chickpeas.

A breath out. Trying to eat because it seemed petulant to refuse when so many had lost so much, Andromeda discovered she was ravenous. She watched the same realization cross her father's face, though her mother picked at the bread without interest. Andromeda wondered where they would sleep and then flushed in the dim light to be thinking about such a minor thing when half the kingdom was underwater.

A breath in. The sound of men's footsteps hurrying through the halls, her father's head turning as he leaped from his seat, the three-legged stool clattering over. But these men weren't coming to warn of another tidal wave. Andromeda could hear the difference between purpose and panic, even if her father no longer could. The steward had returned, but this time he was accompanied by two priests from the temple of Poseidon. One was wearing an ornate headdress, and held himself with the air of a man who wanted to seem comfortable speaking to his king in a palace storeroom. The second man stood just behind him, like a fearful shadow. Cepheus recognized them both and waved them to come inside. But they stood awkwardly in the doorway instead. Andromeda did not know whether to stand herself, but stayed seated as her glassy-eyed mother showed no sign of moving and she did not wish to draw attention.

A breath out. Do you bring news from the god? asked her father. We do, sire, said the chief priest. His eyes darted around, seeking any possible route for escape. The message has come from Poseidon and it is unmistakable. Unmistakable, echoed the second man. We are punished for a crime committed in this palace, said the priest. Here? Cepheus's bafflement was complete. What crime, when?

Seated behind him, his wife let out a harsh, keening cry.

Elaia

Oh, come on. You must have realized an olive tree was the way Athene won Athens. We're an integral part of the city's identity. We're even on the coins. Well, just behind the owl. We still grow here now, everyone knows us: our grove is sacred and has been since that day. And we're not just important to Athens, we matter to the whole of Hellas. What do you think of when you think of Greece? Don't pretend. Fine, you might think of blue oceans lapping sandy shores, yes. Sure. But when you want to recreate the feeling of Athens, it's olive trees you see in your mind's eye, and olive oil you taste. To pretend anything else is foolish and insulting.

Now where were we? That's right, the gods' decision. The Olympians looked at the sea Poseidon had created and they looked at Athene's magnificent olive tree. They saw another expanse of salt water, as if any part of Hellas required another drop of brine. And they saw a sturdy tree with silver leaves. Then – because they are gods – they saw us in the spring, covered with tiny white stars. Then they saw us in the autumn, our boughs sagging under the weight of our fruit. Then they saw the olive presses. They saw their temples flickering in the light of torches burning olive oil. They saw offerings made of honeycomb and grapes with oil poured over the top. They saw the bodies of athletes gleaming with oil, they saw funerary rites performed with oil. They saw men consuming the oil and cooking with it too. They saw huge amphorae filled with liquid gold. They realized that there was no future for this city without us.

No, it wasn't a unanimous decision, since you ask. But it obviously should have been, and it was perfectly clear to all of us that the gods who voted for Poseidon had an ulterior motive.

Athene voted for us, obviously.

Poseidon for his stupid sea.

Demeter for us, because how could a goddess of agriculture not vote for the best tree? She loved us the moment she saw us.

Aphrodite for the sea, because she said (limpid eyes full of insincerity) she owed it to Poseidon having been born from the foaming deep herself. I mean, if you want to pretend that's a reason to vote for anything, then there's no arguing with you, is there?

Apollo voted for us. He's always had a weak spot for trees. Ask Daphne, she'll tell you. Well, no, I suppose she won't tell you, because she turned into a tree rather than be raped by the Archer. And even then he couldn't resist tweaking her leaves. Trees have a word for that sort of behaviour.

Artemis voted the same way as her brother, of course she did. The two are almost inseparable on Olympus, but when they are separated here, she roams the mountains of Boeotia with her women and her pack of wild deer. Do you know what deer like to eat? Leaves. So, obviously she was on our side.

Ares went for the sea. Why? I'll tell you why: we are sacrosanct in war. Do you hear that? We are so precious, so irreplaceable, that when an army invades, they burn the crops. They cut down men like so many stalks of wheat. But they do not touch the olives, because we are too beautiful and perfect. So of course the war god resents us. Pathetic.

Hephaestus voted for us, a hopeful expression on his face as he moved towards Athene. She turned away from him, and stepped back.

Hera went for the sea, out of spite for Athene. Why change now? Hephaestus was suddenly filled with anxiety that he had done the wrong thing. But he couldn't change his vote.

Hestia voted for Poseidon. We couldn't prove it, but I don't think there has ever been a clearer example of someone failing to understand the question. Our wood burns even when it is wet. What more could the goddess of the hearth require?

Zeus voted for Athene because he loved her more than Poseidon, because she was his daughter and she complained less. And also because we were clearly better.

Hermes saw that he could make it a draw, if he took Poseidon's side. So he did, because he is a petty god whom no one likes.

Zeus realized that his strategy had failed, and sighed. He waved his hand and suddenly there was one more figure standing on the hillside, by our beautiful trunk. This man didn't introduce himself, but we already knew who he was: Erichthonius, the first of the true Athenians. The child spawned by Hephaestus and nurtured by Gaia. The one Athene brought here in a basket to be raised by the daughters of Cecrops.

Don't say you've forgotten him already. I'm sure it is very confusing when someone is a baby one moment and a grown man the next, but you must have understood by now that the gods don't feel time the same way you do. To them a life takes no longer than drawing a breath does to you. So some years had passed, and none of the gods had thought about him, and now he was a man.

The stories you may have heard about him were (largely) untrue, by the way. He didn't have a snake's tail, like people said. That was just the rumour that reached across the city when the daughters of Cecrops died so suddenly. Some said the basket they had so unwisely opened was full of snakes (which was half-true). Some thought the child himself was a hybrid of man and snake (which was not true). Some said he was cursed (obviously wrong), some that he was divine (half-right). But everyone believed he was protected by Athene, and that she had sent snakes to destroy the girls who had disobeyed her. And so the Athenians admired and feared him in equal measure, and when he overthrew the previous ruler, they made him their king. And they felt a little closer to his guardian goddess and wondered if she might also become theirs.

Did Zeus know this, when he summoned Erichthonius to the sacred hill to be his judge? Of course he did: Zeus knows whatever he chooses to know. And he wanted his daughter to be happy, or at least happy enough never to discuss this again. Poseidon would soon be carping about something else, so there was no gain for Zeus in trying to please him now. Or ever. Whereas Athene would be grateful to him for this intervention, or something approaching grateful. Besides, he had already voted for her trees and he saw no reason to be on the losing side in this battle. The other gods should have followed his lead.

Erichthonius was a small, neat man who – Zeus imagined – made a perfectly adequate king. On this occasion he appeared somewhat dazed, but mortals always did when gods interacted with them directly, so no one was surprised that he was temporarily silent. Zeus explained the contest and the tied votes (with a hard stare in Hermes's direction) to the king, who nodded bravely. Erichthonius, a mortal man, was suddenly in a position of judgemental power over – Zeus had to repeat himself at this point – his own protector goddess or the god of the sea.

And though Erichthonius seemed stupefied, he knew he could not make this decision unless he was protected from its consequences. He murmured to Zeus, unaware that every god could hear every syllable, and so could we.

'If I must choose one of these deities,' he said, 'what is to stop the other one from drowning me the next instant?' Excitement rippled over the hill: he would choose Athene.

Poseidon raised his mighty head and stood tall.

Erichthonius quaked, but did not collapse.

Zeus frowned, because it had not occurred to him that there would be any consequence for the little king beyond the immediate reward from his patron goddess. But now he saw the man's expression, and noticed that he was shaking uncontrollably, he could see that for some reason the king was terrified. Zeus thought for a moment then made a promise to the man that he would suffer no ill-effects from his decision.

And Erichthonius chose us. Chose Athene.

Poseidon slammed his trident into the ground and distant cities sank beneath his raging waves, never to be seen again. He slunk off into his puny sea, determined to take his revenge on someone, even if he couldn't punish Erichthonius.

Athene planted the rest of this olive grove, to celebrate her victory. In case you didn't know, victors in competitions in Athens (sporting, theatrical, you name it) are still given olive wreaths as prizes. We are the most jubilant of trees and everyone loves us for it.

The other gods disappeared now there was no hope of a further conflict. None of them cared very much when Poseidon was angry, but all wished to consider what the consequences might be for his failed bid to take the city.

Erichthonius became the first true king of Athens (we don't count the ones that came before him, because Athens wasn't really Athens until it belonged to Athene, and until we were here). The king ruled well, married wisely and was succeeded by his son.

Athens flourished as no city has before or since. They built a huge temple to Athene on their most advantageous spot. The colossal statue of her that they placed inside was famed across the whole of Hellas. They built a smaller temple to Poseidon on a lower hill, further away, with excellent views of most of the city and unrivalled views of the temple of his niece.

Zeus congratulated himself on a successful outcome to an awkward situation.

Poseidon lurked in the briny depths and loathed every mortal and half the Olympians. He would find a way to wreak havoc on someone, even if Zeus was protecting the hated Athenians now.

Athene considered how she might punish the gods who had voted against her. But mostly, she showered love on her new trees for how we helped her humiliate her uncle.

Andromeda

Andromeda jumped when she heard the inhuman sound. She watched her father do the same, almost laughed to see the alarm she felt appear on his face too. Mirror images, they both turned to see that the source of the noise was her mother, her face a mask of pain and fear.

'Dearest, what is it?' asked Cepheus. Neither he nor his daughter moved towards Cassiope. There was nothing about her expression, her posture, that suggested she would welcome it. Her voice eventually faltered and there was a brief silence, before her body convulsed with sobbing. Andromeda had never seen her mother in distress before: she was always so poised. And she too had felt like screaming when she saw the water running through their halls, sweeping bodies and belongings away.

But she didn't feel like that now: now she was numb with shock and fatigue. The priests stood in silence at the door, beside the steward, all of them staring at the queen. Had the events of the day suddenly crushed her mother beneath their weight? Cassiope's hands were clawing at the air as she tried to take a few juddering breaths. Andromeda felt quick irritation seize her in its warm grip. Her mother could even make a disaster on this scale all about her.

'Dearest.' Cepheus had broken free of his stupor and kneeled before his wife, taking her face in his hands. 'Please, enough of this. It has been a long, terrible day. But you are safe and we are unhurt and tomorrow we will begin to rebuild our kingdom.' Cassiope's racking sobs began to subside. Cepheus held her gaze and stroked her hair.

'These men will tell us what we must do to appease the gods,' he said. 'All will be well.' He paused. 'Or at least, all will be better.' Andromeda felt the same as her father: no longer able to be certain of things. Cassiope renewed her weeping, and Andromeda wondered if she should tell the steward to escort the priests to somewhere safe and dry enough and offer them refreshments. But she felt uncomfortable issuing orders with both her parents present: the whole dismal wedding proposal had made it all too clear that they didn't trust her to make decisions for herself. So she stood awkwardly, while Cepheus murmured comforting words to his wife.

'Tell me how I can help,' he said. 'The priests did not mean to upset you, I am quite sure.' Andromeda watched the visitors in silence. They offered no reassurance.

'The crime was committed here, my lord,' said the chief priest. 'There can be no doubt.'

'What crime?' asked Andromeda. The two men looked at her in alarm, unused to being addressed by a young woman, even if her father was the king.

'The blasphemy,' said the older one.

'The provocation,' said the younger.

'Someone has offended Poseidon?' asked Andromeda,

wishing that they would just say what they meant. They nodded vigorously. 'In word or deed?'

'Speaking the words is a deed,' said the younger one. Andromeda wondered how the god tolerated such servants. Then she wondered if that was the sort of thing that counted as blasphemy.

'Speaking which words?' asked her father, groaning slightly as he stood up again.

'She knows which words,' said the older man. Andromeda felt a shock of fear, thinking he meant her. But both men were staring at her mother. Cassiope began to shudder, first in her hands and then her whole body. The stool on which she sat rattled against the stone floor. Andromeda could not bear it and moved in to embrace her, holding her tight until the shaking eased.

Her father disliked the priests, Andromeda realized. He wanted to have them both thrown out of the palace, but he did not dare to treat the emissaries of Poseidon with such disrespect. 'When you address the queen,' Cepheus said, 'you will call her that.'

'Forgive me, sire.' The older priest was dripping contempt. 'The queen knows which words. She has offended the king of the waves, and she has offended his queen.'

'She will make it right,' Cepheus replied. Andromeda felt the tension in her mother's body. 'We will make offerings in the temple immediately. Why aren't you doing that now?'

'We have made offerings,' said the younger man. 'That is how we know what has angered him, my lord.'

'This is what you asked us to do,' said the older one. 'It is hardly our fault if you do not like the answer we bring.'

'My wife will make the offering then,' Cepheus said. 'She

will offer her finest jewels and you will sacrifice a hundred oxen.'

There was silence. Andromeda didn't even know if her father still had a hundred oxen, or if her mother now possessed a single jewel. Everything had been washed away: perhaps Poseidon had already taken by force what her mother was supposed to give him by volition.

'That is not enough,' said the younger priest. Andromeda could see how much both men were enjoying this moment, wielding their power so cruelly. She wondered why they hated her mother.

'Then what?' asked Cepheus. He sounded so weary that Andromeda worried he might collapse where he stood. 'What did you say, my love?' he asked his wife.

Andromeda expected her to scream again, or start shaking, but she did not. Instead, Cassiope rose to her feet and stared at the men who were so enjoying her downfall. Both men tried and failed to meet her gaze. 'I made a mistake,' she said.

Andromeda could not recall hearing her mother ever say these words before. Cepheus nodded. Everyone made mistakes. 'What did you say?' he asked.

'I told my reflection that I was more beautiful than a Nereid,' said Cassiope.

Andromeda watched the spasm of fear and sorrow pass over her father's face.

'I see,' he said.

'I understand what I have done,' Cassiope continued. 'I must pay for my hubris, of course.'

'Of course,' said the older priest, still unable to look at her.

'I will give myself to the sea.' The queen stood tall and

proud, and in that moment Andromeda thought she might have been right. She was more beautiful than anyone – goddess or mortal.

Cepheus closed his eyes. He could not save her and he could not look at her.

'That won't be necessary,' said the younger man, reassuring words seasoned with the cruellest smile. Her father understood; she saw his shoulders slump.

'It isn't you they want,' said the priest.

Medusa, Sthenno, Euryale

Medusa did not dare leave her cave. She would not unbind her eyes; she only unwound the cloths to sleep and even then she kept them right beside her, wrapped lightly around her hands. No matter what reassurances her sisters offered, she was plagued by one thought: what if she could turn them to stone?

'It's impossible,' said Sthenno. After all these years of being scared for her sister, she could not be scared of her now.

'We're immortal,' added Euryale. 'Your gaze would have no more impact than a sword thrust or a twisting knife.'

'You don't know that,' said Medusa, her head turned to face the wall.

And she was right: they did not know.

So Medusa had a choice which was – to her – no choice at all. Risk harming one of her sisters, or rob herself of sight so there was no danger to them at all. She did not share their confidence that they would be impervious to her lethal stare.

The scale of her loss was undeniable. She missed the sun

243

and the sand and the birds and the sky and the sheep and, above all, the loving faces of her beloved Gorgon kin. She had learned to take some pleasure in the mewing of the gulls and the uneven clattering of hooves on rocks but she felt so isolated in the dark. And she had no one to tell, because if either sister had suspected the depths of her loneliness, they would have refused to allow her to go another day with her eyes covered. As it was, Euryale kept suggesting experiments to test the power of her gaze. Try staring at the wing of a cormorant, she said. We need to know if its eyes have to meet your eyes, or if your look alone is enough.

'What if I turn one of its wings to stone?' asked Medusa.

'Then we'll know more than we knew before,' said her sister.

'What did the cormorant do to deserve a stone wing? And how do we ensure I don't lay my eyes on anything else?' Medusa was immovable on the matter: she knew, though she could not say how, that her eyes must meet those of her prey for the petrification to occur. But she didn't want anything to be her prey. Nor did she want to answer any more questions about how her new power worked. She put off her sister's suggestions by saying that brightness made her head ache anyway, and she did not want to make it worse by allowing in any more light if she could avoid it. Sthenno put one hand on Euryale's shoulder and advised her sister that they leave Medusa to do what she thought best.

But it was so hard, when they had taken care of her as carefully as they could, yet she had still come to harm at the hands of Poseidon and now again at the hands of Athene.

Euryale, Sthenno knew, wanted Medusa to want this lethal power. It had always been painful to the two of them to see their sister as a fragile creature who needed their protection. And here, Euryale thought, was a chance to make that right.

'She can turn any living thing to stone!' Euryale muttered to Sthenno, long after Medusa was asleep one night. She was turning the stone scorpion in her hands, tracing her claws along its segmented body. 'Anything.'

'Yes,' Sthenno said. 'I think that's right.'

'Do you understand what this means?' said Euryale. 'It means she has strength that rivals ours. At last.'

'It does.' But Sthenno's voice was filled with doubt.

'She can protect herself!' Euryale said. She couldn't understand why her sister wasn't as happy as she was. Why neither of her sisters seemed to be happy.

'She can't do anything else,' Sthenno hissed.

'What do you mean?'

'Power is something you can control,' Sthenno said. 'Medusa can turn anything to stone, yes. But she can't not do it, if she doesn't want to.'

'Why wouldn't she want to? I don't understand what you're saying.'

Sthenno took a pause, and organized her thoughts. 'I'm saying that she can't avoid turning something to stone, even if she wants it to stay as it is. She just looks at it and it's gone.'

'Yes! A mighty power.'

'And a terrible curse,' said Sthenno. 'Because she cannot look on any living creature without destroying it.'

Euryale stopped turning the stone scorpion in her hands,

and considered it. 'It's only a scorpion,' she said. 'There are dozens in the caves. Hundreds, probably.'

'And Medusa could kill every one just by turning her head.'

'We were always worried a scorpion would sting her,' Euryale continued. She was beginning to see her sister's point, but didn't want to give up this giddy feeling. 'Now they never can.'

'No, they never can,' Sthenno agreed. 'But she can never look at a bird again. Or one of our flock. Or a mortal girl. She can't befriend anyone or love anyone unless she is blind to them. Because if she tries to catch even a glimpse of any living thing, she will kill it.'

'Stone dead,' said Euryale.

'Yes. And so she withdraws to her cave and covers her eyes and consoles herself that she will never see again.'

'She could look at us.'

'She won't. She's terrified she would kill us.'

'She can't be. She knows we're undying.'

'She knows her new power comes from an undying source. She doesn't know how it would affect us, that's why she's bound her eyes. So she can't hurt us.'

'She could test it,' Euryale said.

'She won't. You know she won't. She loves us and she will never take the risk of hurting either one of us.'

'She can't live in the dark for ever.'

'That is exactly what she plans to do.'

Euryale let out a low wail. 'How do you know all this? When she doesn't say anything?'

'The same reason you know it,' said her sister.

Athene

The cliff split and splintered ahead of him and Perseus had no idea which way he was supposed to go. He saw a reasonably flat boulder and sat on it, panting. Helios was high overhead and hurling his brightest rays down onto Perseus's aching head. He thought of Hermes wearing his angular sunhat when they met on Seriphos, at the sacred grove of Zeus. It seemed so distant – in both time and space – that Perseus was filled with a sudden melancholy. He didn't think he had failed on his quest yet, but it was so hard to keep track of the days. How long had it taken him to reach the Graiai? How long had they spent travelling from there to the garden of the Hesperides? It had felt instantaneous, as though the world had simply reordered itself before his eyes. And yet he had arrived at each new place exhausted, ravenous, parched. So perhaps the journeying had taken many days, and the gods had simply addled his mind so he didn't notice.

He could almost hear the corrosive scorn in Athene's voice if she knew what he was thinking. As if he needed any more derision from her. A bright green lizard darted across his foot, and he started. He wished he had Hermes's sunhat, rather than the cap he was carrying in his bag. And – now he thought about it – he wished he wasn't carrying the bag either. It was so heavy, it left dark red marks on his shoulders. There were thin white streaks of salt on his tunic, where his sweat had formed echoes of the straps, so that even when he wasn't carrying it, he was thinking about it. Not that there was ever a time when he wasn't carrying it, he thought. Apart from when he slept or rested, like now. The first night he spent with it, he had tried to use it as a pillow with his cloak folded on top of it. Despite many unpleasant evenings since he embarked on his quest, it was the least comfortable night he had ever spent. The bag hated him, he had decided. It didn't want to be used by him, or even borrowed by him. It grew heavier with every hour, and resentment was the only cause he could name.

He dug around in the bag for his water-skin and raised it to his lips. The liquid tasted warm and gritty and he was no less thirsty when he stoppered the skin and put it away again. He knew he would come across a stream at some point, but not when or where. He felt his cheeks burn and this had nothing to do with the heat of the sun. It was the persistent shame he experienced at being so unsuited to adventuring. He could not shake the belief that another quester would know how far he had travelled and which path he should take. Perseus felt like he just blundered from place to place until the gods intervened. Of course, he reminded himself, it was a sign of his heroic prowess that the gods intervened on his behalf. A lesser man would not have such powerful allies. But this didn't raise his spirits for long. Zeus was his father, yes, but that was down to his

mother, whom Zeus loved. He, Perseus, was almost inci-
dental. He had never even met his father.

And now, here he sat. He could clamber down the rocks
that seemed to lead him closer to the sea. Or climb higher
and hope to find fresh water and supplies further inland.
He wondered again how far he was from the Gorgons and
felt another rush of anger that he knew so little but was
expected to achieve so much. He muttered a brief but heart-
felt prayer to his father.

'Well, you shouldn't have picked him, then, should you?'

Perseus jumped at the sound of Athene. He turned and
lost his balance, sliding off the rock he had been perched
on before realizing with relief that she wasn't shouting at
him. Nor was she looking at him, which meant he could
pick himself up without further embarrassment.

'You can't possibly mind.' The disbelief in Hermes's voice
was entirely at odds with the rage of Athene.

'What do you mean, I "can't possibly mind"?' she shouted.
'Why wouldn't I mind? It was my city for the taking and
you tried to give it to him.'

'I didn't do anything of the kind,' he replied. 'My vote
wasn't enough to change anything, and you know it.'

'It was enough to make it a draw!' she said. 'So that
Father had to get an independent judge to decide.'

'Not quite independent,' Hermes murmured. She stared
at him. 'And anyway, my vote wasn't worth more or less
than any of the others. Why aren't you arguing with them?'

'Because they aren't here,' she snarled. 'And you were
last. And you enjoyed it.'

'Everyone enjoyed it,' he said. 'What difference does it
make that I was last?'

Perseus could see he should keep quiet.

'It meant I thought I might win,' Athene said. 'I thought you might choose me, since we've been on these trips together.'

'I'm the messenger god,' he replied. 'I've been on trips with everyone.'

'Well, I thought you liked me.'

'Why?' he asked.

There was a pause.

'I don't know,' she said.

'Why does it matter if I do or not?'

'Well, do you?'

Perseus glanced up from the stone-strewn ground, which he had been studiously considering. Hermes was facing Athene, his smirk less pronounced than usual. Athene looked exactly like she always did, Perseus thought, but more so.

'Not really,' said Hermes. 'I think Zeus spoils you. It makes you petulant and prone to shout.'

'Well, then, I don't like you either,' snapped Athene.

'Then you can't mind who I voted for or why,' said Hermes.

Athene turned and looked at Perseus. 'Do you like me?' she said.

Perseus wondered if he should simply throw himself off the cliff before things got any worse. 'Er, yes?' he replied.

'You see?' Athene turned back to Hermes. 'I'm likeable. He doesn't think I shout. Do you?'

'No,' said Perseus. 'Not unless you want me to.'

Hermes began to laugh. 'He's scared of you,' he said. 'He'll say anything he thinks you want to hear.'

'Are you scared of me?' she asked.

'Yes,' said Perseus.

'Good. But you also don't think I shout?'

'No,' he replied. 'I don't suppose you could help me again, could you?'

Athene rolled her eyes. 'I knew Zeus had sent us for a reason. What is it now?'

Perseus tried not to wince as she shouted at him. 'I don't know which way I'm supposed to go,' he said. 'Or how far it is. Or where I can get fresh water. Or whether those berries are safe to eat.'

Athene looked at Hermes. 'You aren't going to pretend this is me being petulant?' she said.

'No, this is him.' Hermes spoke slowly to Perseus. 'Follow the line of the coast,' he explained. 'Like Athene told you to. You'll know you've reached the Gorgons when you see Gorgons.'

'But I don't know how far it is!' Perseus said. 'What if I miss them?'

'Miss them?' Athene said. 'You think you might just wander past the Gorgons and not notice them?'

'I don't know,' Perseus said. 'I mean, I don't . . .' Faced with two scornful gods, his words tailed off. Perhaps now was not the time.

'You don't what?' asked Hermes.

'Nothing,' said Perseus.

'Zeus sent us here for a reason,' said Athene. 'There must be something you need to know.'

'Well, it's just, I haven't been told,' Perseus said. 'So I don't know what the Gorgons look like.'

Hermes and Athene stared at one another, all animus forgotten. 'You don't know?' the messenger god said.

'No.'

'So you came on a quest for the head of something you couldn't identify?' Hermes asked.

'Yes.'

'Did you think to ask anyone before you set out?' Athene said.

'No.'

'And it didn't occur to you that you'd need to know?' Hermes was shaking his head.

'It did,' said Perseus. 'But I didn't know who to ask.'

'How about the king who set you on your quest?' suggested Athene. 'Polydectes. Remember him?'

'I couldn't ask him.' Perseus was horrified. 'Then he would have thought I was stupid.'

'Yes, I can see how that would have put you off,' Hermes said. 'You could have told us you had no idea what you were doing when we found you.'

'He did seem like the kind of person who might embark on a quest for a Gorgon's head without knowing what a Gorgon was,' Athene said. 'Now you mention it.'

'You already thought I was an idiot,' Perseus said. 'I didn't want to make things worse.'

'They're worse now,' Hermes replied. 'Now I think you're much stupider than I would have if you'd said something at the outset.'

'Right,' said Perseus.

'I probably don't,' Athene added. 'But that's because I thought you were incredibly stupid when we met, and there wasn't much scope for me to think less of you.'

'Yes,' said Perseus. 'I appreciate that.'

'So you've been walking along the coast, wondering if whatever you see might be a Gorgon?' Hermes checked.

'Yes,' said Perseus.

'Like gulls or sheep or prickly pears?' Athene asked.

'Well, I know what all those are,' he said. 'But otherwise, yes.'

'So you just asked Zeus for help, and the help you need is to know what a Gorgon looks like?' Hermes said.

'I'm sorry.'

'No, I just wanted to be sure. I could just tell you anything was a Gorgon, and you'd believe me?'

Panic flooded Perseus's face. If the gods decided to trick him, he would have no way of knowing until he reached Seriphos. He could see the vicious disdain in the eyes of the king as he revelled in Perseus's failure, hear the mockery of his courtiers. He felt suddenly short of breath, even after sitting on the rock to recover from his climb. Perhaps Zeus would intervene to save him, he thought. Or, failing that, perhaps Polydectes wouldn't know what a Gorgon was either, and he could just bluff it out. Even as Perseus thought this, he acknowledged it was unlikely.

'Gorgons are immortal creatures,' Athene said. 'Did you really not know this?'

'No,' said Perseus. 'Well, yes, I suppose I would have guessed they were something like that, because the Graiai mentioned they were sisters.' He tried and failed to suppress the shudder that afflicted him whenever he thought of the hateful hags. If he had been brave enough, he would have told Athene that he hoped they were exactly like the Graiai. Because then he would not struggle to behead one.

'They are indeed sisters to the Graiai,' said Hermes, and Perseus supposed that his pomposity was just part of his nature and had to be tolerated.

'But they are far more deadly,' Athene explained.

This was not what Perseus had been hoping to hear. 'More deadly?' he asked. 'How much more?'

'Well,' said Hermes, leaning on his staff. 'A lot more. The Graiai are old, and blind, and only have a single tooth between them. Had, I should say. The Gorgons are predators.'

'Like wild cats?' asked Perseus. 'Or eagles?'

'No,' said Athene. 'Like dangerous creatures who would swallow you whole if you irritated them.'

'I see,' said Perseus. 'Lucky the Hesperides gave me this sword.' The harpē was the only thing he hadn't complained about since he received it.

'Lent you this sword, I think,' said Hermes. 'It belongs to your father, and he will want it back.'

'What do they look like?' asked Perseus.

'You really need to worry about the tusks,' said Hermes. 'They have huge, sharp teeth and they could crunch your bones in a beat of your puny heart.'

'Right,' said Perseus. 'Avoid the teeth.'

'They also have wings,' Athene said.

'So they can fly at me, with their teeth?'

'Yes,' she said.

'They're incredibly strong,' added Hermes. 'As strong as a god, really.'

'So it's not just the tusks I need to avoid?' Perseus said. 'It's more the whole creature?'

'That would be ideal,' said Hermes.

'Except I need to decapitate one.' Perseus thought for a while. 'Perhaps I could sneak up on one from behind?'

'Yes and no,' said Hermes.

'Why no?'

'The snakes, of course,' snapped Athene.

'They live somewhere surrounded by snakes?' Perseus asked. He hadn't even begun to think about the environment in which the Gorgons might live. He'd been too busy concentrating on what they might be.

'No,' Hermes said. 'They are surrounded by snakes.'

Perseus sighed. He wasn't afraid of snakes, he didn't think. But it probably depended on how many snakes there were, and this didn't sound good.

'The Gorgons are all surrounded by snakes?' he asked. 'Do they just sit among them or . . .'

'The snakes are part of them,' Athene explained.

'I see. I don't suppose they're at ground level, are they? Where one might usually see snakes?'

'No,' said Athene. 'They have snakes for hair.'

'Oh,' said Perseus. 'So right by the head, really?'

'Yes,' said Hermes. 'You couldn't sneak up behind one of them. Because the snakes would see you.'

'And the snakes can talk?' Perseus wondered how much worse this could get.

Both gods looked at him as though he were an imbecile. 'Of course they can't talk,' said Athene. 'They're snakes.'

'Then how do they communicate with the Gorgons?'

'They hiss,' said Hermes. 'I suppose that might sound like talking to them.'

Perseus felt foolish, and vaguely aggrieved. 'So would the snakes see me if it was the darkest hour of the night?' he asked.

'Yes, I think so,' Hermes said. 'Snakes can see in the dark, can't they?'

Athene nodded.

'I don't know how anyone could decapitate one of these deathless monsters!' Perseus cried, and he slumped forward.

'I struggle to believe sometimes that you're the son of Zeus,' said Hermes. 'Although he believes you are, so it must be true.'

'Why?' Perseus asked. 'Everything you've told me makes me certain that this task is impossible. They can eat me. They can fly. They're stronger than me. They are covered in snakes.'

'You have the cap of Hades,' Athene reminded him.

'I have a hat,' Perseus agreed.

'That belongs to Hades,' Hermes said. 'And renders the wearer invisible.'

There was silence.

'I suppose that does help with the snakes,' said Perseus. 'So I can sneak up on the Gorgons after all.'

'They have excellent hearing,' said Athene.

'Right,' said Perseus. 'But perhaps I could approach them while they sleep.'

Again the gods looked at one another. 'Gorgons don't sleep,' said Hermes. 'They're Gorgons. Well, one of them might sleep, but the others? No.'

'Oh,' said Perseus. 'I thought they might need to lie down occasionally. To rest their snakes and so on.'

'No,' said Athene. 'They don't do that.'

'So they're always awake, always alert?' he asked. His voice was quavering a little.

'They're rational creatures who don't want to die,' Hermes explained. 'You have a sword, loaned to you by your father. And a cap of darkness, borrowed from Hades himself. You can't expect everything to be easy. Otherwise you wouldn't be completing a quest at all, would you? You could have just stayed on Seriphos and one of us could have fetched a Gorgon head for you.'

Perseus had thought for some time now that this would be the ideal solution to his problems but something about Hermes's tone made him refrain from saying so.

'I thought you said they were immortal.' He frowned. Every time he gained something – a sliver of knowledge, a little divine assistance – he seemed to lose something else.

'Two of them are immortal,' Athene clarified. 'One of them is mortal.'

'So I need to behead the mortal one?'

'Yes, obviously,' replied Hermes.

'They will defend her, if they can,' said Athene quickly. 'She is much loved.'

'Why would anyone love a monster?' asked Perseus.

'Who are you to decide who is worthy of love?' said Hermes.

'I mean, I wasn't . . .'

'And who are you to decide who is a monster?' added the messenger god.

'She called them monsters,' said Perseus, pointing at Athene.

'No, I didn't,' she said. 'I called them dangerous creatures, which they are. You're the one who thinks anything that doesn't look like you must be a monster.'

'They have snakes for hair!' Perseus cried.

'Snakes aren't monsters,' said Hermes.

'And tusks.'

'Wild boar aren't monsters either.'

'And wings.'

'I'm sure even you don't think birds are monsters.'

'I have to fight one and take its head,' said Perseus. 'They sound monstrous enough to me.'

'You won't be able to fight them,' said Hermes. 'I thought we'd established this already. You need to close in on the mortal one while her deathless sisters are elsewhere.'

'How will I even know which one is the mortal one?' Perseus asked.

'She doesn't have tusks,' said Athene. 'Her wings are smaller and her snakes are younger.'

'Well, that's something,' said Perseus. 'At least I'm trying to behead the least dangerous one.'

Hermes nodded. Athene allowed her perfect brow to crease just for a moment.

'There is one more thing,' she said.

Andromeda

Andromeda had not screamed or struggled when they told her she was the sacrifice Poseidon demanded. She didn't want the hateful priests to see her afraid. Besides, her mother – once she had broken her silence – had not stopped crying and pleading. She was occupying the role Andromeda might have taken for herself, and in the moments when she was alone, Andromeda resented it. How dare her mother decide that she was the innocent victim in all this, when her stupid thoughtless boasting had cost so many lives already? And when the one life spared by the sea nymphs she had offended was her own?

But she even held her resentment in check. She was losing her mother anyway: what would she gain from raging at her first? She cried quietly when alone, and otherwise she behaved as though this awful end to her young life had been decreed by the Fates, and not incurred by her mother's foolish pride. She was, if she was completely honest, delighted to discover that her uncle (and unwanted future husband) was nowhere to be seen. Her father had sent messengers in every direction, and no one was able to say where Phineus was or what had happened to him. There was no confirmation of his death, no body had been found, and his home lay inland from the water's reach. Andromeda took a grim pleasure in the remaining few days of her life having her expectations of the man both met and surpassed. He really was only interested in a young bride and greater proximity to royal power; he really did have no interest in Andromeda herself. Her father expressed concern at first, for his missing brother. But as the hours slipped by, even he could see that Phineus had no intention of supporting his family. Wherever he was, he planned to stay there until there was no danger of being embroiled in their crisis.

Andromeda did not gloat about having been right and her parents having been wrong: there seemed no point when she had so little time to enjoy it. But she did find herself wondering if by some divine intervention she survived whatever punishment was deemed necessary, her parents might allow her to choose her own husband. There would have been so much pleasure to be derived from all this. If only Andromeda had more time.

*

On the morning of the sacrifice, she awoke early and sent away the slave-women who came to help her dress. She picked out a chiton she didn't much like, but which had survived the flood undamaged. It was creamy-white with a pair of dark dotted lines down the front. Vertical stripes also dropped from under her arm to the hem on each side. She added a necklace of large carnelian beads and earrings made of delicate gold spheres, pressed together into a circle.

From each disc hung three gold and carnelian drops. She slipped her feet into the sandals she had been wearing when the water came, because they were the only ones she hadn't lost.

The women did help her with her headdress, which was ornate and heavy, and had been locked away until today. An undulating pattern of lotus leaves was carved around the outside. Her hair was loose beneath it, covered by a transparent veil, fringed with tiny weighted beads that held it in place.

She knew she looked spectacular, a worthy enough sacrifice for the nymphs her mother had so enraged. When her parents saw her, they both wept. They had imagined seeing their daughter dressed in such finery on a festival day, perhaps her own wedding. Even the younger priest looked downcast when Andromeda stepped out from the palace into the harsh morning light. The older one, if anything, was enjoying himself even more than when they first brought the news to her father. The more her mother wailed – her once-beautiful eyes now swollen and puffy – the more joy seemed to emanate from him. Andromeda gazed at the priest steadily through her veil, noting his anger that she dared to meet his eyes and did not look away.

There was quite a procession, she saw, to accompany her to the place where she would die. Her father had always been a popular king, but his people knew they had been punished by Poseidon himself. They would not forgive the queen for a long time, Andromeda guessed: the priests had made no secret of the cause of Ethiopia's ruin. The citizens were too bereft and exhausted by their sorrows now to demand vengeance on their queen. But only when there was no one left alive who had been bereaved that day would her mother's name be spoken without a curse.

Andromeda began her slow walk towards the new shore, following the two priests. She was braced for anger and derision but the gathering people were quiet. Instead of jeering at her, they walked alongside her. She couldn't tell if it was a gesture of solidarity or a desire to see the princess get what she deserved. But she was grateful not to be alone when the ground fell away ahead of her and she could see the impossible: desert made sea.

How had the priests decided where she should be bound and left to the ocean waters? she wondered. Had they chosen a spot where they were sure she would drown at the earliest possible moment? Or were they hoping she would survive for long enough to watch the water rise in another tidal wave, taking her only when it chose? As she drew closer, she found herself realizing they had picked this place because it had a pair of dead trees standing close together, beside a large boulder. The older priest could barely contain his pleasure as he ordered his younger colleague to tie the princess between the two withered trunks.

Andromeda stared dully ahead as he passed the rope around the point where a dead branch protruded – one, two, three, four times – and tightened it against her right wrist. Her arm was slightly raised, and she could feel it pressing into the thin, splintered bark. She knew his eyes were fixed on her face, but she wouldn't meet his gaze. He tied the final knot and she flexed her fingers to see if she still could. The priest stepped behind her to tie her other arm to a branch on the second tree.

In front of her stood the makeshift altar: a wooden box

with tendrils and circles carved into it. On top of this was a calathus, woven from willow rods, ready to contain the offerings they would pile into it. Andromeda wondered why they had made an altar from a box and a basket, but she already knew the answer. These men didn't care about Poseidon, for all that they served in his temple and grew fat on his offerings. They didn't revere him in celebration, they lived only to punish those who blasphemed.

And the daughter of those who blasphemed. Andromeda could hear her mother behind her, still weeping extravagantly, and she looked out over the sea that would consume her. She half-wished the priest had blindfolded her, so she couldn't watch death arriving. Sometimes they did that, with animals. She had seen it. Rather than risk a heifer shying away from the shining blade, they bound its eyes so it would meet its destiny calmly. Would Poseidon raise the sea to drown her? She tried to imagine how it would feel to see the water coming ever closer. And then wondered if it would be worse only to hear it, never to be quite sure until it touched her. Or would she just be left here until she died from thirst, or hunger? Shunned by the sea rather than claimed by it. She shivered, in spite of the heat.

Her parents were drawing nearer: she could hear her mother gabbling, trying to negotiate with the older priest. Let me offer this, Andromeda heard, and this, and this. There was the clattering of metal landing on metal, and Andromeda took a moment to realize her mother was pulling off necklaces, bracelets, earrings, every piece of gold she could carry or wear. She was piling them up in her hands, offering them to the priest to try and buy back her daughter's life. Andromeda felt the tears come.

She did not want her parents to see her cry, didn't want to add to her mother's guilt and sorrow. But now the tears had arrived they flowed down her face. She tensed her wrists against the ropes without thinking, reflexively trying to raise her hands to wipe her eyes. The tears itched on her cheeks, the ropes bit at her wrists.

And in that moment, Andromeda decided that she might not die quietly after all.

Athene

'I am sorry,' said Perseus. 'I think I must have misunderstood.'

'I'm not sure you have,' said Hermes. He had resisted taking a bet from Dionysus on how long this son of Zeus would last, because he had believed the king of the gods would take it amiss. But now he felt a brief surge of an emotion it took him a moment to identify as remorse. If he had only known!

'I think I must have,' Perseus repeated. 'Because I thought you said that the mortal Gorgon, the one I have to behead because the others are immortal so can't be injured and could crush me like a stack of dry twigs, that one? It sounded to me as though you were saying she now has the power to turn me to stone with a single glance. And that can't be right, can it? Because if that's what you meant . . .'

The two gods stared at him.

'Usually a mortal runs out of breath before saying that many words,' said Athene.

'I wonder if they aren't normally facing certain death?' said Perseus.

'Your face has gone all red,' she replied.

'Because I've failed,' he shouted. 'How can I fulfil my promise to my mother now?' He covered his face with his hands and wept.

'I don't even have a mother,' said Athene. 'I'm sure she won't mind.'

'She will lose everything if I fail in the attempt,' he said. 'I either go home now, without the Gorgon head to buy her freedom. Or I die trying.'

'I think that option is worse for you,' said Hermes. 'I mean, relatively.'

'Yes,' Perseus agreed. 'And worse for my mother.'

'It's really the same for her,' Athene replied. 'She marries the king either way, doesn't she?'

Perseus dropped his hands and looked at the goddess. 'I hate to disagree with you,' he said. 'But it's not quite the same, is it?'

'Isn't it?' asked Hermes.

'No,' said Perseus. 'Because one way she loses her freedom and happiness. And the other way she loses her freedom and happiness and her only son.'

'Oh yes, of course,' said Hermes. 'And she would mind that more?'

'Yes,' Perseus replied. 'She would.'

'I think you're being a bit melodramatic,' said Athene. 'You're behaving as though you'd have had a better chance if you didn't know about the Gorgon's power.'

'No,' said Perseus. 'I'm behaving as though I have been clambering over a terrifying rocky island and negotiating with horrible old hags and pleading with nymphs who are laughing at me and trekking along a desolate coastline for days and it's all been for nothing.'

'You're going red again,' she said. 'And you hadn't really faded from the last time you forgot to breathe.'

Perseus took a deep breath but it didn't improve matters at all.

'How will I face her?' he said. 'How will I arrive back at Dictys's house and tell her I've failed?'

'I would suggest that it'll be a lot easier to do that if you aren't made of stone.' Hermes was still smarting about the untaken bet. Why did Athene never tell anyone when she'd cursed someone like this? No wonder half the Olympians preferred Poseidon, even though his perpetual sense of grievance was so tedious.

'Yes, thank you,' snapped Perseus. 'You make an unarguable point.'

'I was going to offer you the advice you need to complete your quest,' said Athene. 'But perhaps I shan't bother now.'

'What advice?' asked Perseus. He could not raise his hopes again, only to have one of these icy immortals dash them to pieces.

'Oh, I see,' said Athene. 'Now you want to know.'

'Yes, I do,' said Perseus.

'Because before you were all screaming about how you were going to die,' she said.

There was a pause.

'Yes, I was doing that,' Perseus admitted. 'It was difficult news to hear.'

'So you've changed your mind?' she asked. 'And you want help again?'

'I think I always wanted help,' he replied. 'I just thought perhaps you would have mentioned the help, if there was any, at the same time as you mentioned the death-stare.'

'You're quite annoying,' she said.

Hermes looked from the golden and impervious Athene to the red-faced, blotchy Perseus and shook his head. 'No one would believe you two are related,' he said.

Athene glared at him. 'It's hardly comparable.'

'I wouldn't want to presume—' said Perseus.

'Good. Don't,' she replied.

'But perhaps you might give me the advice you mentioned?' he asked.

Athene sighed. 'Everything about you makes me regret we're helping you. But since we promised Zeus, this is the advice. The Gorgon can only kill you if you meet her gaze. A reflection wouldn't be enough. Do you understand?'

'Yes,' Perseus said. 'So I should behead her from behind a mirror?'

'Perhaps a shield?' said Hermes.

'Right,' Perseus said.

'And the mortal Gorgon sleeps,' Athene added.

'Unlike the immortal ones?' Perseus asked. 'The ones that can also kill me?'

'Yes.'

'I'm not sure how this helps me,' he said.

'She closes her eyes when she sleeps,' Athene explained.

'Oh, I see!' Perseus finally looked less miserable. 'So I just have to wait till she's asleep and then behead her? While her sisters are distracted?'

'Using only Hades's cap of invisibility and my winged sandals,' Hermes replied. 'And the curved sword you have from Zeus himself. And advice from the goddess of wisdom.'

'I suppose it's a start,' said Perseus.

Medusa

Medusa saw her cave much as she always had. She could feel every part of the smooth rock as she traced her fingertips around the walls. She could hear every corner and crevice as the creatures that inhabited its darkness moved across its sandy, stony floor. The touch and the sounds created pictures in front of the bindings on her eyes and, as she tried to recover from the curse, she moved with almost the same confidence she'd had before. And even though she had made her own eyes blind, she had acquired many more.

The snakes were patient at first, because they knew no other life. But they longed for heat and light. The cave bored them and they wouldn't pretend otherwise. They belonged to Medusa and she belonged to them, and they sighed and seethed until she accepted that she could not hide away from the light they craved.

And then the snakes relaxed because they had the light she needed. It was not – they had realized – in Medusa's nature to hide away. However protective the Gorgons were of one another, she could never have sustained herself by hiding in the cave. Sthenno wanted to welcome Medusa back outside, but Euryale shook her head. Medusa needed to find her way back to life step by step. She had lost so much so quickly – her body, her hair, her sight – that she could repair herself only slowly.

But she did. The snakes were her eyes now, and although she was less sure-footed outside the cave, she had little fear of falling or injuring herself: she had wings, after all. And the mass of snakes could look in every direction at once. It took time for Euryale to stop shadowing her sister as Medusa felt her way around the shore, but gradually she did. The sheep took fright at Medusa's changed appearance, but they too grew used to the metamorphosis. This Gorgon now resembled the others more closely, and the sheep knew that Gorgons were no threat to them.

The sisters settled into a new life that was closer to the old life than any of them had imagined could be possible. Medusa saw all she needed to see and it was enough.

'We are one and we are many,' said Sthenno, as she pulled hot puffy bread from atop the charred wood and gave it to her sister. Medusa's snakes would not approach the fire at all, and anyway, cooking for her sister was Sthenno's passion. Euryale nodded, and Medusa raised her head towards the light of the evening sun.

'Are we still one?' she asked. 'Even after everything?'

'We will always be one,' said Sthenno. 'One family of Gorgons.'

'But I've changed so much,' said Medusa. Sthenno could hear the frown that the bindings covered.

'You've changed every day,' said Euryale thickly. She liked the taste of warm bread even if she didn't need it. 'Since you were a baby.'

'I suppose so,' said Medusa.

'It's true,' replied Sthenno. 'You were so small and could hardly move. And then you grew longer and then you stood up and grew taller.'

'The noise,' Euryale added.

'You used to cry,' Sthenno agreed. 'And then you learned to talk.'

'But I was always me,' said Medusa. 'I never changed.'

'You always changed and never changed,' Sthenno said.

'Then how did you know I was still Medusa?'

'Because of the ways you stayed the same,' Euryale said. 'Everything changes except the gods. We don't think the sheep have stopped being sheep because we sheared them.'

Medusa ate in silence for a while. 'But you always had each other,' she said. 'And you never change.'

Sthenno looked at Euryale and smiled, her outermost tusks pointing in towards her nose. 'We do change,' she said. 'You changed us, when you came here.'

'And you didn't mind?' Medusa asked.

'No,' said Euryale. 'Gorgons aren't supposed to be like gods. We belong here, in the place between the land and the sea, not on a lofty mountain. They put our image on the outside of temples, not within. We look out on mortals, not down on them. When Phorcys delivered you to our shore, he brought you to where you needed to be.'

'So I wouldn't die, or embarrass him,' said Medusa. The Gorgons had discussed this a great deal before.

'Yes,' said Sthenno. 'And so we would become three, as we were meant to be.'

'How do you know we were meant to be three?'

'Because we are three now,' Sthenno replied. 'You ask so many questions.'

'So was I meant to have snake hair? Was I meant to be more like you?' Medusa asked. And this, Euryale realized, was the question that had been gnawing at her sister's heart.

'No,' she said. 'That was just Athene, finding a clever way to punish you. Clever, as she thinks of it, I mean. She would have been so pleased with herself, punishing you by making you a monster, like your sisters.'

'You aren't monsters,' Medusa said.

'Neither are you. Who decides what is a monster?'

'I don't know,' said Medusa. 'Men, I suppose.'

'So to mortal men, we are monsters. Because of our teeth, our flight, our strength. They fear us, so they call us monsters.'

'But they don't know who you are.' Medusa stopped eating and turned from one sister to the other. The snakes never stopped swirling around her head. 'Men call you monsters because they don't understand you.'

'I don't mind being a monster,' Euryale replied. 'I would rather have power than not. I like being what scares them.' There was a pause. 'I like you having snakes,' she added. 'I didn't like how they hurt you at first. I didn't like how you lost your hair. But I don't see this change as any different from the others, except we know who caused this one.'

'I don't mind the snakes as much now,' said Medusa. 'I do miss my hair.'

Panopeia

He is almost upon them, though he doesn't know it. He has travelled across the sea and along the coast, and he has never stopped petitioning his father for aid. He knows he cannot do what has been asked of him without divine assistance. Some people, I know, find humility an endearing trait. Others might wonder why one bastard child deserves so much attention.

And now he is closing in on the Gorgons, ready to kill a creature that has done him no harm just to acquire a trophy for a man he despises. Men often kill for trophies, I suppose: animals, certainly. But not the children of gods. Not often. And not with the help of other, mightier gods.

It makes me wonder – and I never wonder because I see it all – is no one going to rouse Phorcys? Will no one call to Ceto? Will these immortals not rise up from the deep to protect their daughter? Perseus wants to save his mother from marriage: will neither of these sea gods intervene to save their daughter from death? From mutilation? Are they afraid of Zeus or has no one told them she is in danger?

Her sisters don't know what's coming, of that I am sure.

Neither would blink before she defended Medusa from a son of Zeus, no matter how much power he had. Euryale would tear his head from his shoulders and take the consequences without fear.

And perhaps she will. Because I have watched Perseus for many days now, and he is as likely to fail in his quest as succeed, I would say.

From the water, all we can do is watch.

Athene

'But we only just got back.' The goddess scuffed her foot against the perfect marble floor.

'Well, how fortunate that you can be anywhere more or less instantly,' said Zeus.

'I know, but . . .'

'But nothing. He is my son and I'm asking you to go and help him.'

'We have helped him,' Athene snapped. 'If it hadn't been for me he would have drowned in a box years ago.'

'He is praying to me all the time,' said her father.

'Because he can't do anything for himself,' she replied. 'Because we keep helping him.'

'Then one more visit won't hurt, will it?'

'He doesn't learn if we do everything for him,' she said.

Her father shrugged. 'He's human, he doesn't have time to learn anything important.'

'Then just let him die,' she said. 'So I don't have to put up with Hermes again.'

Zeus sat on his throne, gazing into the middle distance, as though he were considering her suggestion. But she knew this was a deceit he usually practised on Hera, who never believed it either.

'I can see you aren't actually thinking about it,' she said.

'He's your half-brother,' Zeus replied. 'You could show a little familial loyalty.'

'When does anyone show familial loyalty to me?' Athene asked. 'I have helped Perseus three times already. Maybe he should do something for me.'

'Dearest,' said her father, who couldn't be tired because immortals didn't sleep. 'He can't help you because you are a goddess and he is a man. What could he possibly have that you would want?'

'Nothing,' she replied. 'That's why I'm sick of helping him. He can't do anything for me, he can't do anything for himself, he's useless. He's just a bag of meat wandering round, irritating people.'

'I think that's a little harsh,' said Zeus. 'He's handsome, isn't he?'

'They all think they're handsome,' she said. 'I've seen better.'

Zeus looked rather offended but tried to conceal it. 'What would you be doing instead?' he asked.

'I could go to Athens,' she replied. 'I want to see how my temple is looking and make sure they all know that they are mine and I am theirs.'

'That's very sweet,' said her father. Athene frowned. 'You can do that as soon as you've helped Peri—' He broke off.

'Perseus,' she said. 'I knew you didn't know.'

'Of course I knew,' he said. 'I was just testing you.'

'Why?' she asked. 'I've spent more time with him than his mother has lately.'

Zeus shifted his weight and she stared.

'That's it, isn't it?' she said.

'What is?'

'You still want his mother,' she said.

'Don't be ridiculous, she's too old.'

'Well, that's what I would have assumed,' said his daughter. 'But that's it.'

'No.'

'Well, if you don't want her for yourself any more, you still don't want her to marry some king.' Athene refused to let it go.

Zeus sighed. 'No,' he admitted. 'I don't want her to marry that king.'

'Or anyone else.' Now she had puzzled it out, she was triumphant. 'That's why you washed her up on Seriphos with that man who doesn't desire women.'

'Coincidence,' the king of the gods replied.

'It is not,' she said. 'You forgot he had a brother, that's all.'

'I am omniscient,' he said. 'I don't forget things.'

'You just forgot your own son's name.'

'Will you please go and help him decapitate one single Gorgon?' bellowed her father. 'It is hardly a difficult request, is it? Is it? I knew Hermes would only do half the job because that's always the problem with him. Takes the message, doesn't bother with the task at hand. But I thought you would help me. You are my daughter. I supported you in your petition for Athens. And now you throw obstacle after obstacle in my path.'

Athene couldn't believe what she was hearing. 'I have already helped him three times,' she cried. 'Why don't you go and do it?'

'Because I am ordering you,' he shouted.

'Well, then I have to, don't I?'

'Yes,' he said.

'I want the chance to help a mortal man I like in return,' she said.

'Fine,' Zeus replied.

'Anyone I want,' she said.

'You can choose whoever you like,' he agreed.

'Even if the other gods are against him?'

'Yes.'

'Whenever I decide?'

'Yes.'

And with this agreement, she left Olympus and reappeared behind Perseus, out of sight.

Herpeta

α: We sensed him coming. We could feel his uncertain steps on the rocks; we felt them in our bellies as we nestled on the sand.

β: We sensed him coming. She was asleep. We were awake, but she was asleep. It's important that you know this, because he will try to claim there was a battle. But there is no battle to be had between an armed man and a sleeping girl. Don't forget.

γ: We sensed him coming, but we didn't know what to do. The sisters were outside the cave entrance, as always. We could hear them murmuring to one another and we could smell the charred meat left on their fire.

δ: We sensed him coming. We should have woken her. I wanted to wake her but the others wouldn't let me.

ε: How did we stop you from waking her? I don't remember you saying anything about it.

ζ: We sensed him coming. He was drawing closer and we could feel something was different about the way he moved.

δ: That's what I'm saying. I felt something different. Different and dangerous.

ε: You felt a man creeping across the rocks and tiptoeing through the sand. You hadn't heard a man here before. You'd heard Gorgons and sheep and small creatures, birds and so on. The only thing you felt was that this was new, that he was new.

δ: New things are always dangerous. If you'd listened to me, she might have been safe.

ε: You are such a liar.

η: We sensed him coming. And there was someone else, too. Someone behind him.

ε: We didn't sense her.

δ: Of course we didn't sense her, she's a goddess. And the goddess of wisdom, sly and determined. How on earth would we sense her if she didn't want us to?

θ: We sensed him coming, but we thought the Gorgon sisters were just outside.

ε: We didn't notice they had gone.

δ: Where did they go?

ε: Oh, I thought you knew everything without being told? Didn't you sense that as well?

δ: There's no need to be unkind.

ι: We sensed him coming. And he would have been stopped before he came anywhere near our cave if the sisters had stayed nearby.

ε: They were tricked by a goddess. Athene took them away from the cave.

δ: How did she do that?

ε: She made them believe their flock was in danger. She drew Euryale away and up the shoreline. She howled and raged like a wild dog, and Euryale thought her sheep were lost if she didn't fly straight to them.

δ: Is that what that noise was?

ε: Of course.

κ: We sensed him coming. We didn't know she was in danger but we knew something was wrong. His weight was wrong. He was carrying things a mortal could not carry.

δ: Where did the other sister go? Sthenno?

ε: She was tricked by Athene too.

δ: How could she be in two places at once?

ε: She's a goddess. She can do whatever she chooses.

δ: So there was never any hope?

ε: I don't want to talk about it any more.

β: We sensed him coming but she was asleep. You must remember, you must promise.

α: We sensed him coming but he was far away and then suddenly he was very close. Very close.

ε: Because he had the cap of Hades. We couldn't see him because he wore the cap of Hades and he was darkness in the dark.

γ: We sensed him coming but we thought the sisters were still there, guarding her like always.

δ: We should have been guarding her.

ζ: We sensed him coming but he had the curved blade. How could we guard against a weapon of Zeus? How could we save her?

θ: I don't know any more if we did sense him. We didn't sense the sisters leave.

ε: We were tricked by a goddess renowned for her cunning. What were we supposed to do?

δ: I thought you didn't want to talk about it.

ι: We thought the sisters were outside. They were tricked and so were we.

α: We can see in the dark.

All: We can see in the dark.

θ: But we couldn't see him.

ε: Because he wore the cap of Hades.

θ: Why didn't we see his footprints?

ε: Because he was wearing the cap of Hades. It wasn't a cheap trick, it was magic.

δ: Was it really?

ε: Yes.

β: She was asleep.

ε: We know, don't worry.

β: It's important no one forgets.

α: Everyone will forget.

β: We can't let them.

γ: He was in the cave and she was sleeping close to the entrance.

δ: Was that our fault? Because we liked to be near the embers of the fire?

ε: No, it wasn't our fault. I'm sorry I was cross with you.

η: We couldn't fight a man who had a goddess on his side.

ε: No.

κ: He drew his blade in silence. We didn't hear it.

β: It was already drawn. There was nothing to hear.

α: She slept facing the cave wall that night, curled up with her arms folded in front of her.

δ: Like a child.

ε: Yes.

η: He sighed with relief when he saw she was facing away from him.

ι: He was a coward.

γ: It didn't matter. He didn't need to be brave to kill her while she slept.

β: Thank you for reminding them.

α: She was asleep until he held the sword above her neck.

β: She was asleep.

δ: Not then.

β: She was, I'm telling you she was asleep and he crept up on her while she slept and then he brought the blade down on her neck.

α: She woke when he was standing above her. He kicked two stones into her back and she woke.

β: Don't say that, when you know it isn't true.

ε: It is true.

β: No, you're lying. She was asleep.

α: Until the final moment she was asleep.

β: If what you're saying is true, why didn't she open her eyes?

ε: You know why.

δ: You know why.

β: I don't.

α: Because she wouldn't kill him.

Stone

There is no statue here; there is only an empty plinth. But if the statue were here, it would look like this.

A young man stands with his weight on his right leg, toes flexed. The left foot is slightly raised, so you can see he is on the verge of moving forward. If he were real, he would be on the point of walking into you. He is well-muscled: his biceps are clearly defined and his shoulders are straight. He wears a knee-length tunic beneath which are slender calves. He is strong but not yet a warrior. He has no shield nor does he wear armour.

His cloak is fastened at the neck with a simple round clasp. The cloak has a thin dark border that forms a solid line all around the edge. It is a plain travelling cloak: it looks warm and serviceable. On his feet are sandals which must have been very difficult to carve. They have leather straps, and they come up high: to mid-calf. And they are decorated with wings, one on either side of each ankle. Each feather is distinct and you might reach out to touch them because they look so soft. But they are hard stone, like the rest of the piece. Your eyes have been tricked by the skill of the sculptor.

There are more feathers on his cap: a soft hat with a folded brim. There is a small bird's wing on either side of that, too. They taper into gentle points above the young man's nose, if you look at him in profile. His jaw juts out almost as far as the turned-up brim. He is determined to carry out whatever task he has been given. His curls spring out from the back of the cap. You can imagine if he were to take it off, his hair would lie matted against his skull.

You can see dozens, hundreds more statues of young men and you will never see another one wearing a hat or shoes like this one. It is a plain traveller's cap, but the wings make it unique. The sandals would look more at home on the feet of a god, surely.

In his right hand, he carries a sword with a short curved blade. It is like a scythe. If you didn't know better, you'd think he was about to cut wheat. But – although only a small part of it is visible beneath his clenched hand – he is clearly holding a weapon by the hilt rather than an agricultural tool by the handle. The blade is curving away from him, as though he does not know from which way the attack will come.

This impression is further reinforced when you notice that he is looking behind him. How odd. Has he just heard a sound that has captured his attention? His sword hand is raised, but he is looking away from where he would strike, if he were to swing his arm. It seems a rather indiscriminate way to go about things. Perhaps he is consulting with another figure behind him, but we do not see her.

And nor, as I said, do we see him. Because this statue was never made so only the idea of it exists.

Part Five

Stone

Gorgoneion

How did they know so quickly that she had died? There must have been something in Sthenno's belief that they were one because the first thing I remember hearing was the beating of wings, and the first thing I remember feeling was the rush of air as Euryale landed outside the cave entrance, where their fire had been. It was immediately extinguished by her clawed feet: she wasn't looking at where she landed, and anyway, the heat was nothing to her. And then Sthenno, a moment behind her, another pair of feet standing on the sand.

Are you wondering why I was looking at their feet? I'm sure you've worked it out by now: I am the Gorgon head, the head of Medusa, born (or perhaps I should say created) in the moment she died. And I have a much lower opinion of mortal men than she did, for reasons which I would assume were obvious. In case it is in any way unclear, I am looking at their feet because I was determined not to look at their eyes. But I had to keep my eyes open, for the chance to lithify the one with the sword. I didn't yet know his name was Perseus. But I did know he deserved to die.

They could see nothing of him, of course. He wore the cap of Hades and he was invisible even to those beautiful bulging Gorgon eyes. I could see him, because that is the trick with things that belong to Hades: they have no secrets from one another. And now I was dead, I was a servant of Hades too, in a way. Not the way that would ever see me obey him, you understand. Just in terms of categories, to keep things simple for you. Medusa is dead, I am dead. But I'm still the best narrator for this part of the story, because I was there for all of it, and because I am not a lying deceitful hateful vicious murderer.

It's important to keep these things clear. If you're wondering how come I am able to see and hear and tell you what happened after Medusa died, the answer is simple. I was a Gorgon, a child of Phorcys and Ceto. We cannot speak of Ceto yet, so let us focus on my father for now. I was, I am the daughter of a sea god, and even though I was fated to die, I was hardly an ordinary mortal, was I? I had wings, for a start. Do you have wings? No, I didn't think so. Here's something else I have: the ability to retain my memories, my faculties, even after death. I really wasn't like other girls.

All this is a long way of telling you that I could see Perseus, no matter how much he believed that Hades kept him invisible. And I wanted to stare unblinking into his vacuous eyes and turn him to cold, pale stone. Are you feeling scared yet, of the monstrous head with no heart? Perhaps you should. Because what have I to lose, at this point?

Two things: my sisters.

Are they still my sisters, now I am just a head?

Euryale has found my decapitated body and her mouth is open in a silent scream. Not my body any more, her body. On the sand, resting on her hands. The legs are folded beneath her. I could still be asleep if it weren't for the thick black blood that flows from her neck.

Perseus is terrified when he catches sight of them both. I don't know which gods prepared him for his violation but they have not warned him of the size of Gorgons, or the strength, the speed. He is shaking as he stands there, terrified to move in case they hear him. He wants to run but he doesn't dare.

And then Euryale finds her voice. She will never lose it again. She opens her wondrous mouth wide and she howls. Perseus almost drops me where he stands. He had not thought he would be in danger after he had killed me, he had focused all his energy on getting to the Gorgon cave and killing a snake-haired monster with a death-bringing gaze. It hadn't occurred to him that escaping might be harder than arriving.

A fat drop of blood falls from my neck – and I mean my neck, not Medusa's – onto the sand beneath me. Sthenno's sharp eyes see something fall, but a snake wriggles across the sand and she believes that is the movement she noticed. Perseus feels the next drop land on his foot and I hear him retch beside me. He is pathetic. Suddenly, he seems to remember that someone had prepared him for this moment and he reaches round and opens a gold bag that he's carrying on his shoulders. He puts me inside it and everything goes dark.

I can still hear, though, so don't think this is an end to my part of the story: it isn't. And I have been waiting a long time to have my say so I'm not giving it up now. The bag is a thick and heavy blackness so I open my eyes wide to see and the material still moves around me, so I haven't turned it to stone. This is another thing I've learned, then: objects are safe from me. It's only the living that need fear me. Perhaps you think I should have known that already, but remember Medusa had spent almost all her time with her eyes bound or inside a cave. The cave is made of stone already, obviously. So this is when I found out.

Perseus is numb with fear as he stands unseen before Euryale. I can hear her mighty jaws working as she bellows her rage and grief. Medusa would have comforted her, but now she cannot and nor can I. I wonder if he feels any remorse at all as he hears my sister crying no, no, no, no, no.

Of course he doesn't. He saw Medusa as a monster and he sees Sthenno and Euryale as the same. If he had the power to kill them too, he would. All he hears is danger from this creature that wishes him harm. He doesn't hear sorrow or loss. He claims to care about family (it will be later that I discover this) and I wonder how his mother would feel if she saw his decapitated body lying on the sand before her, where moments earlier she had left him asleep.

Just to be clear, even that act of imagination makes me more human than him.

*

I can feel her, even though I can't see her or hear her. Athene, I mean. I know she's nearby somewhere. Don't ask how I know: how do you think I know? If someone had ripped out every hair in your head and replaced it with living snakes, do you think you might be alert to their presence in future? Just maybe? I can sense her and the oddest thing is, I'm not surprised or even especially angry. This goddess – to whom I have done nothing and who has gone out of her way to torture me and conspire in my murder – is right here and all I can think is: of course she is. Why stop now?

And the next thing I think is: who else is helping you to destroy me? Because the cap belongs to Hades, that I knew straightaway. Death knows death when she sees it. And Athene is standing by, encouraging him. The bag I'm now inside, this is a divine object for sure, but someone else has lent it to Perseus unless we're all imagining that Athene has a helmet, a spear, a shield, a breastplate, and a backpack. Which we aren't – or I'm not. So he's also been given this by a god. What else? The sword, of course. Well, I just listed Athene's weaponry collection, and I didn't mention a sword. And such a nasty sword, too, with its cruel curving blade. Designed to embrace the neck of the sleeping woman he decided to kill. I don't know who it belongs to and I'm not sure I want to. I'd like to know why they wanted me dead, of course.

I can feel his body shaking as he hoicks the bag back onto his shoulder. Euryale still issues her mighty cry; no wonder he's afraid. He stands stupefied at the noise and it's clear he has no plan for what to do now. And then I hear her, hear the voice of the goddess who assists him, and she tells him to run. I think, interesting. She must want him dead, because there is no chance that he could outrun either of Medusa's sisters and certainly not both of them.

But, of course, I haven't seen the sandals he's wearing

and I won't until later, so I don't know that he has the assistance of yet another god in his quest to murder me and escape unpunished. The sandals belong to Hermes, I'll recognize them when I see them. Ornate twisting leather, with a neat pair of wings on either side of the ankle. So when Athene tells him to run and this jolts him from his horrified trance, he has another advantage. He tenses his shoulders and begins sprinting towards where the sun will rise. I conclude this from the way my head bangs against his ribs as he moves. The snakes cushion it, of course, so it doesn't hurt. And anyway, it wouldn't hurt because I have already been severed from my own body so what difference will the bruising make now? Gods, I despise him.

Euryale sees not the man, not Perseus. But she sees the indentations in the sand as he runs across it. And although she has no idea how he is there and also not there, she knows that the man who killed her sister is running across the shore right in front of her and she lets out a curdling roar and suddenly I hear the beating of wings and I feel the night displaced as Euryale rises into the air and flies straight at Perseus. Even through this golden prison I can feel the movement and I hear a strangled scream from the murderer as he pumps his legs, trying to speed up. He twists his back and I wonder if he is about to jettison the weight of me, but he is just looking to see how close she is behind him, and he would have been better off not knowing, because she is gaining on him as fast as thunder, faster. And I know Euryale will not miss her prey, not now, not ever. She could catch a bird in the air in full flight, Medusa saw her do it more than once.

And I feel a surge of something – not joy, because I can't

feel that, not vengeance because I haven't reached there yet – but I want her to snap her jaws around his pathetic trunk and break him into two halves. I want her to catch the bag as his unfeeling hands drop it and I want her to hold it, to hold me as he expires before her and she drags her clawed feet across his twitching body. I want her to carry me back to Medusa, back to Sthenno, back to the cave. I want to be buried where I fell. No, where I was cut down. I want to stay with her, I don't want to be carried away by my killer in the darkness, I want it all to be over.

But what I want has no effect on what happens. Athene intervenes of course. Perseus is suddenly shoved to one side: he has climbed the rocks by our, their patch of the coast. Or rather, the sandals climbed the rocks. Perseus is panting from the exertion or more probably from fear. Nothing I have subsequently observed about Perseus has changed my original opinion of him: he is spineless. Euryale can no longer see his footsteps in the sand, she has simply followed the only line of ascent he could have taken. And Athene – who must have been watching this whole time – pushes him hard and he stumbles and loses his footing and crashes down onto his knees and I am gratified to hear a muffled cry of pain and I hope it hurts. Although realistically, it is unlikely to hurt as much as having your neck severed.

Euryale flies over us, I feel her quickening wings – she is so close I believe I could reach out and touch her but I can't, of course. And then she is gone, and I will never see my sister again, or hear her, or be held by her. Sthenno is still on the sand, I think, because I hear her keening cry and I know that she is holding my broken body and cradling it in her arms. I wish I could comfort her.

Athene directs Perseus to follow her and he gets back on his feet, complaining about his injuries and the way she pushed him, and I hear the anger in her voice when she responds, though he seems not to notice. He continues to speed away from the Gorgon home: I hear the sea but it is far below me. He twists his other arm through the straps of the bag, so I am tightly held, like a precious object.

Which, it will soon be revealed, I am.

Reed

One thing people rarely know about Athene is that she invented the flute. It isn't the most important thing about her, as far as most people are concerned. Mortals pray to her for wisdom, for advice, for her help in their battles. When they want music they turn elsewhere: to the Muses, to Apollo. Her interests are well-documented, and she has rarely shown any passion for song. But on one occasion she heard a noise so remarkable that she longed to be able to emulate it so she could hear it again.

The flute, then, was inspired by the Gorgons. Specifically, it was inspired by the sound Euryale made when they found the body of Medusa. Piercing, atonal, bellicose. Athene had never heard anything like it. How could she make such a sound on a battlefield? She experimented for days. But even with all her divine power, and all her cleverness, she couldn't come close.

She sat, disconsolate, by a quiet riverbed, not very far from her beloved Athens. She considered going back to the Gorgon cove and asking the sisters to teach her how they roared. She could sense there was something about this plan that was flawed, although she couldn't quite place the weak spot.

Her frustration was mounting – if she hadn't helped Perseus kill the Gorgon, she would never have known what she was missing, and if she had let the Gorgon kill him, she might have had more time to study her battle cry – but she did not know what else she could do. And then she felt the gentle Zephyr breeze gathering strength. It whipped through the reeds beside her and the quiet riverbed was transformed into a wild cacophony.

Athene looked around her in astonishment as she realized here – all around her – was something that could help her achieve her desire. She took a sharp little knife and hacked at the plants, cutting a large hollow reed that she hoped would create the noise she wanted. She bored small holes into the stem so she could adjust the note with her fingers. (Later flutes would be decorated with burned rope held against the body of the reed, but this was the very first and it was quite plain.)

When she blew into the top of it, the reed made exactly the penetrating scream she demanded. Musicians – satyrs, in the first instance – would come along later and bend the instrument to their talent, creating the far sweeter sound we associate with the flute today. But Athene was no musician, and nor was she looking to play a tune. The first flute therefore sounded exactly like what it was.

The desperate cry of a reed that has been severed from its root.

Gorgoneion

He escaped, of course. With the aid of all his gods, Perseus escaped. And, though no one ever thinks of things this way, so did I. I left behind the mortal body that had made me weak and vulnerable and I escaped into what, exactly? A new life? Please, this isn't life. It's death. You can't have forgotten how Medusa was sliced in two by this man, this hero. Now she is dead and mourned and loved by her sisters and I am, well, I am this: the stolen head. The hidden trophy.

The snakes are wrapped tightly around me: they protect me still. But we are all hidden in this golden kibisis, carried by Perseus to keep him from danger. He complains all the time, about how much the bag weighs. There isn't even anyone else here to listen to him. He just moans into the breezes about how heavy and awkward it is. What I would like to say to him is that if it is so inconvenient carrying someone's head around in a bag, perhaps you should think about that before you decapitate them. So I do say it. He doesn't respond and I assume he hasn't heard. Perhaps the gold muffles sound or perhaps he can't hear any more after

Euryale shouted in his pathetic mortal ears. But he stops complaining, so perhaps he heard me after all.

He is walking from wherever Athene abandoned him and he probably wants to complain about that too, but he is still wearing the sandals of Hermes so these steps must take no effort at all. He wants to return to somewhere, because he keeps muttering about getting back to Seriphos before it's too late. I don't know where or what this place is, so I ask, and again he doesn't reply. But now he is worrying about finding a boat, so it is across the sea. An island? A port? I wish I knew.

No, that isn't true, is it? That's a last little trace of Medusa, who really did care about what mortals wanted and where they might want to go. Me? I don't care if Perseus lives or dies, let alone where he's trying to get to. What difference would it make? If he opened the bag now, and I turned him to stone, what would happen to me? I'd stay here in exactly the same condition. If I don't turn him to stone and he reaches his destination, it's the same, isn't it? I am still the Gorgoneion, Medusa is still dead.

So I have only a slight interest when he sees a shepherd and shouts at the man to please tell him where he now finds himself. The shepherd explains that he has reached the kingdom of Atlas, where the land bridges the sky. Perseus asks if he may have shelter with the shepherd, but the man refuses him. There is a nervousness in his voice and I believe it is caused by me. The shepherd has not seen me, of course, but he can tell there is something dangerous in front of him. He has honed his instincts, perhaps, protecting his sheep from unseen predators.

I hear the sheep bleating as Perseus walks into their

midst. They remind me of Euryale's flock. He asks the man again for a bed and food and the shepherd replies that he is in the service of the king, so strangers must petition him if they need shelter. Perseus asks which way he should go to speak to this king and the shepherd tells him the way. The directions are complex and involve many landmarks. I can feel Perseus growing irritated by the details the man is giving him, and I am just wondering why he asks for help when he is so ungrateful about receiving it when he shrugs his shoulder so the strap of the bag slips down and he reaches inside. I see his fingers grasping at my snakes and I know what he is about to do and I think he is being extraordinarily petty.

He lifts me out into the open air and I blink once, twice at the sudden brightness of the sun which I have missed more than I can describe. When did my eyes last look into the light? I have no way to measure time any more, and nor did Medusa once she was cursed. I feel warm and alive, though I know I am neither. I see everything at once: the vast sky, the rock-strewn ground, the fluttering trees. I feel the warmth of the sun and the cooling breezes and the fingers of Perseus gripping my snakes and brandishing me like a torch.

I see the shepherd man.

He sees me too. For just a moment our gazes meet, and his face forms a silent mask of fear and then he is stone, frozen at the point in time when he encountered Perseus. I hear him – Perseus, now a double-murderer – gasp as he sees how swift and lethal I am. He stuffs me back into his kibisis and I feel a huge surge of energy. The shepherd is dead, all thanks to my power. How can I not revel in this strength now I have it?

Perhaps you are wondering what the shepherd did to deserve such an abrupt end? What do any of us do? What did I do? He was in the wrong place and met with the wrong man. Could I have averted my gaze? you're thinking. Could I? Yes, probably I could. But obviously I didn't. But couldn't I have saved him from Perseus and his nasty little temper?

I don't feel like saving mortals any more. I don't feel like saving anyone any more. I feel like opening my eyes and taking in everything I can see whenever I get the chance. I feel like using the power the goddess gave me. I feel like spreading fear wherever I go, wherever Perseus goes. I feel like becoming the monster he made. I feel like that.

*

Perseus is terrified of me. I can tell by the way he holds the bag now, much more careful. I'm sure he didn't doubt whatever Athene had told him about my power but who believes what he has not seen? Even I didn't know how fast it would be, how entire. I had glanced at a bird, a scorpion, and made them stone. But a man? It was dizzying how quick it was to petrify him. And in that moment between his death and my return to darkness, I saw his face held in the expression he wore when he caught sight of me. It thrills me now, thinking of the way the energy fizzed between us, tiny motes in the air that somehow travelled from my eyes to his and took his life.

If you were waiting for me to feel guilt, you will be waiting a long time.

And now, Perseus has followed the shepherd's directions,

though he gets lost and has to retrace his steps many times. I wonder if this will be a lesson for him: to be careful who he kills, because he may need their assistance later. He doesn't strike me as the kind of young man who learns lessons, however. And even from inside the bag I can feel the air grow cooler as the sun drops. Perseus eventually accepts that he must spend another night under the open sky. He puts the kibisis down so carefully that I almost laugh. Perhaps I do laugh, in fact. We have yet to ascertain whether Perseus ignores the sounds I make or whether he cannot hear them when the bag is closed. But he has decided he doesn't want to antagonize me. Or perhaps he has decided my value to him is so great that he must take care not to damage me. I wonder if the irony is lost on him. I imagine so.

*

The next morning, he is full of hope that the king will receive a wandering hero with every kind of celebration. And perhaps he would have done, had Atlas not been a fearful and suspicious king. But he is and he always has been.

Atlas owns many beautiful things in his expansive kingdom. He cherishes each of them, from his lovely flocks to his wonderful orchards. He probably even cherished the shepherd, but he doesn't yet know the man is dead. He especially loves a grove of trees that produce the most remarkable fruit, golden apples.

Atlas considers these apples to be the most perfect food imaginable. He can eat whatever he chooses whenever he likes (he is the king, after all), but it is always the apples he waits for each summer, like a child. He employs men to

305

watch the trees and nurture them all year round. If the weather threatens to disrupt them, he makes offerings to Aeolus, lord of the winds, to send the offending cold spell elsewhere. As the summer days lengthen, he goes to visit his trees first thing each morning to examine their burgeoning fruit.

Atlas has never feared invaders would steal his crops or damage his trees. He lives without aggression from neighbouring tribes for one reason: he is a Titan, one of the old gods from before the Olympians, before Zeus. What mortal would be so foolish as to pick a fight with a god? Well, I'm sure you have already guessed the answer.

When Perseus arrives at the enormous dwelling, he is bad-tempered from the night he spent sleeping under a tree. He still doesn't blame himself for killing the man who could have guided him here more quickly. He is briefly chastened – I feel the hesitation in his step – by the size and grandeur of the palace he now sees. But he raises his chin and tries to convey his heroic stature that way. I am mocking him from inside the kibisis, of course. He continues to be unaware. A steward is standing by the gates and Perseus asks if he may meet the king and discuss matters advantageous to both. A child could see through this ruse, and the steward is not a child. He explains that the king is occupied elsewhere and will return at an unspecified time. Perseus, aware he is being dismissed, tries another tack. Tell him it is the son of Zeus who asks, he says. And at this, the steward disappears: I hear him scurrying away down a long corridor, his footsteps echoing.

As he listens to the man retreat into the deeper recesses of the palace, Perseus assumes he has done something right. He has impressed a stranger with his heroic connection and he has asked for shelter as a hero might, by offering something in return. He has not yet worked out what it is he could offer that Atlas might find advantageous, but it doesn't matter because there is something else (one of many things, as I'm sure you have noticed) that Perseus doesn't know.

Atlas did not always live here in this wide-reaching kingdom. Once he travelled across Greece with his Titan siblings. He retreated here after the arrival of the Olympians, once Zeus had waged war on the Titans and gained power for himself.

Atlas was not an ambitious god so he was only too happy to withdraw to his palace and his flocks and, above all, to his orchard. But he did retain one connection with his old life, which was a fondness for the goddess Themis, who was highly gifted in the arts of prophecy. Themis had once told Atlas that he would one day lose the gleaming fruit of his tree to a son of Zeus. Atlas had remembered this ever since. At first, because he assumed its meaning was metaphorical and he would have a son who would die at the hands of a demi-god. Latterly, he had come to realize the prophecy was literal and his beloved trees were at risk.

So the one thing he has told every servant, every subject he has is that they must beware the son of Zeus and bring any news of such a creature to him. The shepherd, had he lived to discover his murderer's identity, would have run across the land in the darkest hours of the night to tell Atlas that the man whose coming they all feared had finally arrived. And now the steward is doing the same thing: better late than never, he thinks, as he rushes through the colonnades.

And when Atlas hears that the son of Zeus is right outside his gates, demanding an audience and pretending he has something to offer in exchange, he is horrified. Does he dare kill the child of his ancient enemy, one who exceeds him in power in every way? But if he does not, will the man steal the apples, the golden apples that Atlas so cherishes and loves? He paces up and down as the steward watches anxiously. What should he do? How can he preserve his beloved trees?

Atlas spends a great deal of time thinking; Perseus has almost given up on any hope of food or shelter. He has refilled his water bottle three times and he now sits in the shade, leaning up against one of the palace walls, with me beside him. Eventually, Atlas sends his men to guard the orchard, assuming that this is where Perseus will choose to attack. Perseus – of course – has no idea the orchard exists, and if he did he would be unlikely to visit it. He has no interest in the natural world that I have noticed: he seems unmoved by birdsong, he doesn't slow his pace when faced with a beautiful vista. He is keen to complain about his aching feet and shoulders, his hunger and his thirst. But when all these wants are satisfied, there is no corresponding enthusiasm for any of the sights and sounds he has witnessed since he created me.

So, perhaps you are wondering if Themis had made a mistake when she told Atlas of the prophecy? Or was she making mischief, as gods sometimes like to? Of course not: Themis is never wrong and less likely to make trouble than most. She told the truth, but Atlas was too early in his suspicions: it would be another son of Zeus who stole the apples from Atlas's orchard and that day is far in the future.

Eventually, Atlas rises from his throne and strides along

the colonnades of his palace. His brow is creased, and he pauses. Should he visit his orchard and see his protected trees one more time? He shrugs off the thought, embarrassed that he has even considered losing a fight to some puny demi-god. I hear him coming long before Perseus does. He does not feel the shaking of the earth as the Titan advances upon him, he notices very little. But when the steward comes pelting through the gate ahead of his king, even Perseus realizes something is happening.

'All this fuss?' he asks the panting steward. 'Your king is not very welcoming to strangers.'

The steward doesn't have breath enough to respond, but it doesn't matter because Atlas has appeared behind him.

Perseus takes an unwitting step back. The Titan king towers over his unwanted visitor.

'What do you want?' asks Atlas.

'Shelter, food,' says Perseus. These are reasonable and humble requests and yet something about the way he says the words would make anyone want to shove him into a river.

Atlas shares my view, it seems, because he sighs loudly and does not reply. Perseus has grown so impatient waiting that he is whinier than usual. 'I am a son of Zeus,' he says.

'And what makes you think I owe anything to a son of Zeus?' replies the Titan. 'Even if you are who you say you are.'

'You fail to respect the king of the gods?' asks Perseus. His voice is high-pitched, querulous.

'I have to respect the king of the gods,' Atlas says. 'But I don't have to respect a man who claims to be his bastard son.'

'I have slain a mighty Gorgon,' says Perseus. 'And what

about your obligations? You should offer a traveller food and a place to rest, whether you respect them or not.'

Atlas snorts his contempt. 'What obligations? I don't owe you anything. You appear at my gates with no warning. Why should I play host to you when I know why you've come here? I know what you're planning and I won't allow it.'

'I'm not planning anything!' Perseus is incapable of planning anything, so it's no wonder he sounds so aggrieved. 'I have come from attacking the Gorgons in their lair. I will return to Seriphos as soon as I can. I need shelter before I continue on my way. Who are you to refuse me?'

'I am the king of everything you can see and a thousand times a thousand more that you cannot,' bellows Atlas. 'I do not answer to you or to anyone. You are a thief and you're not welcome in my palace. Now leave before I kill you.'

Perseus is already reaching into the kibisis. He grabs at my head and I feel his fingers groping blindly to feel my nose or mouth so he doesn't accidentally cover my eyes.

'We could have been guest-friends,' he says. 'But you refused. So let me give you the gift you deserve.'

He draws me out of the bag and holds me up to face the Titan. His own eyes are closed in fear and horror.

Even I am surprised by what happens next. Because Titans are not mortal creatures, so they do not turn to stone the way the birds and the scorpion did, the way the shepherd did. As I stare at Atlas, I don't know what to expect. I feared for my sisters' lives when I had sisters, even though they were immortal. But I don't fear for Atlas: he seems like a petty king and why should he have life when I have death? So I open my eyes wide and meet his gaze.

His expression is quite different from the shepherd's: he

has seen worse than a Gorgon head in his long life, I suppose. His steward is the first to change, and he is stone before I have even noticed him. But Atlas does something else. There is a deafening crash, like a great rock fall. Atlas raises his arm to knock Perseus to the ground or perhaps he hopes to grab me from his opponent's outstretched hand. But Atlas cannot move his feet, he is pinned to the spot. And then there is another smash of rock against rock and he is turning to stone from the feet upwards. But as he lithifies, he grows. The Titan king is now a huge mountain: his limbs becoming shelves of rock, his hair sprouting into vast pine trees. He is immense; his head is lost in the clouds that surround the newly formed peak. We stand halfway up a mountain the gods must have decided to create. Because surely I cannot have so much power on my own?

Perseus is astonished by what Atlas has become. He has no regrets that I can sense: he returns me to the kibisis and congratulates himself on the effective way he has bested another enemy. I am almost dazed by the enormity of what I have just created. The heavens themselves now rest on Atlas's shoulders: the world has changed because of me. I wonder if Perseus feels anything for the men and women who lived and worked in Atlas's palace, and who are now surely all dead. But I don't wonder for very long, because I know Perseus cares for no one but himself, and his precious mother.

*

The apple orchard survived, incidentally. It continued to grow on the lower reaches of the Atlas mountains and this brought the Titan some pleasure every day. He nurtured a dragon to protect the trees because all his men were dead. But then another son of Zeus came along and purloined the beloved apples, just as Themis had predicted, and Atlas lost his last remaining delight. So all that was left to him was to hold up the weight of the sky.

Andromeda

The princess of Ethiopia was beginning to think that her mother had offended Helios, rather than Poseidon. She drooped as she stood with her arms wide, squinting into the glare. She tried to straighten her back as the pull on her bound wrists was making the ropes bite. But the heat emanating from the red boulder behind her was almost as intense as the dazzling rays hitting her from above. Her lips were cracking and she felt as though every part of her exposed skin was ablaze. She looked from left to right, hoping someone might bring her water or shade or something to ease her discomfort. But the priests had ordered everyone to stay back.

Andromeda knew the gracious thing to do was to be silent. She knew it would make things less agonizing for her parents if someone could tell them that their daughter had slid away into unconsciousness before her death. Or perhaps they were still there, watching from whatever distance the priests would allow. She could stay mute until her throat swelled and her voice was lost for good. Would that be the dignified thing to do? She felt it was. But that

313

was before she saw the dark shape rippling in the water beneath her feet.

At first she thought her eyes were tricking her because nothing that size could be so close to the land. It could not have swum this far from the old shoreline in so short a time. Sweat dripped into her eyes and the stinging left her blinded for a moment. She waited for her vision to clear and looked again at the water. How deep was it? she wondered. Had this been a valley until Poseidon's greed took it away? She had lost all sense of place because nothing looked familiar at all. Robbed of the landmarks she knew, she recognized nothing. So perhaps she was imagining things. But again she thought she saw a huge flickering mass and she stifled a scream.

She began praying to a god she hated.

Gorgoneion

Perseus has discovered that his sandals grant him the ability to travel across the sea as well as the land, so he is flying – as much as a human in winged shoes can – back towards Seriphos. One dead shepherd, one dead Titan, time to go home. He doesn't know the way, of course. He isn't sure where Seriphos is because he arrived there as a baby and he left there with the help of the gods. I asked from inside the kibisis if he even knows where he is now. He gave no answer so I concluded he does not.

He soars above the water complaining now that the shoes might help him fly but they don't choose a direction. I already despised him so nothing changes. He scours the skies and the seas one way, and then another. He also – I find out – doesn't know what he's looking for because he has never seen Seriphos from above. He claims to be in a great hurry to get back to his homeland and rescue his mother from an unwanted marital entanglement. But she could have married and had three children in the time he wanders fruitlessly.

He is covering an area I am convinced he's travelled before

when I hear a sound. I think it is the voice of a woman but I can't be sure at first because I only hear a few words and then it is silenced. Even Perseus seems to hear something. He pauses, turning slowly in the air. I hear it again, and this time the noise is louder. This time it is a scream.

Andromeda

Andromeda was not sure if it was her voice she could hear, or that of her mother. And then suddenly it was every voice, male and female, screaming as one. The monster rose from the deep. It was dark and glistening in the devastating light and everyone who saw it was afraid. This beast would surely not be satisfied with a single offering but would consume them all. The panic spread and Andromeda heard the priests trying to convince their reluctant worshippers that the monster was sent by Poseidon and demanded one life and one alone. But behind her she heard a stampede of un-believers. Were her parents still there? she wondered. Would they stay to watch her taken by the beast?

*

Uncertain in its new environment, the monster swam one way and then another, trying to identify its whereabouts. It raised its huge head briefly and was surprised by what it saw. It had never swum to this part of the sea before, but Poseidon had ordered it to come here and it had obeyed.

He had given further instructions but the creature was distracted and disoriented and could not remember exactly what the god had said. If it turned to its right it could swim back out to the ocean depths it recognized. But then, would it be disobeying the king of all the seas?

It raised its head again and saw an unexpected sight. A mortal woman, bound between a pair of tree stumps in front of a large boulder. The monster dropped back beneath the waves. Was this what Poseidon had meant when he described an offering? Was the mortal woman the prize for the lengthy journey the monster had made? It was a paltry reward. Was it an intended insult? Or had the mortals promised Poseidon a better offering and then reneged?

It circled the deeper water, considering.

*

Not every Ethiopian fled upon seeing the mighty beast. Many were determined to appease the gods after the devastating flood, but some felt nothing but defiance. Why should they see their princess eaten when they had already lost so much? It was humiliating. So when they saw the sunlight glittering off the muscular body, they picked up their spears, and moved to defend Andromeda.

Gorgoneion

I take in the whole scene so quickly; it feels like I see every part of it at once. But time is different for me than for you, so let me try to describe it in a way you can understand. Perseus has approached another shore, and I know this because I hear the water lapping against rocks, I hear the weeds moving. There is peace here, as there always is by the sea. Even for those who have come, as Medusa did, to hate it.

But I also sense something else: fear and readiness. It was a woman's voice I first heard but now it is many voices. Some are expressing fear, some are shouting threats. Some are praying. Others say nothing but I hear them just the same, the way they prepare themselves to act: leather on skin, wood on stone, metal on metal.

There is another sound, and it is one I recognize but do not know. It's impossible to explain this contradiction, so much so that I can hold onto it only for an instant and then it is gone. I feel something grab at me and I cannot place that either. Is it a memory or a thought, a connection or a burst of pain? Is it warm or cold? I cannot say. I'm not even sure it was there at all, because it disappears completely.

Then there is the familiar sensation of Perseus opening the kibisis and grabbing at my snakes. One of them bites him but it doesn't stop him from balling his fist around three of them and pulling me out of the bag. The glare is dizzying after the darkness and I blink twice. I am faced by a crowd of mortals but they are not looking up at Perseus, or at me. This is how so many of them are still alive. They are instead looking at the water beneath me. It is a large crowd spread across a wide area: men armed with spears, women holding rocks that they are ready to throw. Two of the mortals are dressed in great finery. At first I mistake them for the leaders of these people, but then I see their headdresses and I realize they are priests. I cannot identify a king or queen; perhaps they are absent.

Perseus is to the side of the shore. Beneath him, in front of the rest of her people is, what? A queen? A sacrifice? She is wearing a diadem, a bracelet: both are gold. But she is tied in front of a large rock and she is screaming. Luckily she is not looking to her right so she doesn't see me. Then Perseus whirls in the air and now we are facing what the sacrificial offering is facing. Which is a calm sea, marred by only a few ripples.

And yet something must have made her scream. The mortals behind her are now advancing towards the water. There is the sound of men arguing and pleading. It is the priests, I think, trying to persuade their people not to attack. The water is stirred and something appears on its surface. If it was much smaller, it could be a dolphin. It is a quick dark body glistening in the light. An eel? But it is vast, whatever it is. A second creature appears far across the bay: there are no fins or gills, just a dark tentacle unfurling. And then a third, a fourth, a fifth: this is a huge shoal of fish or dolphins. There is a sudden plunging sound, as these giant fish all descend at once and another rises in their midst.

And then I understand why she screams. Because it is not a shoal of creatures, it is one immense creature. I have never seen anything like it and nor has Perseus because he gasps. Obviously, he is scared of everything so this isn't a reliable indicator. But if I took breaths, I would gasp too.

Men will tell you that Gorgons are monsters, but men are fools. They cannot comprehend any beauty beyond what they can see. And what they see is a tiny part of what there is. So for Perseus the only difference between this great creature and Medusa and her sisters is one of scale. They terrified him because of their claws and teeth and wings, I terrify him with my gaze. The beast in the water terrifies him because of its size and its mighty jaws. But he has me to fight the creature so why is he still afraid? Because he is a coward, and even when he fights with the assistance of the gods, he never stops fearing for his life.

So why has he decided to come here and defend the woman who is tied between those tree stumps? There are several reasons I could give you, and each of them is part of the truth.

*

He did not know what he was getting himself into when he flew here. He heard a woman screaming and imagined himself a hero and then he arrived and saw a creature that

321

terrorized all who laid eyes on it (all but one) and it was too late then to just flap his shoes and fly away. So now he is stuck with trying to attempt an audacious rescue.

He was frustrated by his many failures so far, and by his inability to complete his quest.

He is testing his father's love for him, by fighting a creature that can obliterate him with a single bite.

He is getting a taste for adventure, rather late in the day. He is heavily armed and favoured by the gods and he wants to take advantage of this.

He has already destroyed a Titan and left a great stone monument to its destruction. What else could he achieve?

He sees a woman in danger and he tries to save her.

He is malevolent and he wants to kill.

*

The people armed with spears and arrows are letting them fly at the monster they fear as it towers above their sacrifice. Mortals are perplexing: why did they tie her up if they didn't want her to be eaten? The creature shows no sign of feeling the few arrows that hit their mark. It shrugs them off. Spears hit the side of a huge tentacle, but they too bounce, useless, into the water. The beast drops back beneath the surface and the men pick up their second spears, nock more arrows. They jeer, thinking they have scared it away. Perhaps Perseus is not unusually stupid, by mortal standards.

The water churns and the creature rises up and drops immediately back. The resulting wave rushes inland and knocks its assailants off their feet. When the water retreats, their weapons are drawn back into the sea. The men are left lying on wet sand, little knowing that the beast has chosen not to create a larger wave and take them too. The girl bound in front of the rock is drenched: her tunic is ragged, her crown askew. She screams again, as the water begins to surge.

Perseus has no spear or bow and his curved sword is no good to him here unless he flies much closer, which he is unwilling to do. He manoeuvres himself to a place next to the rock and slightly behind it. He drops to just above the height of the water, and raises his hand. The hand that holds me.

I look out over the ocean, the expanse sparkling before me, and I feel no fear, not of Poseidon, or Athene or the creature. And then it rises again, dark limbs everywhere. I look to the centre, because that must be its head, but it is hard to tell as each part of it looks like the rest: a rippling mass of muscle. The light falling on it is so bright it is dazzling and I cannot tell if I am looking into its eyes or not.

But I am. Its gaze has met mine and it is frozen into stillness. I wonder, how will this one die? Will it turn into a statue like the birds and the shepherd? Or a mountain like the Titan? Will it be left here for ever, a tribute to my great power? Or will it be remembered as a marker of Perseus's power? Will it sink beneath the waves? I don't want Perseus to be remembered at all, but it is too late now because the creature is petrifying limb by limb, from the tip of each tentacle towards the core. Its glittering black flesh becomes dull grey stone and I know I have saved the life of the sacrifice even if Perseus claims the credit. The creature writhes as its extremities go numb and I see that the weight of each limb is dragging it beneath the waves. It has only moments left before it is solid rock.

And suddenly I see its eyes. And I recognize them.

Andromeda

The princess stood with her mouth agape. All thoughts of the discomfort of her tied wrists were gone. The salt water that had washed over her moments earlier had left her eyes stinging, but she didn't think about that either. The proximity of death had pushed everything else from her mind, and then suddenly she was saved by a stranger. Or by whatever the stranger was holding. She looked at his back and tried to blink away the water that obscured her vision. But nothing changed what she thought she had seen: a flying man holding a handful of snakes which had apparently turned the monster to stone.

As her eyes focused, she still saw a man seeming to hover over the sea, as he pushed his snakes back into a golden bag slung over one shoulder. The monster was slipping beneath the surface and, now that the danger was past, the man turned back towards her. He was, she saw, very young. As young as her. Half the age of Phineus. His hair was a damp black mess, but she suspected he had curls. His short tunic revealed muscular arms and legs, in every way unlike those of her uncle. And he had rescued her from certain death.

He flew to her and untied her hands. Even if she had had the strength to stand, she would have fallen into his arms. Exhaustion, gratitude, and the absolute need to convey that she was no longer promised to a much older man: all these contributed to her collapse.

'Thank you, sir,' she said. And he smiled.

'How did you end up in this position?' he asked. She liked his dark, darting eyes and the way he seemed to have no other interest but her. He didn't even know she was a princess. He had not even seen her mother.

'The priests made me sacrifice,' she said. His brow creased. 'I mean, they made me into their sacrifice,' she clarified. 'They didn't ask me to make a sacrifice and everything went wrong.'

He nodded. She assumed he was befuddled by her beauty, but she wasn't sure until he reached up and straightened her diadem.

'I am Andromeda,' she said.

'I'm Perseus,' he replied. 'Who is your father?'

'Cepheus, king of the Ethiopians,' she said.

'I see.' He brightened. 'I will kill these priests for you, and then perhaps you would introduce me to your parents?'

Andromeda thought about saying that killing the priests was unnecessary, and that she would rather he met her parents straightaway. But on brief reflection she realized she did want the two priests to die, so she nodded in happy agreement. Perseus helped her to a smaller rock so she could sit and recover. He liked the way she accepted everything he said. Finally someone took him seriously. The first time since he had left his mother. And all he had had to do was save her from certain death. Killing two more men would not be hard, he thought. It was perhaps rather crowded here to use the head, but he had his harpē, and that would be enough. They could hardly outrun him when he was wearing the winged sandals.

'Wait here,' he said. 'I'll return shortly.'

Andromeda watched his tunic fluttering as he stepped away from her. She half wanted to disregard him and see the priests meet their premature end. But she didn't want Perseus to think she would be the kind of wife who ignores her husband. It would be better, wouldn't it, if he thought she was the kind of woman who needed rescuing, and to be kept away from killing? Perhaps it would even be better to be that woman, rather than merely to be thought so. Her mother had taken an influential role alongside Cepheus, and look where that had got everyone: half the kingdom lost and Andromeda almost dead. Andromeda must be more careful than that. And anyway, she didn't want to scare the boy.

Panopeia

Now the place where Ethiopia meets Oceanus has changed. The furthest sea reaches further than it once did. But still, Perseus has found his way here. Andromeda is saved, which will not please the raging Nereids, not one bit. They finally persuade Poseidon to act as they demand, and their sacrifice is stolen at the last moment. So what happens now?

The Nereids might ask for another sacrifice, but Poseidon will not heed them a second time. He has his larger sea, which is all he wanted. Even the angriest Nereids – though they may not like it – will have to accept that their chance for retribution is gone, because it is the son of Zeus himself who has taken their prize away. They will not set themselves against the king of the gods and nor will Poseidon, on their behalf. Their grudge may be unsatisfied, but it is over nonetheless.

And what of the sea itself, which has lost one of its mighty guardians? Monster to Perseus, but goddess to us. How do we grieve her, now she is stone beneath the waves? Will no one seek justice for her? Has Phorcys just let his wife die with no retribution?

But who could he make pay? He cannot hope to outwit Zeus, who will surely protect his son no matter what.

He could take his grievance to Poseidon, of course. But it is Poseidon who sent Ceto here in the first place. If Poseidon had not ordered her to the shallows to feast on the Ethiopian princess, Ceto would have been hidden as always in the furthest recesses of the sea. Phorcys might not even know why the sea lord chose Ceto, over all the other creatures, for this task.

I know why, of course. And perhaps you do. Poseidon hurt the Gorgons the first time when he decided to rape Medusa. And perhaps if they had accepted the injury and pretended it was trivial, the matter would have ended there (perhaps not: Athene's anger was already roused). But they fought back. Euryale took his sea and forced it away from her shore. And of course, Poseidon did not consider this fair punishment for what he had done to Medusa. He saw it as an unprovoked insult.

And so he wanted revenge on the Gorgons for their refusal to respect him and to live in fear. But he could hardly rape Medusa again, could he? She was hidden in a cave and he was sulking in the depths of his diminished waves. Instead, he came up with this plan, which was so clever I doubt he can have thought of it unaided.

He sent Ceto precisely because he knew the son of Zeus was nearby, flitting about on his convoluted journey home.

He knew Perseus possessed the head of Medusa, everyone knows that is all that is left of her. We watched her sisters mourn her, lay out her body, weep for her. We saw them fold her wings around her, and build her pyre. We grieved for them as they burned her rather than return her to the ocean. The water would not touch her again, they swore. And they kept their word: Euryale flew days inland to bury her ashes as far from Poseidon's realm as she could. We listened as she told Sthenno of the trees growing in the oasis she had chosen.

Poseidon saw this as a further insult, naturally. And then the perfect solution presented itself. He would punish the remaining Gorgons by ordering Ceto, their own mother, to ravage the Ethiopian coast and consume their hapless princess. Did he guess that Perseus would be unable to resist a woman in crisis? He is his father's son, after all.

Whatever the outcome, it was pleasing to Poseidon. Ceto might kill Perseus and destroy the head of Medusa, taking her back to the water after all. Zeus might lose his son, but that was too bad. Poseidon had let him live once before, when he was a baby, placed in that box and put out to sea with his mother. If he died trying to rescue Andromeda, well, Poseidon was merely settling an old debt. Zeus wouldn't thank him, but Hades would be grateful, and they are all brothers alike.

The second possibility was that Ceto would be killed by Perseus using Medusa's head. What better way for a malevolent god to take his revenge on the two surviving Gorgons? Their mother is dead; his hands are clean. It wasn't him: it was Zeus, or the son of Zeus, anyway. Poseidon has lost one of the oldest goddesses of the ocean, it's true. But he has more goddesses and Nereids than he is comfortable with so he can easily afford to lose one.

I see everything but I don't know everything.

I don't know if Ceto knew it was the head of her own

cursed child – unrecognisable to most, but surely not to her – that Perseus used to kill her.

Did she look into her eyes deliberately? Because she could not harm the last remaining piece of her daughter's body?

The sea gods keep their secrets deep; they always have.

Gorgoneion

No.

It cannot be true.

But it is true. I lost her in the very moment I found her. No, not lost. Lost would be the word to use if someone else had killed her. So the Gorgons lost Medusa, lost their beloved, when Perseus took her life and her head.

But I did not lose my mother: I killed her.

Oh, Perseus killed her, that's what people will say, isn't it? That's what he will say, murderous little thug, desperate to impress everyone with his courage and his strength. One man standing alone against a giant sea monster. He would have been dead as soon as she saw him if I hadn't been there.

He thinks anyone who is not like him is a monster: have you noticed? And any monster needs killing. I wonder if he told himself the priests were monsters too. They were far more monstrous than Ceto, as I see it. But they're all dead, just the same.

How long did I look at her before I realized she was my mother?

How long did she look at me? No time at all. A heartbeat, if either of us had a heart left to beat.

There is one question that devours me still.

Why didn't I close my eyes?

Andromeda

The princess walked along the corridor towards the large hall of her father's palace. The salt marks had been washed from the walls, and the tapestries and couches had all been taken outside to dry. If there was a faint aroma of damp, that was all there was. She hurried to her parents, hoping that Perseus was being well looked after in his rooms. Would he be impressed by her family and her home? He must be, of course.

She found her parents waiting for her at the table. Her father lounged almost as comfortably as he ever had. Her mother looked drawn.

There was a silence between them that Andromeda intended to resolve.

'You know I will marry him?' Her eyes were bright with the challenge. There had still been no word from Phineus, even now his niece was free.

'Yes, my dear,' said her father. 'It appeared that way when you allowed him to grab you in front of all our subjects.'

'He'd just saved my life,' she remarked. 'So I thought it best to confirm to everyone that he is the kind of man I would like as my husband, rather than an absent coward.' There was a pause. 'An old, absent coward.' Her mother flinched, but did not speak. 'He is the son of Zeus,' Andromeda continued. 'This is a match you should both approve.'

Her father nodded. 'I can hardly refuse him,' he said. 'After he appeared so impressively and saved you when I could not.' There was a tremor in his voice and Andromeda wondered why. It was a little late, as far as she was concerned, to be wishing he had done more to save her now. He had done nothing when it mattered. Perseus had done everything.

'He will ask you for permission to marry me tonight,' she said. 'I am certain.'

'I'm not sure he asks for permission,' said her father. 'But perhaps he will, since he is a guest in my house.'

'I don't know why you don't like him. He saved my life when no one else would, or could. He didn't fear a monster, he didn't fear Poseidon, and he didn't care what those vile priests said. I would have thought you'd be happy for me to marry such a man.'

'I would be,' said her father. Andromeda waited, in case there was more. But her father simply ladled out more wine.

'You don't seem very happy,' she said. She took her place on the next couch, leaving plenty of room in case Perseus wasn't sure where to sit when he arrived.

'If you are happy, we are happy,' said Cepheus. 'I cannot pretend I'm anything other than deeply ashamed of my brother's continuing absence, and his cowardice. Although I do find his age more forgivable than you do.'

'I see,' Andromeda said.

'Your mother and I chose a husband for you because we

believed he would be good for you. His behaviour has made it clear that he would not. I would like to be able to choose you a new husband myself, rather than have one swoop in from the skies who we don't know and who you don't know either. But we have discussed the matter and both of us feel that we cannot stand in his way if he wishes to marry you: we barely survived the wrath of Poseidon. We cannot incur the anger of Zeus the Almighty.'

Andromeda looked at her mother, who stared into her cup, tilting it gently so the wine flowed around it.

'And what about what I want?' asked Andromeda. 'You behave as though I have no say in the matter at all.'

Her father smiled. 'No,' he said. 'But you had made up your mind the moment he appeared, I believe, so we didn't worry about that when we discussed it.'

'I don't think that you are pleased with this marriage, whatever you say,' she replied. 'You sit here in silence as though we were preparing for a funeral. Which you very nearly were, although I would have been conspicuously missing.'

'No.' Her mother's voice was creaky from lack of use. 'We are grateful to him for saving you from my folly. He is a child of the gods and well-favoured by them. I have only one reason to be unhappy today, and I hope it will fade with time.'

'What is that?' asked Andromeda.

'He enjoyed killing the priests so much,' her mother replied.

'Why shouldn't he have killed them?' Andromeda said. 'They wanted me dead. You can find new priests easily enough.'

'I don't disagree with you, my dear,' said Cepheus. This was what he invariably said when he did disagree with someone. 'We wanted to placate the gods and we thought we had to do as they demanded. But your young man comes with a higher authority, from Zeus himself, if he is to be believed.'

'Why shouldn't he be believed?' Andromeda was beginning to wonder if her parents would rather she'd been eaten alive. 'Why would you question his parentage like this?'

'I'm not questioning it,' Cepheus replied quickly. He didn't want to blaspheme against another god. 'I am just not accustomed to meeting sons of Zeus, I suppose.'

'It's been quite an eventful time for everyone,' Andromeda said. 'I don't see how the father of my future husband is more surprising to you than a wandering ocean, or a sea monster. And what did you mean when you said he enjoyed killing them? He was saving my life. I don't imagine enjoyment came into it. There was hardly any point in killing the creature that had been sent to eat me if he was just going to stand back and let the priests issue orders for some other god-demanded death. At least he stood up for me.'

There was a long silence.

'He is not king of all the Ethiopians, my dear,' her father said. 'I was their king before I was your father.'

'Well, now I have the chance to marry a man who thinks of my needs before those of his people,' she replied. 'Which is more than could be said of the man you wanted me to marry.'

'He relished the killing,' said her mother. 'You didn't see it but we did. His eyes were full of excitement when he swung his sword into the old priest's throat. He was happy.

337

I'm sure you're right that he would never put other people's needs before yours. But he will never put anyone's before his own.'

'That's not true,' Andromeda said. 'How can you say that, when you have barely met him?'

'You're agreeing to marry him and you've barely met him,' her mother retorted.

'He's on a quest to save his mother from being forced to marry a man she doesn't like,' Andromeda replied. She and Perseus had discussed everything important on the walk back to the palace. The things she didn't already know about him she was sure she would love as much as everything she did know. How could she resist someone who was trying to save his mother from the very fate she herself had faced?

'So he explained,' said Cepheus. 'He said it's very urgent. A most perilous quest.'

'Which the gods have assisted him with, because he is the son of Zeus and enjoys their favour,' said Andromeda. 'Which will make a nice change for me. Enjoying divine favour.'

'And yet,' said her mother, 'he delayed his journey home so he could save you.'

'Yes!' cried Andromeda. 'I don't know how you can think that reflects poorly on him. I can only assume it's because it reflects so badly on both of you.'

'You said he wouldn't put anyone else's needs before yours,' her mother replied. 'But he chose to put the needs of a stranger – you – before the interests of his mother, to whom he is so devoted. Why was he not hurrying to save her? Why was he diverted from his journey home?'

'Because he loved me the moment he saw me,' Andromeda said.

'He'd already abandoned his mother before he'd seen you,' said Cassiope.

Andromeda stared at her in furious silence. Her father looked at the floor.

'I hope I'm not late,' said Perseus, as he stepped into the dining room.

Gorgoneion

I don't know where it is that he stops after he leaves Ethiopia. It's a coastline unlike any I have ever known. An island, then? Or the other side of the sea that lapped up against the Gorgons' shore? I don't know. I don't see the land, because he takes me from the kibisis and puts me on the ground, facing the sea. He is still afraid of me, which is something, I suppose.

He doesn't put me down carefully enough: he can tolerate gripping my snakes but only for a short time before he is repulsed by the sensation of warm reptile bodies writhing in his hands. The sand is as hard as the rocks in Medusa's cave. The pain shoots up through my neck and I set my teeth. And the man who has not responded to anything I have said notices my discomfort. He walks away.

I wonder if he will leave me here. There are worse places to be, apart from the hardness of the ground, and I could get used to that. I have grown used to everything else, after all. I would stay here for ever, then, looking out over the waves and thinking about all I have lost: my sisters, my mother, my once self.

But then I hear his footsteps returning. He lifts me from the sand, and there is a rustling noise beneath me. When he puts me back down, the spot is softer. He has piled up leaves or seaweed fronds and made a cushion for my raw neck.

No.

You cannot be feeling affection for him at this point. You cannot. Can I remind you that my neck wouldn't be raw if it weren't for him? Gratitude is not something I can or will ever feel towards Perseus. But still, I rest on the seaweed mat and I look at the water and he also rests, because travelling with divine help is exhausting work, apparently. And when he decides it is time to travel to Seriphos at last, he opens the bag and lifts me into it. The seaweed cushion has hardened to a delicate sculpture of rock: I catch a glimpse of it before I am in darkness once again.

Danaë

Danaë had counted off the days her son was gone. She tried not to feel anxious because Zeus had always looked after her before. But she was not as young as she had been when she first caught his eye, and (unworthily, she said to herself, trying not to offend him even in her mind) she worried that she was now too old to have his attention and thus his help. He would be eyeing new girls now; how would he remember the mother of Perseus, whom he had saved from a prison and from a box and from the sea? But even if he didn't remember Danaë, he would remember Perseus, she hoped. Zeus was generally proud of his sons, and defended them staunchly. And yet, why did they always need his defence? Because Hera was set against them and her fury was as uncontrollable as a raging ocean.

But, the hopeful side of her nature reasserted itself: Hera had not punished Danaë before. It had been her own father, Acrisius, who'd locked her up and then left her to drown. So if Hera was not angry with her, perhaps Perseus was safe and she was safe. And her son would come home and she would not have to marry a pompous old king who smelled of stale wine and self-regard.

But another day passed and she watched for the boats to return. Every time she hoped that Dictys would somehow have found Perseus sailing alongside him, heading for home. But each day, she watched his boat bobbing back towards the shore alone. And she knew that wherever Perseus was, he was not about to run up the hill to their house, desperate to tell his mother about whatever huge creatures they had seen in the ocean (Dictys had always been looking the wrong way at the crucial moment so missed the great monsters of the deep). And she smiled and shook her head: she was remembering a far younger Perseus than the one who had set out on his quest almost two months ago.

The planned wedding was now imminent, and the hated king sent messengers each day with one thing or another: a dress she must wear, a bracelet she would like. Dictys flinched with every new arrival. Danaë piled them up in a corner and put an old fishing net over them so they didn't have to see his brother's influence as they went about their day. She supposed the dress would smell of fish now, but she was used to that, living in a fisherman's home. And she still hoped not to wear it, though her hope was wearing thinner with every hour that passed.

And now so many hours had passed that the wedding was due to take place tomorrow. Polydectes would present himself to his bride in person, the pompous messenger told her on her final day of freedom. She must ensure she had packed any possessions she wanted to take with her (at this point, the messenger could not prevent a sneer as he looked at the humble cottage). Because she would not be returning here and Dictys would not be welcome at the palace. So – he explained slowly, as though she might not understand him – anything she left behind would be lost to her for good.

She nodded wearily and turned to look again at the distant sea, but after the messenger left, she found she could not endure watching for the boats to come in and one man to climb the hill to their home alone. She waited inside to greet Dictys – as she had in old times – willing herself to hide her sadness when she saw his brown, lined face break into a tired smile.

The boats were back later today, she thought, eyeing the shadows as they moved across the floor. She would never see these shadows, this light, again. She picked up a broom irritably. She was not going to cry about the floor. Zeus would save her or he wouldn't and that was all there was to it.

Eventually, she heard his slow footsteps as he approached the house. He was carrying a heavy catch today, she thought, or his stride would be quicker and lighter. She turned to the doorway and beheld the face of a young man who looked as familiar as her reflection and as unknown as a stranger. But she had no time to consider this paradox because he was already in her arms, sobbing with relief.

Gorgoneion

The day of the wedding has arrived but Danaë will not have to marry the king. The light is sharp and ruthless. The king—

Do you even need me to tell you all this? You already know what happens. The king arrives to claim his unwilling bride. His corpulent face is disappointed and astonished in equal measure when he sees Perseus has returned to defend her. He makes snide remarks, but you can hear the unease in his voice. He sent a boy away on a hero's quest, and the fool claims he has come back with the prize.

That would be me, in case you have forgotten.

The king is all bluster and feigned disbelief. Perseus is full of anger. His mother is quiet; Dictys lays a protective hand on her arm.

The king – who is even more stupid than Perseus, or at least equally ignorant – asks to see his prize. Perseus milks this moment, building the tension by taking his time to find the kibisis, to loosen the tassels that hold it closed, to reach inside. He tells his mother and Dictys to turn away. They don't ask questions, just do as he says. There is a perceptible sense of triumph and relief about him since he returned home. This is what he has been missing, then: the simple experience of being heard and heeded. I wonder if he has chosen a wife who will provide him with that, in Andromeda.

The king scoffs at the precautions taken by his brother and his intended. What are they afraid of? Perseus must have really fulfilled his promise, and so on.

And then, as you could surely have guessed, he catches sight of me and he says nothing ever again. Three of his bodyguards are looking in the same direction, and they petrify in the same instant. The others – seeing their comrades are now statues and their king is dead – run for their lives.

As he returns me to the bag, Perseus remarks that he will leave the men where they stand as a warning to others.

The last thing I hear is Dictys, calmly responding to the death of his brother by saying he would prefer it if they took the statues away and buried them under the sand. Perseus agrees reluctantly, but they bury them all, just the same.

Hera

'I wonder if it's a good precedent to set, my love.' Hera stood behind Zeus as she stroked her husband's shoulders, so he wouldn't see her expression of disdain.

'I'm sure it is,' he replied. Hera waited. 'What precedent?'

'Your bastard son,' she said. Even though she could not see his face, she knew his eyes were darting from place to place, trying to work out which one she meant, and whether she had only just discovered him. 'Perseus has just killed the king of Seriphos.'

'Oh, good,' said Zeus. His wife's grip tightened briefly but she didn't speak. Zeus thought for a moment. 'He was a very unjust king,' he said. 'The islanders have prayed for deliverance for some time.'

'I see,' said Hera. 'Well, then, I'm sure I don't need to worry.'

'No,' said her husband. 'Why were you worrying?'

'Nothing, really,' she replied. 'I just wondered if it was a good idea to allow young upstarts to go around killing kings and face no penalty.'

'He's my son,' said Zeus. 'He can do whatever he likes, within reason.'

'I thought this might be without reason,' Hera said. 'The king seems to have done nothing beyond decide to marry some woman, and it's difficult to imagine anyone could have resented that.'

'These things happen,' said her husband.

'I worry that people might start to think they can overthrow any ruler they don't like,' she continued. 'If this behaviour goes unpunished.'

'It runs in the family,' Zeus retorted. 'I myself—'

'You aren't the upstart any more,' his wife said. 'You're the old king.'

'Mortals aren't going to overthrow the king of the gods,' Zeus said. 'They wouldn't dare. Who would attempt such a thing?'

'Not mortals,' Hera murmured, leaning in close.

'Then who? I already suppressed the rebellions of the Titans and the giants. Who is left to rise up against the Olympians, against me?'

'Well, those two aren't quite the same thing, are they?' she said. 'What if one of the Olympians decides to take his chance?'

'None would succeed,' he stated. 'Who?'

'I don't know,' she said. 'I just worried it was setting a bad example.'

'Well, it isn't.'

'That's wonderful,' Hera said, singing to herself as she walked away.

Gorgoneion

Blood is spilled before statues are made. The scale of the wedding massacre surprises even me. I'm not sure why, because he has shown no remorse on any of the previous occasions. But the numbers are dizzying. I don't know if it surprises me that I can kill so many at once – dozens, then hundreds – or whether it is that Perseus cannot even engage in what is traditionally a happy occasion without mass murder.

Obviously, it isn't the fault of Andromeda's parents. Battered by the multitude of disasters that have recently beset them, they keep quiet when Perseus leaves and they stay quiet when he returns (though they have been wishing for their daughter's sake that he will not). They agree politely with the happy couple that this wedding is an opportunity to unite the people of their troubled country after the recent struggles. Andromeda and her mother choose her dress, Perseus and her father choose the guests. His mother will not be attending, he explains, because of the distance involved. But he and his new wife will be heading back to the Greek mainland and they will travel via Seriphos. Cepheus and Cassiope agree to everything, and the day of the wedding goes smoothly until the guests arrive. Unusually, it isn't Perseus who starts the fight.

*

Andromeda had been promised to another, to her uncle Phineus. But he disappeared when the country was flooded and failed to reappear when Andromeda was taken by the priests. Phineus was therefore presumed – by the royal household, at least – to be dead. But Phineus was very much alive, at least until the wedding day. He had been hiding in the mountains, having retreated to higher ground when the water came. Then there was talk of blasphemy and divine retribution and a sea monster, and he saw no reason to leave. If it came as a surprise to find his betrothed had not been eaten after all, it was presumably a pleasant one. But less pleasant was the accompanying rumour, that she now planned to marry her rescuer. Phineus wanted to be sure there were no more monsters coming before he reappeared and asserted his prior claim.

By the time he feels it is safe to do so, Perseus has returned and the wedding day is here. Phineus – incensed by how quickly he has been forgotten – gathers a ragtag bunch of supporters and marches on the wedding as though it is a battlefield. When they first appear outside the palace, no one is quite sure if they are uninvited guests or a disgruntled army.

Inside the halls, the torches flame brightly. Wedding hymns are sung and wine is poured. Outside the halls there is a festering anger. Phineus and his men hold torches aloft and demand Andromeda be given to them as was once promised. The stewards try to hold them off but they are outnumbered, and the men swarm through the palace, shouting their demands.

Cepheus and Cassiope rise from their couches and tell Andromeda that they will deal with everything. They rush through the halls and come face to face with Phineus. He has no control over the men he has brought here, which is hardly surprising. Everyone knows he is a coward, after all. So while Cepheus tries to reason with him, the men are running in all directions, determined to find the wedding feast and the wine.

Cepheus speaks softly and apologetically and Cassiope is quiet. The last month has taken all the fight out of her. Cepheus explains to Phineus that he is quite wrong to be angry with them. That they had not chosen Perseus as a preferable son-in-law, but that the gods had chosen him and they could not disagree. They have learned how costly it is to offend the gods in any way.

But Phineus is not interested in these excuses. He has been cheated of his bride and cheated of his place in the line of succession and he will see justice. Cepheus tries to buy him with gold and cattle but Phineus is drunk and besides, he can already hear the fight breaking out. It is too late for bribes, he says. He wants his wife. Cepheus – who has no idea how to deal with one more catastrophe – tells him he must take this up with the Nereids, with Poseidon, with the sea monster. And to bear in mind that the contest he hopes to win is against the son of Zeus himself.

Phineus strides off towards the large hall, where the battle is already underway. Perseus has leaped to his feet and is swinging a large knife at anyone who comes too close. Andromeda is screaming because she really has had enough of things going wrong, and anyway someone has spilled wine on her saffron-coloured dress. And then she catches sight of her hated uncle as he comes through the doorway and she grabs Perseus and points at the older man and screams right into her husband's ear that this is the man he has saved her from. Perseus looks around at the upturned tables and couches and the men wrangling with one another. He realizes that he has no idea who is fighting for Phineus and who is fighting against him. They are all strangers to Perseus, except for one. He presses Andromeda to his side and hopes her parents have removed themselves from the fray. He reaches down for the kibisis that is never far from him and tells his bride to close her eyes. She screws up her face and buries her head in his shoulder as he reveals me to the room.

He cries out and men turn to look at him, which means they see me, which costs them dear. One man is turned to stone as he jabs a short sword into his countryman. The dead man – whose eyes had glazed before he could turn his head – has to be lifted off the statue which had killed him. Blood is shed, but there are dozens of bodies amid hundreds of statues.

*

When Andromeda opens her eyes again, she does not scream. She looks around and tries to comprehend what has happened: the loss of almost everyone she knows. The girls with whom she had planned weddings are all dead. Their brothers and parents are dead. Her uncle and all his men are dead, but she doesn't notice because she is desperately searching the rooms for her parents. Perseus has replaced me and hooks the bag over his shoulder and wonders at the clean resolution he has achieved. No more men demanding his bride as their own. No more fighting. He wonders why Andromeda isn't more grateful, like she was after he killed the sea monster.

He thinks of Dictys, and how he had been so concerned about burying the statues in the sand of Seriphos, rather than leaving them on show for all to see what happened when you crossed the son of Zeus. Perhaps that is what is bothering Andromeda, who now appears in the hall again, holding on to her parents as though they might run off. Perseus supposes they have lost a lot of slaves with the floods and now the fighting and so perhaps she and her parents are wondering how they can empty their halls of the statuary. He will help them, of course: there's no need for them to look so stricken. He doesn't like her parents. Perhaps he will just take Andromeda away with him and leave them to clean up the mess.

Athene

'I don't know why you want him to stop,' Athene said. 'It's the first interesting thing he's ever done and now you don't like it.'

'Hera advises me that he should give up the Gorgon head,' said Zeus. He stroked his beard so his daughter would know he had given it a great deal of thought himself, and decided to heed his wife's advice.

'Because he killed a few Greeks,' said Athene. 'Hera doesn't like competition, that's all.'

'I don't think it was just the Greeks that concerned her,' Zeus replied. 'It was the culling of so many Ethiopians. The Gorgon head wiped out more than Poseidon's tidal wave, and his sea monster too.'

'He has ensured a trouble-free succession for generations to come,' said his daughter. 'It is the only time he has ever reminded me of you.'

Zeus nodded slowly. He was torn in this matter: it was always easier to do what Hera wanted, and it was certainly the case that he could do without Poseidon complaining about being overshadowed by a mere mortal. He knew that would be coming if he failed to act now. But at the same time, it was a moment of some paternal pride. That his son – a mortal who had needed divine assistance just to get off his own island – had managed to slaughter hundreds of people. And at a wedding! When they might least have expected it. There were always good reasons for reducing mortal numbers. Imagine how many lightning bolts Perseus had saved him with a quick flash of the Gorgon head.

'Do you think he would still remind you of me if he gave up the Gorgoneion?' he asked Athene. She tilted her head slightly, as she thought about it. She reminded him more and more of her precious owl.

'He would be dead in a month without it,' she said. 'If he carries on picking fights the way he has been. You can't be petulant and angry all the time if you haven't got a much more powerful weapon than everyone around you.'

Zeus frowned. 'That doesn't answer my question.'

'Oh, doesn't it?' Athene asked. 'Well then, yes, in some ways he would continue to remind me of you. He's not like his mother at all: she isn't interested in killing anyone as far as I can tell. She didn't even try and kill the king of Seriphos, she just waited until Perseus came and did it for her.'

'I see,' said Zeus. 'I don't suppose you could go and tell him not to use the head unless there's no choice?'

'He already does that,' said Athene.

'Really?' her father asked.

'Yes, he's quite cowardly and stupid, so he can hardly ever choose to do something difficult or brave,' she explained. 'The head really has made all the difference.'

'He might learn to be brave.'

'No,' said Athene. 'He won't. He's more the kind of person who doesn't learn anything. He takes easy shortcuts whenever they're offered and gives up when they aren't.'

'Take it from him.'

Athene nodded. 'Very well,' she said. 'And then what should I do with it?'

Zeus had already lost interest. 'Whatever you want,' he said.

Iodame

Her father had built the sanctuary to Athene before she was born, so she was a priestess from the beginning. She grew up shadowing the footsteps of the women who served the goddess, hiding in the recesses to witness their observance. She wanted so much to serve alongside them, she would stand on her tiptoes whenever the chief priestess walked past, determined to be older. Iodame loved her goddess and loved her temple.

As a junior priestess, she worked harder than anyone. The older women loved her, even when they grew tired of the questions she always had about one or another part of their religious practice. No one could fault the child for enthusiasm, they would say. And she enjoyed even the hardest, most painstaking tasks. They had her carding wool for months at a time, so they could weave the finest and most beautiful robe for their goddess. She never complained that her hands were scratched by the burrs, or that the grease from the wool was staining her tunic. When the carding was completed, she sought to learn spinning, so she might be closer still to her goddess.

Boys came sometimes, from the surrounding neighbourhood. They watched the young priestesses as quietly as they could, knowing that the moment they were discovered, one of the old women who swept the sanctuary steps each day would be after them with her broom. But the lure of young women who had turned their back on future marriage was too great, and the boys would return even when the bruises from last time had yet to fade. Some of the girls would encourage them, but not Iodame. She had a brother: boys held no mystery for her.

And anyway, she loved Athene. She had little interest in anything else. She felt a great warmth towards her parents that they had given her this life, even as her siblings rejected it. Let them lead the lives they chose, Iodame thought. The life of the temple was the one for her. The older priestesses were so impressed by her focus that they taught her to weave: the youngest girl ever to assist in the making of Athene's robe.

Each year, they made a new peplos for the goddess they served. Her statue – larger than life, if Iodame could think such a thing about her goddess – was taken from the temple, paraded through the streets for all to see her lapis eyes and golden skin. Every year on this day, her dress was made anew, so she was always as perfect as she could be, in honour of their always-perfect goddess. Music was played by her devotees, although Iodame had yet to learn the flute. She could sing, at least, and she would be a flute-player next year. The music teacher had promised her.

*

Iodame wove the finest, neatest cloth she could make. She worked until it was dark and then by torchlight. She knew if she made it perfect – or as close to perfect as anyone who was not Athene could achieve – she would see the dress adorning the statue for a whole year, a dress she had helped to make. Even flute-playing could wait. When she finally completed her work, she knew it was good.

On the morning of the festival, she watched the priestesses draw the old dress over the statue's head. They were careful not to snag it on the helmet Athene wore. They had to remove her spear and return it to her grasp once the new peplos was in place. Iodame felt oddly impertinent, seeing the statue naked. But the light reflected off the goddess's golden skin and Iodame glowed like the one she served. She had told her family that her weaving would adorn the goddess this time. Her father had squeezed her shoulders, mute with pride.

The ceremony was formal and joyful. It was the moment when the priestesses were closest to the people who lived around them, and when the people were closest to their goddess. When the statue was finally returned to the precinct, the shadows had grown long and the cicadas were adding their own hymn of praise. Athene stood in her recess once again, spear in hand, helmet tilted back at the characteristic angle.

The priestesses now had their own, more private celebrations. They poured wine and made offerings to their goddess, and then they ate and drank together in her honour. Iodame was tired and elated in equal measure. She did not want the day to end, and yet she could not keep her eyes open. She edged away from the other women and hid herself behind a pillar. She sat leaning against it, its warm curve fitting neatly into the curve at the base of her spine. She allowed her head to droop until her chin rested on her knees. She closed her eyes just for a moment.

When she woke, the precinct was dark. The music had stopped, and the torches had died. She wondered if she was in trouble. But how could she be? She felt suffused with love for her goddess and she could not believe she was anywhere she was not supposed to be. She crept around the pillar and blinked. She looked up at the sky: it was cloudless, but the moon was only a sliver. An owl flew overhead, pale in the dim light. She smiled: she always loved to see Athene's favourite bird.

Iodame looked again across the precinct. She must still be dreaming. Because she could see, quite clearly, the back of her goddess standing in the middle of the sanctuary, admiring her statue's new dress. Athene mirrored her mannequin perfectly. Iodame thought it must be a trick of the light, and she crept up the colonnade, trying to untrick her eyes. But the goddess did not disappear or resolve into a mass of shadows. Iodame was now almost level with her, and she could see Athene's face in profile.

The other priestesses had talked about Athene sometimes coming to visit her sanctuary, but Iodame had thought they were speaking of their hopes, and nothing more. She stood gazing at the goddess in silence. Her jawline, her nose matched the statue exactly. Iodame felt her devotion more powerfully than ever, but there was another feeling too. She was disconcerted by the uncanny sense of the familiar. The goddess was right there in front of her, and she knew her intimately. Yet she was also a stranger, huge and imposing.

She didn't know whether to hide or reveal herself, to worship or retreat. When the goddess turned her head, Iodame stood her ground. She did not run or fall to her knees. She bowed her head and then returned the bright blue-grey gaze. Athene smiled. 'You're my priestess,' she said. 'The one everyone loves.'

Iodame could feel herself blushing in the darkness. 'I think so,' she said.

'You are,' said Athene. 'I wanted to see you for myself. Come here.'

Iodame stepped out of the shadows of the portico. Her goddess shimmered with a golden radiance that the gold-encrusted statue could never match. Iodame looked at the glittering helmet, the glinting spearhead, the braided hair, and she felt pride that their feeble lifeless copy of the goddess was as accurate as it could be, given the impossibility of trying to replicate perfection. But she was especially glad that Athene had chosen to visit on a day when her statue wore a new dress not much shabbier than the one she wore herself. How hard she had worked to contribute to their offerings.

There was only one thing the real goddess had which the statue did not. Iodame was sorry to see that the priestesses had missed a garment the goddess wore over her dress. An aegis, was that the word? Her brother would know. It was armour, anyway, covering Athene's breastbone. It made her look more warlike than ever: Iodame wanted to make one of those next, even if she had to learn leather-working first. But what was the decoration in the centre? A huge mass of snakes? Or was there something else?

But of course, she was stone before she could see.

361

Athene and the Gorgoneion

'Turn her back,' said Athene. 'I didn't mean for that to happen.'

'Neither did I,' replied the head of Medusa.

'Then turn her back.'

'I can't.'

'What do you mean, you can't? You made her stone, make her flesh again.'

'I don't have that power.'

'Well, you should have thought of that before you looked at her.'

'Perhaps you should have thought of it before you secured the head of the Gorgon to your breastplate.'

'It's too late for me to think of that now.'

'Yes.'

'You won't bring her back?'

'I would if I could.'

'It's very inconvenient. She only looked at you for a moment.'

'That's all it takes.'

Athene lifted off her helmet and rubbed her brow bone. 'So you can't look at anyone without them turning to stone?'

'You know I can't.'

'How would I know?

'You cursed me.'

There was silence.

'I didn't know it would be so quick,' Athene said. 'I thought you'd have to really stare at something.'

'Now you know,' the Gorgoneion replied. 'Why did you mention her now?'

'Who?'

'The priestess. That's who you meant, isn't it?'

'Yes, of course it is. What do you mean, why mention her now?'

The head of Medusa stared out over the sea. Athene's breastplate was propped up against the trunk of a wizened olive tree.

'You asked me to change her back as though it had just happened.'

'It did just happen.'

'No,' said the Gorgoneion. 'It happened centuries ago.'

'I don't know what that is.'

'A century is a hundred years.'

'Is that longer than an hour?'

'Yes.'

'Oh.' Athene thought for a while. 'Could you have changed her back if I'd asked you sooner?'

'No.'

'So it doesn't make any difference how long it's been?'

'No, not really.'

'I wish I hadn't turned round,' said the goddess, all the words at once. 'But she'd be dead now anyway, if it's been hundreds of years. They die, don't they?'

'Yes, they do. And the priestesses at your temple have kept a flame burning for her ever since they found her statue.'

'To the priestess?'

'Yes, her statue stands where it was made.'

'In my sanctuary?'

'Yes.'

Athene frowned. 'I thought that the fire was for me.'

'It's for the girl.'

'I suppose that's not blasphemy.'

'Her statue serves yours,' said the Gorgoneion. 'It isn't blasphemous at all.'

'I'm bored of it now. I don't care about the statues any more.'

'Bored of the girl we killed?'

'Yes. And everything else.'

'I see.'

'I don't remember when I wasn't bored.'

'That must be painful for you.'

'It is. Are you mocking me?'

'No. Immortality must be a painful business for you.'

'There's no one to talk to.'

'Because they die?'

'Yes.'

'There are other gods.'

'They don't like me. I don't like them either.'

'You're lonely.'

'I am not.'

'You are. That's why you're talking to me.'

'I don't know who else to talk to.'

'If you're not lonely, then what are you?'

The goddess blinked once or twice as she tried to find her answer. 'I helped so many men find their way home,' she said. 'Because they had lost themselves on a quest or in a war and all they wanted was to return home. No matter what adventures they had, what riches they held, what wonders they saw, what they really wanted was to remember those things from the safety of their homes. Do you understand?'

'I do.'

'That's how I feel.'

'You want to go home?'

'Yes.'

'To Olympus?'

'No, to . . .' Athene watched the waves breaking softly in front of her. 'I don't know where home is. I don't have a home, really.'

'You have many homes: Olympus, Athens, the sanctuary where the girl died.'

'Those are places other people call my home. But they don't feel like it to me. I want to be somewhere else, but I don't know where. And I want to know when I reach it that I have come home.'

'So you're homesick for somewhere you've never been?'

'Yes. Where do you think it is?'

'I don't know.'

'You could help me find it.'

'Perhaps.'

'Now?'

'If that's what you want.'

'It is.'

'I can only take you to one place,' said the head of Medusa.

'And if it isn't home, I can't bring you back. You under-stand that?'

'Yes.'

'Then look.'

Gorgoneion

You have seen this statue before. It has been copied many times. Athene stands comfortably: her weight on her right foot, left heel slightly raised, left knee bent. Her dress drapes over the outline of her knee. If you only glanced at her, you might think she was mid-step. But look at the way her arms fall. Look at how her head is half-turned. She isn't walking anywhere. She is standing as if she has decided that this is the most flattering pose she could think of. And looking at her – youthful, careless, beautiful – you might conclude that she was right.

Her helmet is tilted back, the way she always liked to wear it. Her hair coils beneath the rim, snaking over her ears. Her blind eyes stare into nothingness, her mouth forms a perfect bow. Her skin looks so soft, it makes you want to reach out and stroke the marble to check if it is warm. Although she was never warm to the touch, even when she wasn't made of stone.

Her head is facing down: she is looking at something on her left, on the ground, not far away. People will spend lifetimes arguing about what the sculptor was trying to convey with this choice, this angle. But you know the truth. She is looking down to her left because that is where she had placed her aegis. The one with the Gorgon head at its centre.

And what happened to the Gorgon head? The final part of the story. It was carried out to the sea eventually. It is enmeshed in seaweeds and coral, which have hardened around it, like stone. The Gorgoneion is lost beneath the waves, and no one can reach it, not even the creatures of the sea. It has closed its eyes, one last time.

Acknowledgements

I am incredibly lucky that the person I get to send my books to is Peter Straus. He is the cleverest, kindest man, the finest agent and the most incisive reader. Lena Mistry keeps us both on track – thank you to her too. I'm also very lucky to have my wonderful editor Maria Rejt at Pan Macmillan; constant thanks to her, Alice Gray, Samantha Fletcher, Hannah Corbett, Emma Finnigan (did you not learn last time, Emma? You were so nearly free . . .). Special mention to Ami Smithson for her beautiful jacket designs: she makes everything look so classy. I never thought I would be in a position where I feel like I should brush my hair before I hold one of my own books. Elena Richards myth-checked the manuscript as I was editing: one day she will understand what she is worth to those around her (spoiler: she's priceless).

Thanks to the people who keep the rest of the show on the road while I'm writing – to Pauline Lord, who runs my live performances across multiple time zones without ever breaking a sweat; Mary Ward-Lowery, who produces *Natalie Haynes Stands Up for the Classics* effortlessly, even when we're locked in different parts of the country; Christian Hill, for the website (he has so many better things to do. OK, not better, other); Matilda McMorrow, for running my social media life and sending me pictures of animals every day when I finish work (want to avoid procrastination? Write as though someone will send you a pic of an egret when you finish). To Dan Mersh, of course – my first reader and too much more to put into words here.

Thanks to all the friends and other geniuses who contributed their knowledge to this, including: Helen Czerski for telling me how I could move a sea; Tim Whitmarsh for introducing me to the *Halieutica* (a whole book of which is on sea monsters. This is not the first time Tim has cracked open a huge seam of material for me with a casual remark); Roslynne Bell for her tireless expertise in ancient art and sculpture; Adam Rutherford for his snakes; Edith Hall for continuing support in all matters ancient and modern. One day last year, I texted Robert Douglas-Fairhurst and asked him if it was mad to write a chapter from the perspective of snakes: he called me straight back to say no, and I wrote the chapter that evening. Imagine being the kind of person who fills your friends with energy and focus and sharpens their ideas to their best form. That is him.

I'd like to thank James Runcie for saving me all the palaver of getting married and divorced and being my dream ex-husband anyway. Andrew Copson is both friend and conscience and I am so glad I know him. Rachel McCormack made (not bought, made) biscuits and sent them when I was sad: this is vintage long-distance friend work. Rob Deering and Howard Read never let it go too long before we hang out. My friends at the dojo held me up when I lost my balance and refused to let go until it came back. Special thanks to the majestic Sam Thorp, Adam Field and Jo Walters, who could kill me with her hands, but has chosen not to (so far).

This book is full of sets of three women (Greek Myth has so many of them). I realized as I was writing it that I belong to several trios myself. So masses of love and thanks always to Helen Bagnall and Philippa Perry who love me even when I'm blue; to Catherine Nixey and Francesca Stavrakopoulou for peerless unholy trinity work; to Helen Artlett-Coe and Lottie Westoby, who came to my rescue more than once; to the women of Sezon Gunaikes, who number many more than three, but especially Magdalena Zira, Nedie Antoniades and Athina Kasiou: they still have very hostile intentions and I dearly hope they decide to perform this book too.

Huge love and thanks to my family, as always: my mum, Sandra; my dad, Andre; Chris, Gem and Kez.

Want more from Natalie Haynes? Discover her previous novel, *A Thousand Ships*, shortlisted for the Women's Prize for Fiction 2020.

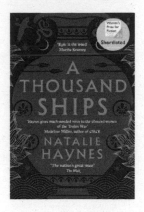

'With her trademark passion, wit, and fierce feminism, Natalie Haynes gives much-needed voice to the silenced women of the Trojan War'
MADELINE MILLER, bestselling author of *Circe*

This was never the story of one woman, or two.
It was the story of them all . . .

In the middle of the night, a woman wakes to find her beloved city engulfed in flames. Ten seemingly endless years of conflict between the Greeks and the Trojans are over. Troy has fallen.

From the Trojan women whose fates now lie in the hands of the Greeks, to the Amazon princess who fought Achilles on their behalf, to Penelope awaiting the return of Odysseus, to the three goddesses whose feud started it all, these are the stories of the women embroiled in the legendary war.

'A gripping feminist masterpiece'
DEBORAH FRANCES-WHITE, *The Guilty Feminist*

One of *The Guardian*'s and *TLS*'s 'Best Books of 2019'